MUERTO

A NIGHT REBELS MC ROMANCE

CHIAH WILDER

Chapter One

M UERTO LEANED AGAINST the bar admiring the way the woman's ass moved as she bent low to take a shot at a ball near the left pocket of the pool table. He was surprised she could even bend in her tight-as-sin jeans, and her top inched up just enough to expose a glimpse of skin.

"She's got a nice ass," Crow said behind him.

"She's a looker, that's for fuckin' sure." Muerto raised his beer bottle to his lips, his eyes never leaving her tight curves.

"She's damn hot, but she doesn't know much about the game." Crow laughed. "She was in the other night and she lost her ass. Last night she did a little better, but she's got a long way to go."

"Most of the guys in here don't play so hot, except for Willy and Gator. I'm sure the guys are playing with her just to get a peek at her tits when she bends over. Hell, I'll play a game with her for that chance." Muerto pushed off the counter and went behind the bar. "How was business the last couple of nights?"

"Steady," Crow said.

Balls and Holes was the pool hall owned by the Night Rebels MC. It was a classic dark and smoky players' hall, not one of the upscale billiard rooms with loud music and video games. It was one of the last of the old-school pool halls, refusing to be muscled out by the new chic ones that had been sprouting around the county and Durango, the large neighboring city.

The pool hall had chalk-covered floors and high-backed wooden chairs against the walls so spectators could watch the game. There were six green felt pool tables at the center of the room, and an old jukebox in the corner. The place was dark with low ceilings, and the smoke from cigarettes and weed curled around the players. No one seemed to care about the law forbidding smoking in public places; they came to play pool and watch people play as they threw back some beers. It was the gathering hole in its most basic form.

Muerto and Crow ran the place, making sure the bar was stocked and the fights didn't get out of hand. The bar had a large selection of beer and hard liquor, and for friends and long-time customers, the brothers would pull out bottles of Jack Daniels No. 27 Gold and Gran Patrón Platinum. For the most part, pretzels, peanuts, and popcorn were the only food served.

"Is Zach working tonight?" Crow asked. Zach was the citizen bartender in the place. They'd hired him about six months back, and so far the twenty-eight-year-old was working out nicely. With his fit body, he was an asset when they needed another hand to throw out an unruly group.

"Nah. He wanted the night off. I knew you and I could handle it tonight." Muerto placed the glasses he'd washed on a towel to dry.

"Two more Jacks and a couple of vodkas on the rocks. Boy, am I beat," Jaime said as she rubbed her neck.

"You need some help with that?" Crow smiled.

Jaime shook her head and turned to Muerto. "You want me to wash the rest of the glasses? That's not really man's work."

"Thanks, but I got it." He placed her drink order on the tray and watched as she swayed her hips. She was one of two waitresses at the joint, and her jeans fit nicely around her body, but she was nothing like the black-haired cutie who had just lost the game.

"That's the way it rolls, baby. Look at it this way—you're doing better than you did the last two nights," a stocky man in his late twenties with a crew cut said while he scooped up the bills on the side of the table.

"You got me. I'm done," her dark, sultry voice washed over Muerto like velvet. He straightened up and gazed at her; she piqued his interest.

"Why don't you play another game with my buddy?" another stocky man with short hair said, placing an arm around the woman's opponent. "What do ya say, Cory?"

Cory nodded. "If you want, I'll play another game with you. Maybe you'll get lucky like you did earlier."

The slender woman glanced at the wall clock. "I don't know. How much are you betting?"

"A hundred bucks?"

She whistled. "That's a lot of money. What about fifty?"

Cory grinned. "You're on."

Muerto turned away. "I'd sure like to squeeze my hand down her jeans and see how soft her pussy is," he said to Crow.

"I'd be right behind you, dude." Crow picked up a box and walked out of the bar. "I'm gonna go over our inventory. If you need me, give me a holler."

Muerto nodded and watched as Jaime approached the bar. When he'd hired her the year before, he thought she was good-looking with her shoulder-length brown hair, brown eyes, and curvy body. But he knew she was off-limits since she worked for the club. The Night Rebels never mixed pleasure with business, not even at their strip bar, Lust. He suspected she had a small crush on him, but it didn't surprise him; most women did. The other waitress, Brandy, was always flirting with him and brushing against him whenever she had to come behind the bar. He knew he could have both of them and probably at the same time, but they were the club's employees.

Six feet of hard muscle turned a lot of women's heads. Add dark, thick hair, a strong jaw, full lips, and intense black eyes and women practically drooled when they saw him. And he loved the attention he got from them. Unlike most of the brothers, he enjoyed going out with citizens, relishing the drama that would ensue when a woman found out he was fucking another one. Whenever that happened, they'd turn on each other instead of him, and he loved that they fought over him; it made his blood boil. But when they got too possessive and started talking about relationships and marriage, he disappeared into the arms and pussies of the club girls who knew the score.

The only downside to angering so many citizen women was that he was constantly changing his phone number, and that pissed off his brothers big time, especially Steel. He figured it was a small price to pay for the challenge of pursuing a woman and getting her into his bed. The club girls were too easy and they were always available. There wasn't any drama except for the usual chick stuff, but they knew they were at the club for all the brothers alike, and that's what they wanted as well.

What he liked about being with a citizen was that she was his alone, and she was totally centered on him until he grew bored and moved on. When he'd go to the biker rallies the club had a couple of times a year in the San Juan Valley, he'd have a bevy of women glaring at him, wanting to tear him to pieces. He'd just wink at them and go his own way, scouting for another woman to conquer. There was always a good supply of enamored, willing women to seduce.

The pretty chick with the cue stick was someone he'd love to seduce. Her ebony hair swayed as she twisted her sexy body to make the shots. He'd love to yank a fistful of her long hair as he slammed his cock into her from behind.

"Muerto? Did you fill my order?" Jaime asked as she placed the tray on the bar.

"What? Sorry. I don't know what the fuck's wrong with me." He grabbed several beer bottles from the refrigerated shelves and popped them open. *I got my mind on her. She's so damn hot.* He placed the bottles and three shots of Jack on the tray. "There you go."

"Thanks." She threw him a warm smile and headed over to the pool table where the woman was playing the game.

"I won," she said as she clapped her hands gleefully.

"See, you got lucky," Cory said as he took the beer from Jaime. "You wanna up the bet to a hundred bucks?"

Muerto jerked his chin at Army and Goldie as they walked in and placed two shots of Jack Daniels No. 27 Gold on the bar. "I thought you guys were at Lust," Muerto said as the two brothers sat down on the barstools.

"We were, but there wasn't anything much going on there. Tuesday nights are pretty slow." Goldie finished his shot. "Fuck, that's good."

"Only the best for the brothers," Muerto said as he poured him another one. "Fiona wasn't dancing tonight?"

"What difference would that make? I went there to check out the women and have a few beers with the brothers." Goldie threw back his shot.

"Fuck that. You went for Fiona. We all know you have a boner for her." Army swung around on the barstool and whistled softly. "Talk about having a boner, check out the chick with the tight pants and luscious ass."

Anger pricked at Muerto's skin. "Cool it, dudes. She's a customer."

Army looked over his shoulder. "And why do we give a shit about that? You've fucked a few customers."

"I mean she's a regular." *Why the fuck am I saying this lame shit?* "We kinda got a new policy in here where we don't mess with the women customers."

"When did you get that policy, 'cause you didn't have it last week when you were fuckin' that blonde in the storeroom."

"Just leave it and *her* the hell alone." Fire began to burn in Muerto's veins as he scowled at Army.

Goldie laughed. "I think what he's sayin' is he wants to fuck her, so stay back."

Before he could reply, Crow came out and the brothers began talking about their favorite thing—Harleys. After a couple hours of making drinks, bullshitting with the brothers, and washing what felt like his hundredth glass, loud voices pulled him away from the conversation with Goldie and Army. He looked over at the table with the hot chick and saw that a large group had formed near it.

"Watch the bar," he said to Goldie. "I wanna see what's going on." He took a few steps toward the table and saw the black-haired beauty's steely eyes as she aimed her cue stick before taking her shot. She aced the ball in the pocket, then went around the table and took another shot. Balls rolled every which way, all of them landing in the side pockets.

He quirked his lips as he watched her, admiring her grace and accuracy as she shot down the cocky bastard who, by the looks of it, bet a wad of bills on the game. When she landed the last ball, she calmly picked up the money, counted it, and tucked it in her front pocket, although he didn't know how it fit in her skintight jeans. *She's got fuckin' nerves of steel.*

"You hustled me, bitch!" Cory yelled.

She looked at him coolly. "You've never lost to a woman before, have you? I won the game fair and square."

"Bullshit." He glanced around the area at the men perched on the high-backed chairs. "Am I right? You all saw it. This bitch conned me."

The only ones in agreement were the player's friends. The other men stared placidly at him.

"Take it like a man, *Cory*," she said. "Next time you may be the winner and have someone accusing you. There's always a winner and a loser in every game." She shrugged on her leather jacket, guzzled the last of her beer, and walked away.

Cory jumped in front of her, his face bloated and red. "I want my money back, you fucking bitch." He grabbed her arms tightly.

Ready to intervene, Muerto laughed when she kicked Cory in the shin. When he raised his hand to punch her, Muerto rushed over and grabbed it in midair. "Hitting chicks isn't allowed." His voice was hard and gravelly.

"Do you allow stealing? The bitch hustled me. She's a goddamn pool shark."

Her throaty laugh fell over Muerto, and he liked that it made his dick twitch. It occurred to him that ever since he'd spotted her rounded ass in those jeans, his dick had been on high alert.

"You must've spent the weekend watching old movies. 'Pool shark,' what a joke." She zipped up her jacket.

"I've been watching you two play for the past few hours. I didn't notice anything. You play a good game, but she played better. You shouldn't bet what you can't afford to lose. Better luck next time, buddy. Go to the bar and have one on me," Muerto said.

Cory's nostrils flared as he glanced at Muerto, then back at his friends. One of them came over and clasped his shoulder. "Let's get another drink and then go find some food."

Reluctantly he started to walk away. "This ain't over yet, bitch. Let's get outta this shithole." He marched away, his two friends in tow.

"Some guys just can't handle losing to a woman. Pathetic." She slung her large purse over her shoulder and headed to the door.

"Not so fast, sweetheart." Muerto cut her off and she bumped into him.

"What the hell?" She rubbed her head.

"We both know you hustled him." He held up his hand. "Don't fuckin' deny it. You're good. I didn't even see you slip your own cue ball in the game or out of it, but I bet if I dig in that purse of yours I'd find it."

She glowered at him.

"Even though you can wear a pair of jeans better than any woman I've seen, I don't want you back in here hustling. If you didn't have tits and curves, my fists would already be beating your ass."

She raised her chin defiantly. "You can't prove shit."

He laughed. "You better wait a while and have a beer. Pretty sure they're waiting for you outside. I'll walk you to your car when I get done sorting out the receipts. The beer's on me."

"I don't need you to play the fuckin' white knight. I can take care of myself." Her gaze went to the glass doors.

"Suit yourself." He spun around and walked to the bar. When she slinked onto one of the barstools, a smile tugged at his lips. "What kind of beer do you want?"

"Give me a shot of tequila with a twist of lime." She placed her shoulder bag on the stool next to her.

"A tequila girl. You're full of surprises, sweetheart."

"What the fuck does that mean? And stop calling me 'sweetheart.' I'm no man's sweetheart." She propped her elbows on the counter and rested her chin in her hands.

"I believe that. Here you go." He placed the shot in front of her. "Let me tell you something, *sweetheart*. You're a shark in a sea of fish, but you keep it up and someone's gonna run a knife right through you. Alina's a small town, and you're playing in dangerous waters." Her flashing eyes shot daggers at him. He chuckled and held his hands up. "Just sayin', that's all."

"I thought the customer was supposed to *ask* the bartender for advice." She drank her shot. "Save your sage wisdom for someone who wants it." She twirled around on the stool, her back facing him.

"You want another?" He poured her one before she answered. "You from around here?"

She looked over her shoulder. "No." She curled her fingers around the glass.

"Where're you from?"

"Everywhere. My pop and I moved around a lot."

"Muerto, I need three shots of tequila, six Coors, and two gin and tonics," Jaime said as she perched on the barstool next to the pool hustler.

"Sure thing." Muerto turned around and grabbed the beers, then made the gin and tonics. "The guys tipping good tonight?"

"Pretty much, but those three guys stiffed me. I think they were gonna tip me but they got pissed at her"—she pointed to the woman seated next to her—"for winning the game."

The woman swiveled until she faced Jaime. "You blaming me for getting stiffed?"

"What? No, not at all. They could've tipped me as they drank. I loved that you put that big mouth in his place. He's always in here bragging about how great he is. He thinks he can beat anybody. Well... you showed him." Jaime giggled.

When the woman smiled, Muerto's dick jumped. He studied her face: nicely arched eyebrows, thick black lashes, a thin silver ring in her nose, and beautiful eyes. He'd never seen eyes like hers before. They were gray, but not an unremarkable gray like that of concrete or stone. They were the gray of the ocean an instant before dawn's first rays hit the water. And when she glanced his way, they ensnared him. She turned away quickly, and he was pretty sure he piqued her interest as much as she did his. He imagined that she was a woman who wouldn't put up with any crap from a man; a feisty woman who'd give a man a real run before she tore up the sheets with him.

She turned back around, as if sensing that he was still staring at her. "Do you want something?" A frown deepened on her forehead and her eyes turned silver, like a well-sharpened knife blade.

"Depends on what you're willing to give me." He leaned forward so his face was a scant few inches from hers. The scent of leather, smoke, and spice wisped around him.

She jumped off the stool and grabbed her shoulder bag. "Absolutely nothing. Thanks for the shots." She headed to the door.

It would serve her right if I let her go out alone. "I'll be right back," he muttered to Crow. Army and Crow whistled as he rushed out after her. In two long strides he caught up to her.

"You don't have to babysit me."

"I know. I just don't want something happening to a customer on my watch."

"Oh," she said.

She sounds disappointed. Maybe I got a chance of scoring after all. They walked to the parking lot, her heels clacking against the pavement. "Which car is yours?"

"The Impala." She pointed to a black car in the far corner of the lot.

As they approached it, Muerto saw two shadows in his peripheral view. He stopped and turned. "You dudes want something?" He clenched his fists in anticipation.

Cory and his friend cleared their throats. "I lost a key around here,"

Cory said as he dropped down to his knees and patted the asphalt.

"I think I found it," his friend said. "It was in my pocket all along." He laughed and Cory joined him as Muerto stood alert with narrowing eyes and clenched fists. "We're good, dude. Later." Cory and his buddy walked away.

"Thanks," she whispered to him.

"For what?" Muerto asked.

She nodded toward the two men disappearing into the night. "For that. I owe you." She slipped her hand in her purse and took out a keychain. The lights went on in her car when she opened the door.

"Yeah, I'd say you owe me. What about dinner tomorrow night?"

"I'm busy. I'll stop by again and we can figure it out."

He came up to her and pressed his body against hers, the scent from her perfume enveloping him. "You can pay me back now."

"In a parking lot? I don't think so." She placed her hands on his shoulders and pushed him back, then slipped into the driver seat. "Anyway, you only helped me out of a potentially sticky encounter. You didn't resurrect me. Maybe dinner, but that's being generous."

He shrugged nonchalantly, but a fire was building inside him. He wasn't used to women telling him no or giving him attitude. "You can come back, but if I see you hustling again, I'll throw you out on your sweet ass. That's a promise."

"I wouldn't expect anything less from you." She simulated a kiss with her full, pouty lips and then closed the car door. All he could think about was her lips around his cock and his hand on her perfectly rounded ass, spanking all the sass out of her.

After the red taillights of her car faded, he stood for a long time looking into the darkness. There was something about the smart-mouthed, tough woman hustler that drew him, and it surprised the hell out of him. He always drew the women in, and he didn't know what to make of it.

He slowly headed back to the pool hall.

Chapter Two

B ARS OF PRISMATIC light wavered against the wall as sunbeams shone through the chandelier's crystals. Raven had fallen in love with the vintage light fixture the minute she'd seen it at the antique store. She loved the way it sparkled when the sunlight hit it, and it lent an air of elegance to her studio.

She rented the front part of a duplex that had two bedrooms and one bathroom—plenty of space for her and Sooty, her tortoiseshell alley cat. The moment she'd seen all the windows in the house, she signed the year lease and the management company handed her the keys. She knew she'd make the back bedroom a studio, and she went to work sprucing up the place with both bold and pastel shades of color.

Raven stretched her arms over her head for several seconds, then brought them down and began rolling her head around to stretch out the kinks. Sitting for three hours hunched over while making jewelry played havoc with her neck and shoulders. When she worked on an order, she usually forgot to take stretching breaks.

She picked up the necklace she'd just finished. It was a silver chain filled with eclectic charms she'd picked up at various thrift stores, garage sales, and antique stores. She made junk jewelry and, much to her surprise and delight, there was a real market for it. She'd get into her car and scour the neighborhoods in Alina and other towns in the county looking for garage sales. Used dominoes, dice, old keys, Scrabble tiles, prizes from Cracker Jacks or vending machines, marbles, scratched medals, spools of thread, buttons, and many more trinkets were the bread and butter of her business. She made charm necklaces and bracelets, earrings made out of pop tabs, refrigerator magnets from vintage jewelry, and so many other things. She'd intersperse beads and semi-precious stones with her more expensive creations, but she mostly created beautiful pieces with things people threw away.

She sold her jewelry online, at craft fairs, through word of mouth, and to some boutiques in the larger cities and towns in Colorado. Tourists loved her bracelets and keychains, and she actually made a decent living selling them. The jewelry paid her expenses and funded her first and ardent love, acrylic painting. She was able to buy canvas, brushes, paints, and sketch pads thanks to her jewelry business. She'd sold a few of her smaller paintings at a Christmas craft fair in Denver the past holiday, and she'd decided that her dream was to own an art gallery one day.

Standing, she shook out her stiff joints and went to the kitchen. She walked over to the sink and her bare feet stepped in a puddle of water. "Shit!" The last thing she wanted to deal with was a plumbing problem. She pursed her lips together and opened a drawer by the stove. Flipping through a stack of cards, she picked up her phone and dialed the management company. *I hope that bitch isn't the one to answer.*

"Hello?"

This isn't my fuckin' day. "Hey, Deanna. This is Raven. I just stepped in a puddle of water in front of the kitchen sink."

"Did you put something down the garbage disposal you weren't supposed to? Remember how I gave you a list of things that can't go in there?"

Patronizing bitch. "Didn't put anything down there."

"Then what's the problem?"

She gritted her teeth. "I don't know. I'm not a plumber. Can you send someone out here to fix it?"

"I'm just trying to troubleshoot."

"That won't work since I don't know crap about this. Please call the plumber and send him out."

"I'll have to call the owner for approval first." She laughed. "I'll get on it right away."

"You do that." Raven slipped her phone back in her shorts pocket and sat down at the kitchen table. She glanced around her small kitchen, smiling when her gaze landed on the colorful planters housing various herbs and flowers in the garden window. When she'd seen the window, she'd been thrilled. She'd always wanted one, and it seemed like it was a good sign. After she'd signed the lease, she'd gone directly to the nursery to pick out her plants. She loved the brightness and taste of basil and cilantro, and the pop of color from the begonias and geraniums made her smile every time she walked into the white kitchen.

A car backfiring made her jump, and Sooty meowed and hopped up on the table, nuzzling her face against Raven's. "It's okay, girl," she said, scratching her cat under the chin. "I freaked out too."

Raven had been jumpy since the previous night when that goon Cory got in her face about hustling him. She'd acted indignant even though the idiot had been right; she was a pool shark. "I may have overdone it last night," she said to Sooty as she purred. "We needed the money and it was so fuckin' easy to take it from him. The macho guys are all alike. They think a woman can't possibly win a game." She laughed and scooped her cat in her arms, tucking its head under her chin.

The owner of the bar wasn't too pleased with her, but it didn't stop him from blatantly checking her out. She threw in a few peeks at him as well, but she'd at least had the decency to not be so obvious about it. *And who the hell is called Muerto? Did his mom seriously name him Death?* She doubted it. His dark, intense eyes flashed across her memory. She had to admit sexiness oozed from him, and he exuded untamed masculinity and confidence. He was definitely hot, and his dark hair, strong jaw, and well-built body made her catch her breath. She loved a tatted guy, and Muerto wore his ink well. Even though all the images of demons, skulls, and daggers were a bit off-putting, the way they curled around his taut biceps and forearms was mighty fine.

His nose was a bit off center like it had been broken a couple of times, but it was overshadowed by his full sensuous lips, perfectly arched brows, and high, sculpted cheekbones. *I bet he doesn't have a shortage of women. And he knows he's hot. He's cocky as hell, but he had on the coolest earrings.* She'd noticed them right away and was pretty sure they were handcrafted. Made of silver with turquoise and onyx accents, she'd admired the crosses and demonic skulls that had dangled from his ears.

The phone ringing stopped her musings about the pool hall's sexy owner. "Hello?"

"You got a problem with the sink? I'm the owner of the place."

"Oh, yeah, I do. There's a puddle of water on the floor in front of the kitchen sink."

His exasperated breath pricked her nerves. "Did you plug up the garbage disposal?"

"What's up with that question? Deanna asked me the same thing. No, I didn't plug the garbage disposal. I rarely use it. I know what I can and can't put in it. I'm not stupid."

A pause. "You're kind of defensive about it, aren't you?"

Frowning, she replied, "No I'm not. It's just that it seems like you all keep think—"

"I'll be over to check it out when I can," he said gruffly, and then the phone went dead.

She held the phone to her ear, not believing that her landlord had just hung up on her. *What a fuckin' asshole!* She pushed the chair back and jumped up, the sudden movement making Sooty dart away. She went to the refrigerator and pulled out a bottle of root beer. Carefully taking off the top, she placed it in a large paper bag on the counter that was filled with bottle caps. She envisioned the orange and brown cap with red beads hanging down from it. *Perfect for earrings.* She took her drink and went back to her studio.

Right in the middle of stringing beads between several colorful religious icons, she heard her front door creak open. *What the fuck?* Her heartbeat raced as the hair on her nape and arms lifted. Quietly she laid down the necklace and rose from the chair. She tiptoed from the room and pressed her back flat against the wall, craning her neck to see into the small living room. She gasped and covered her mouth with her hand. Muerto stood in the middle of the room. *What the hell?*

She rushed into the room, sparks flashing in her eyes. "What in the hell are you doing in my house?"

His eyes widened, then a small smirk played on his lips as he shoved one hand in his jeans pocket, leaned back on his heels, and looked at her. His stare washed over her from head to toe, dripping steadily.

Self-conscious, she crossed her arms over her chest as she shifted her weight from one foot to the other. All she could hear was the pounding of her heart. Fear ricocheted across her skin as a clammy sweat ran down her back. She inhaled deeply. "Well? You haven't told me why you're in my house." Her voice was calm and collected, but her insides were exploding.

With his gaze fixed on her crossed arms, he clucked his tongue. "You said you had water on the floor. I came to check it out."

Shuffling back a couple of steps, she said, "*You're* the owner? That figures."

He shook his head and raised his eyes to hers. "Well, you're not exactly the kind of tenant I'd choose." He started to walk to the kitchen.

"What does that mean?" She followed him.

"You figure it out." Stopping by the sink, he looked around the kitchen. "What the fuck did you do in here?"

"What is it with you and your management company asking me that fuckin' question? I didn't do anything except come in here and step into a puddle of water. Why is that so hard to understand? Am I missing something here?"

His gaze traveled up from her bare feet to her face. He pressed his lips together. "You got a real mouth on you." She rolled her eyes. "I'm not sure what's gonna get you in the most trouble—your sass, attitude, or hustling." He bent down and opened the cupboard under the sink. He felt around the pipes, then straightened up. "You need a plumber." He brushed past her.

"Are you for real?"

He looked over his shoulder, his eyes dancing with amusement. "You know I am. And earlier, I was asking you what the fuck you did to the kitchen walls. You painted them yellow without my permission."

"They were white and boring." She scratched her arm as his gaze bored into her. "What? Do you want me to repaint them?"

"I want you to ask permission next time you want to change shit around here. You're lucky I like women with round asses and nice tits."

Her hand flew to her chest as her eyes widened. "How rude. Who do you think you are?"

"Your landlord." He pointed to Sooty, who was rubbing against her legs. "I also don't allow pets. Didn't Deanna tell you?"

"No, and it's not in the lease."

His lip curled. "When renewal comes along, I'll have to fix that."

"Don't bother. I highly doubt I'll be renewing." Her chest rose up and down. "And next time ring the fuckin' doorbell. You don't have a right to just come in here when you want."

He stiffened visibly and she saw him clench his fist. "I do whatever the fuck I want, sweetheart. Just remember that." A tense silence filled the space between them as they stared at each other until his phone pinged. Glancing at it, he said, "I'll send the plumber out." He strode out of the house and down the walkway.

She went over and slammed the door, hoping she'd break the amber glass in it, but she wasn't having much luck that day—the window didn't even shake. She looked out and saw him on his Harley. He turned to her and flashed a cocky smile, then revved his engine and sped away. As she watched him ride off, she noticed how broad his shoulders were. *Ugh! I can't believe that jerk is my landlord.* Clenching her teeth, she stalked to the kitchen and pulled out one of the drawers. Flipping through numerous business cards, she smiled widely when she found the one she'd been looking for—Dave's Lock & Key. She dialed the number.

"I need someone to come out here and rekey my locks."

By the time she'd hung up the phone, she had it all set up to change the locks on her front and back door. She picked up Sooty and ran her hands over the cat's soft fur. "He's not the only one who does what the fuck he wants." Sooty purred as Raven stroked her, satisfaction coursing through her veins.

Chapter Three

THE SWELTERING HEAT encased Muerto as he rode past the businesses on Main Street. The trees that lined each side of the road stood mute in the summer air. He sped past telephone poles that dotted the dry landscape on his way to the clubhouse. The earth was baked as hard as concrete, and the cracks that zigzagged on it were like wrinkles on an old face. Rain had been sparse that summer, and the usual wildflowers that lent a punch of color to the landscape were in short supply.

The summer sun beat upon his back, forcing beads of sweat down his neck. In the distance, reddish-brown rock with patches of green pines loomed, their craggy peaks absent of the snow they sported most of the year. Muerto pushed his black skull bandana closer to his hairline. *I can't believe the pool hustler with the cute ass is my tenant.* His chest shook as he laughed. *If she fucks the way she moves, this could be a lot of fun.* He had no doubt that she'd end up in his bed, as most women did. He hadn't been blind to the way she checked him out the previous night at the pool hall, and a woman who ran her eyes over a man's body was a woman who wanted that man. That'd always been his motto, and the number of women who'd enjoyed his sexual skills over the years had reinforced it.

As he slowed down to take a sharp turn, he heard his phone ringing. Knowing it could be one of the brothers, he made the turn and then pulled over. A brother had to always be available if there was a club emergency or a member needed his help. He glanced at the number and saw it was his sister. For a split second he debated on whether he should answer it before he placed the phone to his ear.

"What's up, Laura?"

"Where are you? You were supposed to be over here like twenty minutes ago." Muerto racked his brain trying to remember why he was—"You forgot, didn't you?"

"No. Just running behind, that's all." He made a U-turn and headed back to the main road. He'd hoped the reason he was meeting Laura would come to him.

"Okay. I just want everything to be perfect for Ma's birthday, that's all."

The birthday party. That's right. Fuck. "I do too. I'm on my way."

Muerto parked his bike in front of Laura's home in a working-class neighborhood where all of the houses were either red or brown brick and had green squares of yard in the front and back. In the summer, the porches were filled with gossiping mothers watching their kids as they frolicked. Every once in a while the high-pitched tunes of the ice cream truck would pierce through the laughter and the children would scramble over to the curb, fidgeting in place as they waited for the white van with colorful popsicles plastered on it to appear.

As he wiped his face and neck with a rag, his two nephews and his niece came tearing out of the house, waving at him as they raced by. Laura came toward him, shaking her head. "Sorry about that. They heard the ice cream truck."

"What can I say? That's some stiff competition." He smiled at her. "How've you been? You look tired."

She shrugged. "I'm okay. It's just so damn hot. Let's go inside."

He followed her up the porch steps into the house. Cool air surrounded him. "When did you put the AC in?"

"A couple of months ago. It's been a lifesaver. That guy you recommended gave us a killer price. Do you want a pop or some water?"

"A beer would be great."

"In the middle of the afternoon?"

"Yeah." He sank down on one of the cushy chairs and crossed his leg over his thigh. "So does Ma know about her birthday party?"

She handed him a Coors. "No. You didn't hint at anything, did you?" He shook his head and she visibly relaxed. "I'm trying to keep it a secret. It'll be real nice. You said that you'd help with getting a place to have it. I'm thinking of having about a hundred people."

"Really? Fuck, that's a big party. I thought it was just a few close friends and family."

"Well, you know how that goes. If I invite Aunt Martha, then I have to invite Cousin Julia, and on and on it goes."

"I guess. I'll get the place. We've got about a month, right?"

"Six weeks, to be exact. Don't forget to do it. We need to secure a place now before it fills up. A lot of people get married in the summer. And speaking of that, it'd be great if you could bring a nice girl to the party. Ma worries that you'll never get married and have a family. I worry about it too."

"How the hell did this go from me getting a place for a party to you meddling into my personal life? I've told you before to leave it alone. I can guarantee you that I'm not lonely." He took another gulp of beer.

"I didn't say you didn't have women to fill your nights. I'm talking about the quality of the women. I know the type who hang around at your clubhouse."

"What's wrong with them? They're nice chicks. You don't even know them so don't go judging them."

Laura stretched her legs out on the couch. "Would you bring them over to Ma's to introduce them?" He shook his head. "I knew it. Why can't you find a decent girl? Someone you *can* introduce to Ma."

"What makes you think I want a *decent* girl? I like them wild—it's more fun. Anyway, I don't wanna settle down."

"Ever?"

He shrugged. "How the fuck do I know? I'm just not interested in a relationship right now. Leave it alone or I go." He set the can on the end table.

"You're impossible. You're going to wake up one day and be old and alone."

He waved his hand at her. "Yeah, whatever. Are we done here?"

"No. We need to talk about the food and the decorations. I was thinking we could do a theme. I think Ma would love that. Do you have any ideas on that?"

He ran his hand through his hair. "No. Do what you want. I'll get a place for the party and give you the money for it, but that's where my involvement ends."

"Mateo, I need your help."

"No, you don't, and don't call me that. Mateo's been gone for a long time." Eleven years, to be exact. Once he'd hit eighteen, he'd signed on as a prospect for the Night Rebels and he never looked back. He wished his family would accept that part of his life instead of pretending it wasn't real or it was just temporary.

"I refuse to call you Muerto. I mean, do you seriously want people to call you Death?"

He looked at her stone-faced. "Yeah. Fuckin' deal with it." She shook her head. "Then call me M like your kids do, but don't call me Mateo. Only one who can do that is Ma."

"I'm the oldest, so I should be telling *you* what to do. I hate when you do this shit. I mean, you act like everything I do or say is petty. When you do that, you're telling me you think my life is insignificant and a big fucking joke." Her voice cracked and she covered her face with her hands.

Muerto, at a loss for words, sat and stared at her. *What the fuck just happened?* As she sniffled he grew more uncomfortable. He hated when a woman cried, even though he should've been used to it since he'd grown up with a single mom and two sisters. But he wasn't, and it would always rip through him when one of them would cry.

He wiped his sweaty hands on his jeans. "I'm sorry. I didn't mean to upset you. And I don't think your life is insignificant. I mean, look at you. You're a kickass mom, you manage to keep a good home for your kids, look terrific, and have time to make Joe feel like a king in his house. I think you're fuckin' great. I just don't tell you that very often."

Instead of the teary giggles he was used to, she broke out into low, breathy sobs. He stood up and went over to her, gently tugging her to him even though she resisted.

She finally relaxed and buried her face in his T-shirt. He held her as her body heaved and her nose ran. He grabbed a paper napkin from the coffee table and handed it to her. She took it and pulled back a bit, her puffy eyes red and wet as she blew her nose. She leaned back against the couch and smoothed her dark hair down. "Sorry for that. I know how you hate a crying woman." She laughed through her tears.

"No worries. What's going on? You've been on edge since I got here. Are you pissed off at me about something?"

She wiped her nose again and breathed out. "I think Joe's cheating on me."

"Fuck," he muttered under his breath. "Are you sure?"

She nodded. "I found lipstick on one of his shirts yesterday, and I've had at least three hang-up calls this morning. And he changed the password to his computer."

He put his hand on her forearm. "Do you think it's with someone in Alina or when he's on the road?" Joe was a long-distance truck driver who usually spent ten days at a stretch on the interstates. He'd come home for a few days and then be back on the road for another stretch. Muerto admired the way his sister handled raising her children and dealing with the absence of her husband. As he watched her heart breaking in front of him, a slow burn started to ignite his nerves. All he wanted to do was find his fucking brother-in-law and beat the shit out of him.

"I think it's someone local. All the time he's been driving, I never suspected him of cheating. He never gave me a reason to, but for the past few months he's been acting real restless. I know I've been tired and not in the mood, but I've gone back to work to make up for the cut in hours Joe said he's had. Now I wonder if I've been working to help him have some free time to spend with *her*."

"Maybe he's just been going to the strip bar. A new one's opened up in town. I can check it out for you to see if he's been hanging around there." He'd seen Joe many times at Lust, but each time Muerto had been there, he'd never seen Joe act inappropriately with any of the dancers or waitresses. He was just a guy with a couple of his friends enjoying a beer and a few dances from some hot women. It'd always seemed innocent enough to him, and he'd never thought of mentioning it to Laura. He hadn't wanted to start any problems between them, and as long as Joe had kept his hands away and his dick zipped up, he'd been cool with it. But he hadn't seen Joe at Lust in the last few months.

"If you could do that for me, that'd be great, but I don't want you confronting him. I'll deal with this. I'm probably overreacting. It's just been such a hot summer."

He clenched his jaw. "Let me know if you need anything. And quit your fuckin' job. You got enough shit to take care of with the kids, the house, and Ma."

Before she could say anything, his nephews and niece banged open the screen door, the remnants of their red popsicles around their mouths.

"Uncle M," they cried excitedly as they rushed over to him. He gathered Lorena in his arms, and she snuggled against him while Javier and Carlos sat next to him, Carlos wedging in between Muerto and Laura.

After a couple hours of roughhousing with the kids, Muerto glanced at his phone. "I gotta go. I have some stuff I have to finish before I head over to the pool hall." He gave Lorena, Javier, and Carlos a big bear hug and then walked over to the door. Laura followed him outside. He pulled her to him and hugged her. "I'll look into things for you," he whispered in her ear.

She raised her hand up over her eyes, shielding them from the western sun. "I'm sure it's nothing. Please don't say anything to Joe. Promise me?"

He looked away, the fire that had started when she'd first told him about her suspicions still raging inside him. He couldn't promise her what she wanted. "I'll try not to beat the shit outta him if I find out he's been a fuckin' louse." He shook his head when she pushed him back a little with her hands. "That's the best I can give you."

She nodded as she fanned herself with her hand. "Remember to book the place for Ma's birthday party." He pulled out a wad of bills and gave them to her. "What's this?"

"It's for Ma's party and whatever else you need." She tried to hand it back to him, but he ran down the steps. "Stop working. If you need me for anything, give me a call."

"Mateo, I don't need this much money. We're supposed to split the party. Mateo… are you listening to me?"

He shook his head, smiled and waved at her, then jumped on his bike and took off before she reached the curb. He wished Laura would let him help her family more, but he knew she was a proud woman—sometimes too much. At least she let him pay for the kids' private school tuition, but it had taken the intervention of his mother, the parish priest, and all three of her kids before she'd accepted his offer.

He swung a left on Trail Ridge Road and went south toward his rental. He wanted to see what his sassy tenant was up to before he found Joe and ripped him a new asshole. Muerto was so pissed that he knew he'd have to hit the gym to pound out his aggression on a punching bag or else he was liable to use someone's face later that night at Balls and Holes.

When he rode up to the duplex, there was no sign of her and disappointment weaved through him, making him even more pissed than he already was. *What the fuck do I care if she's around or not? I'm just bored.* He spotted Walter rolling up the hose. Walter was the tenant who lived in the back part of the duplex. He parked his Harley and went over to him.

The man looked up and smiled at him. "How are you?" he asked.

"Good. I was just in the neighborhood. Everything going good with your place?"

Walter nodded. "I don't have any complaints."

"You getting along with the woman who lives in the front?" *Why the fuck am I asking him about* her?

The tenant's eyes narrowed. "Did she say something to you?" His voice dripped ice.

Taken aback, Muerto shook his head. "Nah, I was just wondering. She didn't say anything. You good with her?"

His face softened. "Yeah. I rarely see her, but when I do, we get along fine. She seems like a nice girl."

"Cool. Let me help you with the hose." As he rolled it up, he glanced at Walter. He'd been his tenant for the past five years, but he was an odd fellow. He never talked about anything personal, and Muerto wasn't sure if he had a woman or not. He never brought up women or his parents or friends, or anyone. It was like the man lived in a cocoon, sheltered from the rest of the world. He seemed harmless enough, but Muerto thought there was more to him than he was letting on.

"Thanks for helping out," the tenant said as he placed the hose on the holder.

"Sure. The yard's looking good," Muerto said as he started to leave. "If you need anything, let me know."

"Shouldn't I call the management company? Does Deanna still work there?"

"Uh… yeah, you'd give them a call first. Deanna's still there. Why?"

"Every time I call over there, a man tells me she isn't available."

"Maybe she's busy when you call."

"Every single time? This has been going on for over two months."

Muerto watched as the man's face started to redden and his body stiffened. *The dude's real pissed. I'll have to give Deanna a call.* "What do you have going on over here that you need to call that much? Is there a problem in the unit?"

Walter's gaze drilled into Muerto and he returned it. After several seconds, the tenant glanced away, a small chuckle escaping from his throat. "It's really nothing. I've only called a few times over minor things, like the new trash cans the county made us get."

The guy's a fuckin' weirdo. "If you have trouble getting ahold of someone, you have my number. Use it." He turned around and went to his Harley. Glancing over at the window in the front unit, he swore he saw the blinds move. *I bet she's inside, checking me out. Well feast your eyes on what you may or may not get, sweetheart.* At that moment, he'd decided that she'd have to work to get into his bed. He'd planned on making it easy, but a woman who had that much sass and sexiness had to be taken down a couple of notches, and he was just the man to do it.

He revved his cams for effect and then roared away, sensing her eyes on his every movement. Being a landlord had just become a whole lot more interesting.

Chapter Four

RAVEN WATCHED AS Muerto pulled away from the curb. *He's such an insufferable jerk.* She stared a long time at the road, well after he'd disappeared from sight. There was something about him that pulled at her, and it was more than his dangerously good looks. *The last thing I need is to get involved with another asshole. One was enough for a lifetime.*

Raven's ex-boyfriend, Brent, popped into her mind. She'd met him in Las Vegas about a year and a half before, and she'd fallen hard for him. She'd worked in the coffee shop of one of the big hotels and Brent had been in her section. He and a few buddies were in town for six months working on a large construction project. When he'd gazed at her with his dreamy blue eyes, she'd been immediately smitten. Never in her life had the attraction been that intense, so when he'd asked her to join him for lunch the following day, she readily accepted.

For the next six months, they were practically inseparable, and a week before Brent was to leave, he'd asked her to come with him to Alina. Without thinking, she'd told him yes. She worried about her dad being alone, but then he'd met a lady who liked to drink, party, and barbecue—the three musts for her dad. The fact that she was a well-off widow was an added bonus. So she'd moved to Alina with Brent, eager, happy, and excited to start a new chapter in her life.

She'd fallen in love with the town the minute she saw the sun casting golden rays on the red rock formations. The area had a peaceful, spiritual feel to it, and she'd immediately felt like she had finally found her home after years on the road with her dad. She and Brent had settled into a small bungalow that had a huge yard where she grew vegetables and herbs. Brent traveled about two weeks a month on small construction projects around the state. She'd begun making jewelry while continuing to paint, and their time together was idyllic until she'd answered the door one beautiful, late-spring day.

A woman who'd looked to be in her late twenties had stood on the porch, a small boy on her hip and two small girls next to her. She'd introduced herself as Brent's wife and told her the children were his. The weeks he'd told Raven he was away working, he was staying with his wife in northern Colorado. The betrayal had ripped out her heart.

In the past few months, she'd begun to heal. *I'm doing just fine on my own.*

She went to the small mudroom off the kitchen and picked up her watering can, sun hat, and garden gloves. Even though she found Muerto extremely attractive, she hated his "I'm so badass" attitude. Men were good at breaking women's hearts, but the cocky ones were the worst of all. She'd seen plenty of women throw their lives away on a well-built bad boy. A couple of her waitress friends back in Vegas had done that, and they were left with nothing but tears. Raven was done with tears—she'd spent them all on Brent—and swore that no man would ever hurt her again. Besides, she loved being on her own; she was free to do whatever she wanted.

She opened the back door and walked around to the front where she'd planted a small vegetable garden. She adjusted her hat, put on her gloves, and bent down to pull the weeds.

"You're looking good," a voice said from behind her.

Doesn't the creep have a job? "Hey, Walter." She kept pulling without even a sideways look at him.

"Your peppers look good. Very delicious… like you."

Her insides twisted. *He's such a fuckin' ass.* "I'm kinda busy here, you know?" She wiped the sweat trickling down the side of her face.

"I'm just being neighborly."

"I know, but I'm not in a chatty mood right now. I'll give you some peppers in a bit, okay?"

From the corner of her eye she saw him cross his arms. "I hate peppers."

She shrugged and he stalked off. A sigh of relief blew from her parted lips, and she began attacking the weeds more earnestly. A few minutes later, she heard squeaking behind her and turned around. A small shiver zinged up her spine as she met Walter's hard gaze. The guy had placed his lawn chair right behind her, in full view of her butt. Redness crept up her neck as she suddenly became aware of how short her shorts were.

With a beer bottle in one hand, he stretched out his legs in front of him and continued staring at her. Determined not to let him rattle her, she turned back to her task. The asshole unnerved her; he was always staring and watching her every move. It was like she was an insect under a magnifying glass.

All at once, he started breathing heavily behind her, and the resolve to ignore him slipped away from her. She stood up, quickly watered the plants, and then picked up the bag of weeds. Without even a glance, she headed to the side of the house.

"You're doing a great job with your garden, little lady. I know you can hear me. If you don't like me looking at you in your cute shorts, you shouldn't wear them. But I bet you love the attention, don't you? Women like you—"

She slammed the door, cutting off his ugly words and insinuations. *I can't stand that creep.* Ever since she'd moved in, he'd made her uncomfortable. At first she'd thought he was just trying to be friendly in an awkward, socially inept way, but as his movements and words became bolder, she decided he was just an asshole. Lately, he'd begun to make her feel dirty and violated by his words and actions. She wished he'd just stop. Everything about her rental was great except for him.

And the landlord. Raven groaned and Sooty perked up her ears. She still couldn't fathom that Muerto was her landlord. She'd been in the unit for months and had never had any dealings with him. *Maybe I should tell him about Walter.* But what would she say? That Walter stared at her? Muerto stared at her plenty, boldly assessing her and not giving a shit how it made her feel. *How does it make me feel when he checks me out?* Excited. Nervous. Pissed. But she liked it when he showed that he liked what he saw. With Walter, it just made her feel icky.

No, Muerto wouldn't understand about Walter. He'd probably come over and join him the next time she was gardening.

Men... ugh!

The ringing phone interrupted her as she poured some dry food in Sooty's bowl. Setting it down on the floor, she put the phone to her ear.

"Hello?"

"This is Deanna. Did the plumber come out and fix your sink?"

"Yeah, he came out last night. The landlord really delivered fast on this one. I should deal with him directly all the time." She laughed.

"Don't call him. You need to deal with me or Jay. I'll talk to Mr. Ruiz. Do you understand?" Her voice was tight.

Is this the hour of freaks? First Walter and then this one. "He told me to call him if anything comes up, but I'm dealing with you guys. As long as the problem gets taken care of, I'm good."

"He *told* you to call him? Why would he do that?"

Her foot locked under the chair and she dragged it from the table, plopping down on it, a frown etched on her face. "I don't know, Deanna." Sighing, she tapped her foot against the hardwood floor. "Is there anything else you wanted?"

"No. I just want to reiterate that if you have any problems, please call me or Jay, not Mr. Ruiz. We'll make sure he knows if there's a problem. Do you understand?"

Raven clutched the phone. "Well, I don't know, Deanna. It seems kinda complicated to comprehend. I gotta go. Bye." She clicked off, anger riding down her spine. "She drives me fuckin' crazy. She acts like she's in love with him or something." She picked up Sooty and kissed the side of her face. "Today's my day for weirdos. It's better when I stay in the house and don't answer the phone. We don't need them, do we?" She smiled when her cat meowed and moved her ears forward.

She pushed away from the table and went to the back room, Sooty padding behind her. When she picked up her paintbrush and dipped it into yellow acrylic paint, she laughed. "Can you imagine what our landlord would say to what I've done to this room?" Sooty stared at her. "He'd be pissed. A guy that cocky needs to come down from his pedestal a bit. I bet he always gets his way with women." She glanced at the large paint can in the corner. She'd planned on painting the room turquoise, but she'd been so busy filling jewelry orders that she'd put it on the back burner.

She grinned. "Guess what we're gonna do this weekend, Sooty. We're gonna paint this room and I may even paint a goddamn rainbow on the back wall." She had no idea why she was taking such pleasure in defying and goading him, but she was. Something about him made her nervous and excited. She had to make sure to push him far away from her, and what better way than showing him that she was the one woman who wouldn't fall for his good looks and swagger.

Her hand moved over the canvas, creating many small dots of color on the buildings in the city scene to give the illusion of texture. She worked furiously, loving that her unfounded anger at her landlord fueled her on. Each time she saw his smart-assed face in her mind, she stippled faster, and when she remembered his arrogant words, she painted more passionately.

After several hours of nonstop painting, she stepped back and viewed her efforts. The folkloric city jumped off the canvas, and she could feel the pull of the twinkling stars, the brightly lit windows, and the rolling hills in blue, purple, and pink. She smiled as elation spread through her. She was going to have to think about pissing off her landlord more often; it made her paint well.

Chuckling, she gathered her brushes and headed to the kitchen to wash them out and then figure out what to eat for dinner. Maybe she'd take a trip to the pool hall soon. She may even do a bit of hustling; nothing big like the last time, just a few bucks.

And if he gives me attitude, I'll give it back to him tenfold. After all, the cockier they were, the sweeter it was to pull them down.

Chapter Five

MUERTO LEANED HIS chair back against the concrete wall as he watched his brothers sliding into their chairs. Steel had called church to address the issue of the new strip club, the Climax Lounge, off Ash and Cedar.

"Did Zach stay until closing last night?" Crow slipped into the chair next to his.

"Yeah. Jaime stayed extra to help wash the glasses." He ran his hand over his five o'clock shadow. He had such a thick beard that if he wanted to stay clean-shaven, he had to shave a couple of times a day. The women seemed to like the roughness of his beard, so he usually left it for a few days.

"Jaime? She always seems like she can't wait to haul ass outta there after her shift. Did some lucky guy pick up Brandy?" Crow took a gulp from his Dr. Pepper.

"You've got the hots bad for her, dude."

"Wish the feeling was mutual. She's into you. You should try her out sometime. I bet she'd show you all kinds of fun." He raised his eyebrows.

Muerto laughed. "She's an employee, so off-limits. Anyway, she doesn't do it for me. I know she's hot and all, but even if she didn't work for the club, I wouldn't be interested."

"Are you fuckin' nuts? If she offered her primo body to you, you'd turn it down?"

"I'm not saying that. I mean, if she *gave* herself to me, I wouldn't turn her down. I just wouldn't pursue her. There's a difference." Muerto leaned forward on his chair and grabbed a beer that was in a cooler on top of the table. He twisted the top open and took a long pull.

"Well, I'd fuck her good and hard if she even looked at me. I know you got your eyes on that pool shark. What the fuck's her deal? Did she come in last night after I left?"

Muerto's jaw hardened. "No, and I definitely don't have my eye on *her*." The night before, he'd been hoping she'd drop by, but she didn't, and it pissed him off to no end. But what really got him was that he even gave a shit whether she came in or not. *She's nothing to me. Why the fuck do I care if I ever see her again? She's nothing but a mouthy pool hustler who happens to be my tenant. So what if she's gorgeous and sexy? I can get gorgeous and sexy any day of the week.*

"We ready to start here?" Steel's deep voice filled the room, silencing the idle chatter. He raised his bent knee and rested his foot on a chair. "We've got a new strip club in town. It's called the Climax Lounge." Snickers circled around the room. "I know, fucking clever. Anyway, we don't have a problem if another strip bar opens in Alina, but this one happens to be run by Jimmy Delarosa, and we know what a greasy fucker he is." The brothers laughed as they voiced their agreement with their president.

"You think it's a front for laundering? Remember the scam that asshole was doing a while back?" Goldie brought a can of Pepsi to his mouth.

"I thought the attorney general sent him to the pen for scamming all those old people," Chains said.

Paco stood up, whistling loudly through his teeth. The members quieted down. "The slimebag did a two-year stint for screwing old people out of their money, but he's back and running the strip club. Since he's involved, we know it's a slimy operation. The question is who the fuck is backing it?"

"Also, there're rumors that he's hiring underage girls, and that's bullshit." Steel's green eyes flashed. "No way we're gonna tolerate *that* in our county."

"Where are the rumors coming from?" Muerto asked.

Steel leaned forward. "I bumped into Sheriff Wexler when I was coming out of the hardware store yesterday, and he casually mentioned it to me. He told me that he'd been in there but all the women had good IDs. Said a couple of parents have complained that their daughters got hired at the club to clean tables and sweep up."

Muerto pushed his chair back roughly. "I'm so fuckin' tired of the badges wanting us to do their goddamn jobs. Wexler's got a few deputies. Why don't they figure this shit out? They're nothing but a bunch of inept dumbasses with handcuffs. Fuckin' morons." He shook his head as several of the brothers voiced their agreement with him.

"That may well be, and we *do* count on their ineptness, but do I have to remind you that we were able to score a half-million dollars on our last gun run while Wexler and his deputies looked the other way?" Paco darted his eyes to each of the brothers. "We need the badges to stay the fuck outta our business."

"Paco's right," Steel said. "We need to check this out. Delarosa's gotta know we won't tolerate that shit. When he got back in town a few months ago, Diablo and I went over and basically told him that if he wants to keep walking, he'll respect our rules. And that means no scamming the old residents, no messing with girls under eighteen, and no drug dealing. Knowing him, he's fucking up."

"Where'd he get the money to start the club? He must've stashed a shitload of the dough he got from scamming. I heard he'd bilked millions. I thought the government got the bulk of it," Sangre said.

"That's what we gotta find out. You're working on that, right, Chains?" Steel jerked his chin toward him.

"Yeah. So far it looks like Delarosa was a dumb fuck and didn't even try to hide the dough. The state got whatever was left. They've been giving it back to the victims. He didn't put the money into this club, not from what I can see."

"He's too stupid to have done it. He's got backing," Eagle said as he rolled a joint.

"I can snoop around and see about the underage girls. I gotta go in there and check some shit out for a family matter anyway," Muerto said.

"Sounds good. Let me know what you think," Steel replied. "Before we hear from Sangre about the various businesses and their income, I want to let you know that Breanna wants to get a lot more businesses involved in the October biker rally. She wants this year to be the biggest year for the amount of money we raise for Bikers Against Child Abuse. So if you know anyone who has a business and wants to rent a booth, hit me up, or have them call Breanna directly. Now let's go over some routine business…."

Muerto tuned out the rest of the meeting. As long as he got his cut from the club's businesses, he was good. The dispensary was booming in both medicinal and recreational marijuana sales, and the income from the club's other dealings gave him more money than he ever dreamed he'd have. The good income enabled him to help out his mother and sisters, plus buy several properties in and around Alina. Each member had a share in the club's profits, and the rest of the money was rolled back into the club.

Soon church was over and the brothers headed to the large room where the prospects had their drinks waiting for them, and the club girls had their warm bodies ready. The brothers milled around as Muerto went up to the bar and picked up the beer Ruger placed in front of him. Before he could bring it to his lips, Ruby came up next to him, her strong floral scent making his eyes water.

"You interested in a little lovin'?" she said as she rubbed against his arm.

He smiled. "I would be if I didn't have to go to work. Sorry. Another time, okay?" He drank a deep gulp.

Ruby pushed her lips out in a pout. "All you do lately is work. And when you're here, you're too tired because you worked too hard. I'm dyin' here, baby." Long nails scratched up and down his arm, pebbling his skin.

He cupped her chin. "I don't think you're gonna die if I don't fuck you. I already see you eyeing Brutus." He brushed his finger over her lips. "You know I'm right. Go on over to him. I know you both want it."

"You sure you're good?" she asked, though she was already walking away from him. Not waiting for his answer, she hurried to Brutus, who enclosed her in his massive embrace.

Muerto chuckled and then drained his beer.

As he argued with Army and Chains about the hottest women *Easy Rider* had used in its magazine, his phone rang. He looked at it and saw the management company's name flashing.

"I gotta take this, guys." He walked outside and answered the phone.

"Hi, Muerto. I was just wondering if you were going to be at the pool hall tonight."

"Oh, hey, Deanna. Yeah, I'm working tonight. Why? Is something up?"

"I have a lease I need to bring over to you to sign on one of the apartments in the Duncan Street property."

"Can't it just wait until tomorrow? I can swing by the office."

"Tomorrow's my day off, so that won't work."

"Just give it to Jay."

"That won't work either. He's going to be inspecting tomorrow for some of our other clients. What's wrong with me coming by the pool hall? Don't you want me there?"

"No, that's cool. I just thought I'd save you the trip."

"You know it's not a bother for me," she said softly.

He breathed out. "Okay. Then I'll see you later. I'll be there in an hour."

"Perfect. I'm looking forward to it." Her giddiness and excitement pricked his ears.

After she hung up, he slipped his phone in his pocket and ran both hands through his thick hair. Deanna sounded professional, but a tinge of neediness came through loud and clear. About eight months back, he'd made a stupid mistake and spent a week fucking Deanna's brains out. She was an attractive woman and it'd been a cold, rainy night, and when she'd invited him into her house to wait out the storm, he'd accepted.

He'd thought she had a nice rack and a great pair of legs. He loved the way she'd wear her tight skirts that showed off her toned calves and her rounded hips, but he stayed back because she was a professional contact. But that night, in her house with the fire crackling in the fireplace, his glass full of whiskey, and her soft willing body too close to him, he'd thought "What the fuck?"

They had an intense, short-lived, torrid affair, and when he'd decided it was time to move on, he'd thought she was on the same page. It wasn't like he'd promised her anything. As he remembered it, he'd told her it was just a fling and he didn't do relationships or long-term anything, and she'd agreed. But then he'd had to endure several teary, whiny phone calls and meetings until she finally understood.

Women were always doing that shit to him: saying they understood it was just a fling, then cussing him out and accusing him of taking advantage of them when he walked away after the passion had died for him.

As much as he could, he limited contact with her, preferring to deal with Jay. But every once in a while, he had to talk with her, go over business contracts and leases, and even meet her without the benefit of Jay being there.

Going back into the clubhouse, he grabbed another Dos Equis, downed it, bullshitted a bit more, and then headed to Balls and Holes for his shift.

Chapter Six

A LL THE POOL tables were filled, and Brandy and Jaime were rushing around filling orders as Muerto made the drinks as fast as he could. Of course Zach was a no-show. This was the third time that week. He'd called an hour after he was supposed to be at the hall with some inane excuse that Muerto couldn't even remember. *The dude's history. I'm gonna get another bartender. This is bullshit.* He'd started off working out great, but his work ethic was disintegrating.

"You doing okay?" Brandy asked after she yelled out her order.

"Yeah. Zach's ass is history though. I contacted one of my buddies to help out. How're you holding up?"

"Okay. I didn't think we'd be this crowded on a weeknight. I'm not complaining though. I like the tips, but I woulda worn shorter heels if I'd known I'd be on my feet all night. You got my order, cutie?"

He chuckled and placed the drinks on her tray. She smiled seductively at him and hoisted the tray up as she headed over to the tables. *She does have a fine ass. Maybe Crow's got a point. I bet she would be a lot of fun in the sack.*

"Did you finish making my order?" Jaime asked as she came up to the bar.

"Ready in a sec." As he prepared the drinks, he looked her over. "You look nice tonight," he said as he admired her low-cut top.

She blushed a deep red. "Thanks. Brandy told me to wear something more provocative so I could get bigger tips. She always beats me hands-down on the amount of tips we get when we work a shift together. I have to admit her advice is working." She bit her lower lip.

"I can see why. Hell, if you were my waitress, I'd give you a big tip if

I saw you in that top." He winked at her as he put the last drink on her tray.

"Thank you," she said demurely, her cheeks red as beets.

He chuckled as she scampered away.

A bit earlier, he'd texted Skull to see if he could help him out at the bar, and a wide smile spread across his face when he saw his brother walk in. With a pierced lip, eyebrows, ears, and a ton of tattoos depicting all sorts of mayhem, Skull scared the shit out of most citizens. Add the messy blond hair, his six-foot-two height, and a bulk of muscle, and people literally moved out of the way when the twenty-eight-year-old outlaw entered a room. That night was no different, as several men shooting pool stopped and moved slightly to the right when Skull walked toward the bar.

"Glad you could help me out, brother. We're fuckin' slammed to-night." Muerto moved down to the other end of the bar, giving Skull his place at the end nearest the entrance.

"No problem. Any worthwhile chicks here tonight?" He bent down and pulled out a couple of whiskey and bourbon bottles.

"A few. Dudes mostly hang in here."

"Damn, she's a beauty. I'd love to get lost between those tits." Skull stopped what he was doing and stared straight ahead.

Muerto followed his line of vision and spotted Brandy leaning down real low to place a few drinks on a table where three men sat. "She's off-limits. Works for the club."

"Fuck. Let me know if she ever quits." He resumed what he was doing.

"Hiya, Muerto."

He swiveled around and saw Deanna settling on a barstool. She was wearing patterned stockings, a tight, short black skirt, and a low-cut animal print top. In his opinion, her makeup was a bit overdone, but she had a nice figure that he was sure most men would find attractive. "Hey. We're really busy tonight. I'll look over those papers in a bit. I gotta catch up. What do you want to drink?"

"A glass of chardonnay would be lovely. Take your time. I'm not in a hurry."

He poured her a glass and went back to filling the orders that kept coming in. As he worked, he felt Deanna's eyes on him. Thankful Skull was there to help, he finished an order and walked back to Deanna. "So let me see the lease. Did you do the background check on the tenant?"

"Tenants—they're a couple—and I did a background on them." She pulled out a manila folder from her large black bag, took out the lease, and handed it to him. "Here you go. It's the standard residential lease."

He reviewed it. "We need to revamp the leases. Add a couple of clauses about no pets and no painting the walls without my permission. The rest of it looks good. Once you do that, I'll sign it." He handed it back to her. "Want another glass of wine?"

She nodded and grasped his hand. "Yes. Thank you."

Slipping his hand from under hers, he tilted his chin, and then he sensed *her*. Amid all the noise, the crush of people, the clack of balls, he heard her throaty laugh. He turned and there she was, her long hair touching her ass, which was more delectable in dark-wash skinny jeans. Her red fitted top skimmed her body and her four-inch black pumps made her legs look impossibly long. The crystal in her nose ring caught the light and sparkled, drawing his eye. *She looks fuckin' fabulous. And she knows it.*

Looking at her as she walked by, her hips swaying, her hand tossing her hair over her shoulder, he whistled softly under his breath. When she went to one of the pool tables without even shooting him a sidelong glance, he knew she was purposely dissing him. Instead of pissing him off, excitement punched his gut. *You wanna play a game, sweetheart? You're fuckin' on.* Muerto was usually the one who ignored the chicks, acting like they didn't exist. It surprised and challenged him that his sexy tenant wasn't drooling over him. *At least not yet.*

"I do miss you. Why don't you want to go out with me anymore?" Deanna whined.

For the last few minutes, he'd completely forgotten Deanna was there. He'd tuned her and everything else around him out, except for Raven, the vixen who knew how to make his cock jump and his body tense in excited anticipation of wickedly nasty things to come. Deanna's complaining was like splinters in his ears.

"It's over. We've been through this so many fuckin' times. I told you it was just a fling and you were good with that. Then you got all psycho on me. We had a great time. I loved it and you told me you did too. Now it's over. You'll make some guy who wants to settle down a wonderful girlfriend. I'm not the boyfriend type."

"I'm not asking you to be my boyfriend. I'd be fine with being your friend with benefits. That's totally no strings attached, right?"

"Hang on a second. I gotta check something out." He walked away and came out from behind the bar, striding over to Raven, who was sipping a drink while she watched two men play a game of pool. As he stood real close to her, his nostrils filled with her alluring scent: spicy with a hint of vanilla and musk. It smelled like pure sex and wound around him, squeezing him in a good way.

She turned, and with her head lowered she looked up at him, her lips slightly parted. His dick went crazy as he gazed at her. *Fuck.*

"What do you want?" she asked, her voice slinking over him.

He exhaled, willing his hardness to calm down. "Just making sure you're watching the game and not playing."

"So I'm not allowed to play here?" Her deep laugh stroked him.

What the hell's the matter with me? This smart-ass woman with her not-giving-you-the-time-of-day" attitude was igniting a fire in him that was threatening to combust. "Not if you hustle."

She leaned in closer, her lips hovering right over his ear. "And what if I do?" Her warm breath singed his skin.

"I don't think you want to find that out. I can be a real sonofabitch."

"Now you're just tempting me to hustle." She placed her hand on his bicep and grasped it lightly.

He narrowed his eyes and pressed his lips together as he scanned her flushed face. Her lips were begging to be kissed, and her seductive gray eyes were driving him wild. "Be careful in unleashing the beast in me, sweetheart. I don't fuckin' play nice. Remember that. If I see you hustling, your ass is outta here."

She stepped back from him, her face tight. "And I'm sure you mean that."

"My eyes are on you."

"And that's exactly where I want them to be."

Before he could answer, a man in his early thirties approached her. "I've been noticing you since you came in. What're you drinking?"

"We're fuckin' talking here." Muerto shoved his hands into his pockets so he wouldn't throw a punch at the asshole who offered Raven a drink.

The man's face fell. "Oh, I'm sorry. I thought you were alone."

Raven turned to him and smiled sweetly. Muerto wanted to grab her and press her close to him. "I am. He's the owner of the place and is just going over the rules for playing in here. I'd love a whiskey sour. Thank you."

"I'll go to the bar and get you one."

He started to walk away when she gripped his arm, then looked at Muerto. "That's his job," she said to the guy. "Can you please bring me a whiskey sour and…." She looked at her suitor.

"A bourbon and seven."

Muerto shot daggers at the man and growled at Raven while she smiled innocently at him. He turned around and marched back to the bar, the scent of her tempting perfume on his clothes. When he approached the bar, he yelled out to Skull, "Get one of the girls to send over a whiskey sour and a bourbon and seven to the bitch with the long black hair." Skull glanced at Raven and then back at him. "Don't fuckin' ask."

He went behind the bar and noticed Deanna was still there, glaring at him. *Fuck.* He walked over to her.

"Is she your new squeeze?" she said bitterly.

He laughed dryly. "Hardly." He glanced back at Raven who was laughing and holding onto the guy's arm. White heat burned in his chest. He wanted to beat the dude to a bloody pulp and fuck the vixen until she couldn't walk. A couple of beer cans fell on the floor, and he kicked them violently before stomping on them, causing them to explode. Sticky amber liquid puddled on the floor. "Fuck!" He grabbed a large towel and threw it down, sopping up the mess.

"What's up with you, dude? Why don't you take a break?" Skull said as he came over with a mop.

Shaking his head, Muerto breathed heavily. *That woman pisses me way the hell off.* "I'm good." He continued to inhale and exhale deeply.

"Okay." Skull mopped up the floor, smiled at Deanna, and went back to his station at the bar.

"Are you pissed because she's with that guy?" Deanna asked as she looked over her shoulder.

"Leave it alone, will you? I'm fuckin' busy right now. I don't have time to keep you company anymore, okay? Make the corrections on the lease as I asked you to. I'll be over sometime tomorrow to review it. Leave it with Jay."

"Wait a minute. That's the tenant at your duplex, the artist. You've got the hots for *her*?" Her upper lip curled in disdain.

With his nostrils flaring, he said evenly, "I don't have the *hots* for any chick."

"I'm not stupid. I can see you're attracted to her by the way you look at her." She lifted her wine glass to her mouth.

"So the fuck what? I always check out good-looking chicks. I'm done here. Go check out some of the guys in here tonight. You might get lucky." Before she could answer, he walked away.

"Is she giving you a hard time, handsome?" Brandy joked as she nodded toward Deanna. "She's pretty pissed that you were flirting with the black-haired woman."

Sweeping his arm out, he blew out a long breath. "Is it a gene in women to see every fuckin' thing that goes on and then give a shit about it?"

"Why're you so grumpy?" Jaime asked as she laid her tray on the counter.

"His girlfriend is giving him a hard time," Skull said as he placed three Coors on her tray.

"Fuck off." Muerto shot him a sideways look.

"You have a girlfriend? Who is she?" Jaime turned toward the crowd.

"The black-haired one," Brandy said, picking up on Skull's ribbing.

"Although I never thought the words 'girlfriend' and 'Muerto' would be in the same sentence." Skull guffawed.

"Is it the one in the red top and skinny jeans?" Jaime picked up the tray.

"It's no one. And if it were, you'd all be the last ones I'd tell." He threw his rag down. "Fuck this." He started to walk away.

Brandy went around the bar and placed her hand on his shoulder. "We were just joking. I didn't think you'd be interested in a woman who didn't have double-D boobs like mine." She winked.

"You got the tits all bikers love, darling," Skull said. She laughed, placed the drinks he made on her tray, and headed over to the table where Raven sat. "I gotta fuck that one. It'll be worth Steel kicking my ass."

Muerto chuckled. "Keep your attention on manning the bar. After we close you can go back to the club and have your pick of double-D tits—real and fake."

"Brandy had a point about the dark-haired chick. You usually go for bigger racks."

"If I were interested, which I'm not, her tits would fit just fine in my hands, and that's the way I like them." He glanced over at Raven, the vein in his neck twitching every time she swept her fingers over Mr. Bourbon and Seven's forearm. She was flirting up a storm with him, but Muerto caught her sneaking peeks at him at the same time. Wiping down the bar, chatting with customers, and leaning in a little too close to the waitresses, he pretended nonchalance, but a hot fire was smoldering in him.

When they stood up and walked to the pool table, he turned to Skull. "Take care of the bar. I gotta make sure no one hustles anyone." He strode over to the pool table where the guy was racking up the balls.

Leaning against a table, he watched her as she told Bourbon and Seven that she was a pretty good player. They played a couple of rounds which she easily won, and she begged off the next game.

"I'll play you," a tall guy in his twenties said to Bourbon and Seven.

As they racked up the balls, she jumped up on the stool, watching them. Muerto came over. "I didn't think you'd behave, or are you just setting the fuckin' sap up?"

With a placid face, she brought her finger to her lips. "Shh… I'm trying to watch the game. No one should ever talk when a serious game is on." Her eyes darted back to the two men playing pool.

Her words were like shards of glass slicing his skin. Roughly, he gripped her arm and tugged her to him. When she winced, a feral smile curled his lips. "No one tells me what the fuck to do," he said in a controlled tone. "And no one *ever* shushes me."

She tried to yank her arm out of his grip as she stared daggers at him. "And no one *ever* touches me unless I want them to. FYI, I don't want you to."

Bending down, he hissed in her ear, "When you beg me to touch you, I'll remember that."

Muerto dug his fingers into her skin, then shoved her arm away from him. He swaggered back to the bar, fuming. *She makes me so damn mad. Why the hell do I give a shit?* For the rest of the night he made a vow to ignore her, and he did a great job, almost forgetting she was in the place until the end. And when she didn't even give Muerto a small glance as she and Bourbon and Seven walked out, arm in arm, fire ran through his veins.

He'd never met a woman like her. Women came to him, and *he* decided if he wanted them or not. The silver-eyed vixen had his world out of order, and she pissed him off. But she also excited, perplexed, and challenged him. And he planned to see a whole lot more of Raven Harris.

Sneering, he stared out at the dark street. *I'm gonna fuckin' break her.*

He had to before she did it to him.

Chapter Seven

T HE SUN BORED down as Raven schlepped the groceries from her car into the house. The garage door had broken the previous day, and when she'd phoned the management company to report it, Deanna was snippy and demeaning. She really couldn't figure out what the witch's problem was with her. Not wanting to call Muerto after their encounter at the pool hall a couple of nights before, she figured she'd try the management company again on Monday morning and hope Jay answered the phone.

Muerto had been on her mind since Thursday night. She'd purposely given him a hard time, and he'd seemed madder than hell at her when she'd walked out with Dave. *He must sorta be interested in me if he got that pissed off.* Her face flushed a pinkish red when she recalled how much raw sex radiated from him whenever he came up to her. She'd had to force herself to act stoic around him when all she wanted to do was press her body close to his hard one and kiss him deeply.

She placed the perishables in the refrigerator and closed the door. *I'm thinking way too much about him. It's Saturday night, and I should go out.*

When she came back out on her porch, she grimaced; Brent stood against the brick pillar with a stupid grin on his face. She swept away some strands of hair on her face. "What do you want? I'm busy."

"I was just in the neighborhood. How've you been?"

"Good. Bye." She rushed past him and went to her trunk, took out a couple more bags, and slammed it shut. "You're still here," she said as she walked up the stairs to the porch.

"Let me help you with those." He reached out and grabbed the bags. She resisted. "I've got them. You need to go." She placed them down.

"I wanted to tell you that my wife and I have finally split up. It'd been shitty for a long time. I never loved her like I did you. I want to try and make things work between us now. When we were together, we were real happy, weren't we?"

"Until I found out what a lying, cheating piece of shit you were." She rubbed the back of her neck.

"My marriage was practically over when you came into my life. I just stuck around for the kids. I never cheated on you. You always had my heart. Things were so fucked up between my wife and me for a long time."

"A real man would've owned up to it. Told me he was married and let me decide if I wanted to get involved with a cheat. You played me and her. I don't respect cowards." Bending over, she picked up the bags.

Brent took a few steps toward her and grasped her arm roughly. Surprised, she dropped the bags and looked up into his narrowed eyes. "Don't fucking pretend that you didn't love me." His voice filled the small porch.

"I'm not. I did love you and that's why your betrayal was so much worse. I'm over you now, so don't think you can come over here, sweet-talk me, and when that doesn't work, manhandle me. I've moved on. Get the hell off my porch. I want you to stop contacting me. I know it's you e-mailing me those lame-ass love sayings. I don't want to hear from you or see you. It's done. Over."

Yanking her to him, he tried to kiss her as she struggled to wriggle out of his arms. "You don't fool me. You know you want me," he growled as he wrapped his fist in her hair.

"Stop it, Brent. You're hurting me."

"Leave her alone. Now." For the first time since she'd moved into the rental, Walter's voice brought her a sense of relief.

Releasing her, Brent stared at the other tenant. "Who the fuck are you?" He glanced at Raven. "You fucking *him*?" Stepping away from him, she went toward the screen door. Brent glared at Walter. "Butt the fuck out. This isn't your business."

"I heard her tell you to leave. She doesn't want you here. Leave. Now."

Is Walter fuckin' insane? She took in his chubby thirty-eight-year-old body and compared it to Brent's fit, thirty-two-year-old one, knowing he could decimate Walter. "It's okay, Walter. I'm good, but thanks."

"I'm not leaving until he does." He pointed his finger at Brent. "Get out."

"You fucking asshole," Brent replied through gritted teeth. "You're dead." He walked away from Raven.

With her phone in her hand, she said, "I'm calling 911 right now."

Brent paused for a moment but then jumped off the porch, his jaw clenched as he glanced at Walter. "This isn't finished yet," he said to her neighbor as he walked to his pickup. Whirling around, he caught her gaze. "I'm not buying your shit, Raven. I know you. You're still in love with me. I'll be in touch." He got into his truck and sped away.

Raven watched the pickup until it vanished into the distance. Walter was still standing on her lawn in front of her porch. "Uh... thanks for helping me out. He's an ex-boyfriend."

Walter squirmed in place, shoving his hands in and out of the pockets of his pants. Peering at her, he cleared his throat. "If you'd dress less provocatively, you wouldn't have these kinds of problems."

"Believe me, he wasn't bothering me because I'm wearing a simple sundress. Thanks again for the help." Bending over, she gripped the plastic bags and straightened up.

"Do you ever read the Bible?"

For a split second she wondered if she'd made a mistake in letting Brent go; at least she knew what to expect from him. Walter was giving her a major case of the willies. "I've read it before. I gotta go before my groceries spoil. See you."

Taking quick steps, she went inside her house, locked the screen, and bolted her front door. When she looked through the peephole, Walter stood staring at her door. For a long while she watched him until he finally walked away. She shivered. *The guy's a nut.* There was something odd about him. On one hand, he helped her out, but on the other, he basically told her it was her fault that Brent had accosted her.

After she put everything away and fed Sooty, she plopped down on the couch with a bottle of iced tea in her hand. She took out her phone and called her friend Ava, asking if she wanted to try out the new Mexican restaurant that'd opened on Champa Street. When she said yes, Raven smiled broadly.

They made plans to meet at Alfonso's at seven that night. A thread of excitement weaved through her. It'd been a long time since she'd gone out with a friend on a Saturday night. After her breakup with Brent, she'd been so brokenhearted that she'd had no interest in doing anything but painting and jewelry making. But that night, she was restless and had to get out. She wanted to rid her mind of everything, especially Muerto.

As the time passed, Raven became engrossed in a painting she'd started for an art gallery in Denver that had asked her to send two. She painted pop and contemporary art, loved mixing realism with fantasy. Her signature style was the use of bold colors and textures. When she dabbed pink on the canvas, brushing it out to resemble streaks from the setting sun, her phone alarm went off. She'd set it so she wouldn't let the time slip away from her as it usually did when she was engrossed in her craft.

After cleaning her paintbrushes, she jumped into the shower and then sat at her small vanity, applying her makeup. She'd always loved makeup, and experimenting with it had become a passion of hers over the past several years. Inspecting herself in the mirror, she muttered, "Perfect." Her winged eyeliner gave her an alluring, sultry look which she adored. She slipped on a pair of black skinny jeans, a black and white striped crop top, and a pair of patent leather red high-heeled sandals. The marcasite in her feather-and-skull navel jewelry sparkled when it caught the overhead light. She spritzed her neck and wrists with her signature perfume and headed out of the room.

After feeding Sooty and making sure the back door and all windows were secured, she walked out the front door and headed to her car. She so needed a night out.

I'm dying for a margarita. And I haven't seen Ava in such a long time.

Ava owned a small boutique on Main Street, and she'd fallen in love with Raven's jewelry and art when she'd seen them at one of the county fairs. She'd asked Raven to put some things in her shop on consignment, and they soon became fast friends. Ava had been a huge help to her when she'd found out about Brent. Her friend had been her support when her world had crumbled.

As she drove to the restaurant, she cranked up the radio, adrenaline shooting through her. *My days of mourning are over. I'm ready to live again.*

Chapter Eight

ALFONSO'S WAS A charming Mexican restaurant that had recently opened on the corner of Champa and Colusa. The interior resembled a beachside eatery with light blue and yellow walls and paintings depicting seaside towns in Mexico. The cuisine came from Baja California Sur, unlike all the other Mexican restaurants in Alina that served dishes from the states of Chihuahua and Sonora.

"I hear the margaritas are so good here," Ava said as the two women followed the hostess to their table by the window.

"I'm counting on it. I could use one." Raven sat down and took the menu from the lady. "It's really cute in here. I love all the oil and watercolor paintings. It's like we're having dinner by the ocean. A nice change."

"I'm glad you decided to come out tonight. I practically gave up on you ever going out. It's a good sign. Sometimes you have to get away from everything and just have a good time for *you*. Believe me, I know." Ava picked up a chip and dunked it into one of the four salsas on the table.

Raven nodded. "How's your mother?" Ava's mother had just recently come home from the hospital and wasn't doing so well. Ava and her sister took turns staying with her. Raven knew it was emotionally draining and physically challenging for her. To make the situation more difficult, Ava's mother wasn't the nicest patient.

Ava sighed. "The same. It's my turn to spend the night. I told my sister I'd be over by nine thirty." She glanced at her watch. "That'll give us enough time to catch up."

When the waitress came over, Raven ordered a margarita with a double shot of Cointreau and Ava ordered a pineapple margarita. As they talked and sipped their drinks, Raven heard a familiar voice in the distance. Casually, she craned her neck toward the direction of loud, deep laughter. She saw a table of about eight broad-shouldered, good-looking men in leather vests sporting tattoos on their arms. Then she spotted Muerto, a glass of beer in his hand, his hair falling over his forehead. She yearned to brush his hair out of his eyes, feel the smoothness of his skin, and kiss his full lips which were pressing against his glass. An intense craving for him—all of him—kept her from turning away. Then his gaze locked on hers and her insides quivered as she held his stare, mesmerized by him.

"*Camarones baja?*" the busser asked.

"That's hers," Ava said.

The scent of onions, cilantro, and tomatoes pulled Raven away from Muerto's intensity, and she turned and looked down at her dish. The busser placed a charbroiled flank steak in front of Ava, the pungent smell of jalapeños wafting around them.

"This looks so good," Ava said as she picked up her fork and knife. "Your shrimp look fantastic. How are they?"

"Really good. The perfect blend of spices, and they're cooked just right." Raven tore her flour tortilla in half and dipped it in the sauce.

"So who's the gorgeous guy you were staring at?"

Raven groaned. "My landlord, and he *is* gorgeous. I wish he wasn't." She took a sip of her margarita. "And he's so damn cocky it's unbelievable."

"Your landlord's a Night Rebel?"

"What's that?"

"An outlaw biker. It's the name of their club." Ava placed another morsel of steak in her mouth. "This is just so good."

"Outlaw biker? Is this for real? I thought all that had gone away. I mean, I remember reading about the biker wars from the sixties and seventies, and I saw some of the old movies about bikers, but I thought it was all in the past."

"Not in Alina. I keep forgetting you're not from here. The Night Rebels are an outlaw club, and they're hooked up with the Insurgents MC in Pinewood Springs. The Insurgents are like the head club and Colorado is their turf. I'm not sure how the two clubs fit in, but I know no one wants to get on the bad side of the Night Rebels."

"Well, I'll be damned. Mr. Arrogant really *is* a badass. I kinda thought he was, but I wasn't sure if part of it was just bravado."

"It's not. It looks like you're interested in him. What's his name?" Ava gestured the waitress to come over. "I'm going to order another margarita. Do you want one?" she asked Raven.

She nodded. "You're going to love this. His name is Muerto." Ava stared at her for a couple of seconds, then burst out laughing. Raven joined her. "Isn't that crazy?"

Wiping the corners of her eyes with her napkin, Ava shook her head. "Too crazy. I'm glad you're showing an interest in the opposite sex again, but you don't want to start anything with that one. I think you better stay away from him and his club. They're known not to play very nice."

"No worries there. We don't get along too well. He's got a real attitude and I give his shit back to him, so he's not too fond of me. I just think he's good-looking, that's all. I do kinda like the sense of danger that seems to emanate from him. I never even thought about bikers."

"I wouldn't start thinking about them now. I'm sure he's got a different woman warming his bed each night. I've heard they have wild parties and have a bunch of girls living at their clubhouse who have to be available for sex twenty-four seven. And they seem to have a lot of money. I don't even want to think what they're doing to get it." She shook her shoulders in an exaggerated shudder. "Not for me at all."

Raven laughed. "Switching gears, I've come up with a new design for a necklace. I've made a few of them and want to try them out at your store."

"Sounds good. Did you take any pictures of them?"

"Yeah." She scrolled through her photo files and showed them to her. As they talked about business, she heard a chair scrape across the tiled floor. From the corner of her eye, she saw someone sit next to her. She turned her head and met Muerto's gaze. "Oh," she said.

"Hey." He smiled at her and her insides fluttered.

"Did you eat?"

"Yeah. Just finished. I see you're still at it." He scooted his chair closer to hers, and the heat from his body skimmed over her.

"Uh… this is my friend Ava." She gestured to her. "And this is Muerto." Raven took a large gulp of her drink. "Have you been here before?" She set her glass down.

"A couple times. The food's great. What about you?"

"My first time. It's good." Raven wanted to smack Ava because all she was doing was staring at him, her face tight, her eyes laced with fear.

He must have noticed because he turned his attention to her, jutted out his chin, and said, "Am I scaring you or something?" She shook her head vigorously. "Seems like I am."

"It's 'cause of your club. What's the name again?"

"Night Rebels. No reason to be afraid. You haven't disrespected or pissed me off." He raised his eyebrows, and Ava hung her head down and began playing with the garnishes on her plate. He snorted, then turned to Raven. "Are you afraid of me too?"

"No, and I know I've pissed you off."

"Yeah, you have." He laughed.

She loved the way the descending sun's rays bathed his hair in pinkish hues. The tattoos on his powerful arms seemed to glow under the dissipating sunlight. For an instance, she wished she could curl her fingers around his bicep and trace each tattoo with the tip of her nail. Just thinking of touching him and feeling his arms wrapped around her made her cross her legs as a sweet clench ran through her sex.

"Won't your friends miss you?" She cocked her head to the side.

"If you're tryin' to get rid of me, sweetheart, it's not gonna work. I can see those lugs anytime."

Ava cleared her throat. "I should be going. I have to relieve my sister." She motioned for the waitress.

"I thought you said you had to go at nine thirty?" Raven finished the last bite of her dinner.

"I meant eight thirty. My sister gets testy if I'm late. I don't want to spoil your evening, so you stay." She glanced at the bill and took out forty dollars. "That should be enough for my share plus tip."

"I'll leave too."

"No way. I'll call you tomorrow to discuss… your new necklaces. Have a good time." Ava gulped down the rest of her drink, pushed her chair back, and took off.

"Ava, wait. I'm coming too." She started to get up, but his hand on her wrist pulled her back down. "I should go."

"Why? You're not relieving her sister, she is. Anyway, what the fuck's her problem?" Muerto gestured for another beer.

Raven shrugged. "I think you scared her."

"That's bullshit. I didn't do anything."

"I think it's because you belong to that club of yours. And you are pretty intimidating, what with your size and the pissed-off look you usually have on your face. I hope this didn't spoil her evening."

He leaned into her so his arm was pressed into hers. "I'll keep you company. I'm good with that."

"I bet you are." *That's what I'm afraid of. I better stop drinking.*

"Did you want anything more to eat?" the waitress asked after she placed a draft beer in front of Muerto.

He looped his arm around Raven's shoulder and leaned in close to her ear. "You want a *sopapilla*? I'm gonna get one." She nodded. "Two *sopapillas*."

"Dusted with cinnamon sugar?" The waitress picked up the empty plates and glasses.

"Why the fuck not?" He laughed when the woman widened her eyes before scurrying away.

Raven moved her chair closer to the window to create a space between them. She brushed his hand away from her shoulder.

"You don't want my arm around you?" His voice was low and smooth.

"If I did, I wouldn't have pushed it away."

Nodding, he pressed his lips together, then blew out a long breath. "That's fair."

As she finished her drink, the group of guys he'd been sitting with came over to the table. "I can see why you ditched us, bro," one said. Raven recognized him as one of the other men who worked at the pool hall. "How's your pool game been?" he asked her.

Lifting her chin, she held his gaze. "Great."

Smiling, he gripped Muerto's shoulder and squeezed it. "Is my brother treating you right?" He winked at her.

Biting her inner cheek, she quirked her lips. Several of the other bikers fixed their eyes on her chest while a few laughed and patted Muerto on the back.

Are we in grade school? What a bunch of jerks.

"Excuse me," the waitress said as she pushed through the guys and set the *sopapillas* in front of Raven and Muerto. A few of the men whistled when the woman started to leave. She looked behind her and smiled. "Thanks, guys. You made my night." She winked and hurried away. The guys laughed and spoke in hushed voices about her.

A tall, good-looking man with shoulder-length black hair came up behind the men. "Let's get going." He jerked his head at Muerto. "See you tomorrow." Raven noticed his vest had a patch that read "President," with "Steel" underneath it. She watched him leave and go to a wicked-looking Harley.

"We'll see you back at the clubhouse. Ruby will be waiting for ya," a blond, muscular man said as he walked away from the table.

Who the hell is Ruby? As she picked up her *sopapilla*, she watched the men leave the restaurant. A few seconds later, the window shook slightly from the rumble of the bikes as they exited the parking lot. "Wasn't one of those guys from the pool hall? I recognized him."

"Yeah. That was Crow." He took a big bite out of his dessert.

"Do you two own it?"

Wiping the sugar off his lips, he shook his head. "The club does. We just run it." He poured some honey on his plate. Dunking a piece of his deep-fried pastry in it, he popped it in his mouth. "So, how'd you get to be so good at shooting pool?"

"My dad taught me." She laughed when his eyebrows shot up. "Yeah, that's the look most people give me when I tell them that, but it's true. My dad was a pool shark. It's the way he earned his living."

"That can be a risky way to live. Was your mom cool with it?"

"My mom died when I was real young. I don't have any memories of her. It's been me and my dad for as long as I can remember. Now don't go thinking that my dad was like Minnesota Fats because he wasn't, but he could hold his own. We drove around the country while he plied his craft. When things got too dangerous, we'd be out of the county in a flash."

"Did you like traveling that much?"

She shrugged. "I didn't know any other life. I sometimes wished I had a best friend or even a boyfriend, but anyone I met was short-term. I learned not to lay down any roots. I ended up dropping out of high school when I was fifteen, got my GED a couple of years later. I'd spend hours sketching when we'd be driving through expanses of corn and wheat fields, or when I'd spend hours alone in a hotel room. My art became my best friend. Some people keep diaries. I sketched, and the drawings were my journal."

"How'd you end up in Alina making jewelry?"

"My dad was getting older and tired. His health was crap from too much smoking and greasy food. We ended up going to Vegas for a little recreation. Sometimes he hustled away from Vegas, but nothing too big. Then he met Wanda and she had some bucks her old man left her when he died. They seemed to hit it off, so he became a kept man." She laughed. "Just saying that makes me crack up. But they do really care about each other. I worked and went to the community college where I got my Associate's in Fine Art. I discovered and fell in love with acrylic painting. The jewelry making is fun and pays the bills. I ended up in Alina because the man I fell in love with was from here, so I came with him."

A dark look crossed Muerto's face. "You got a man?"

"Correction—*had* a man. I dumped his ass when his wife showed up with their three kids on our doorstep. Never saw that coming." She grabbed her napkin and twisted it in her hands. "Enough about me. What about you? How'd you get mixed up with the Night Rebels?"

He laughed. "I didn't get 'mixed up' with them. I *joined* them, and it was the best fuckin' decision I've ever made. Not much else to tell. I got two sisters. Laura's a couple of years older than me, and Rosa is a few years younger. Rosa's an accountant and works for a big Denver firm. I'm pretty fuckin' proud of her. She's the first one in our family to go to college."

Raven's heart melted a bit when she saw the pride in his eyes. "That's awesome. Are you close to your mom and dad?"

"My mom? Hell yeah. My dad? Hell no. He cut out on us a year after Rosa was born. We'd hear from him occasionally, but he never paid a fuckin' penny in child support. The selfish bastard always made sure to find jobs that paid him under the table. My mom worked her ass off to give us a good, safe life. I admire the hell outta her."

"That must've been real hard on her. I don't know how women can do that."

"When they love their children more than life, they find the strength. My dad eventually moved to Texas, and we haven't heard from him in a long time. And I'm totally cool with that because if I ever see him, I'll probably do something that'll land me in the state pen."

She laughed, but she didn't doubt for a moment that he was serious. "Does your mom live with your sister?"

He shook his head. "She's still living in our same house. Ramon lives with her. She met him a couple of years ago, and I was happy for her. She gave up her life for us for so long, and it was time she started living again, you know? I like Ramon. When my mom told me about him, I found out where he worked and went to the auto shop. I told him that if he respects, cherishes, and treats my mom right, we'll be friends for life, but if he disrespects her in any way, he'll gain the worst enemy. He got the picture. It's all good." Leaning back in his chair, he put his hands behind his head. "I've never talked this much to a chick in my life."

Warmth spread through her. "I've never shared that my dad was a pool shark with any man, even Brent. It must be the margaritas."

He dropped his hands and pressed next to her. "I like it when you're filled up with booze. You're not so...."

"Bitchy?" she offered.

"No, not that. I actually like your bitchiness. You're a nice change from the women who always want to please me. I was trying to say you're not so argumentative."

"I've always had to fight for myself. I guess it's just in my nature." She licked her lips, then smiled softly. "I like getting to know the man behind the arrogance and badass swagger."

"I have a badass swagger?"

She poked him in the ribs. "You know you do, and you *love* having it. I'm sure you worked hard on it all through your teens." Brushing her fingers across his hand, she smiled. "You have it perfected, and when I'm not pissed at you—which isn't very often—I think it's a damn sexy walk."

He smirked.

The overpowering smell of bleach and white vinegar filled her nostrils. Looking around, she noticed bussers and some of the waitstaff spritzing cleansers on the tables and wiping them down.

"I think they're trying to tell us they're closing. The place is practically empty."

Glancing at his phone, he chuckled. "I didn't realize we talked for so long. The time flew by. I enjoyed talking with you."

"Don't sound so surprised," she joked. "I enjoyed it too."

As they walked to the parking lot, she wished he'd take her hand. *What am I saying? I can't go there. He would most certainly break my heart.*

I can't afford that to happen.

"Have you ever been on a motorcycle?" his voice interrupted her thoughts.

"No. I'd be too scared to get on one."

"I'll have to show you sometime that there's nothing to fear. A rider gets into trouble when he doesn't respect the power of the bike. If there's respect, then all goes well. I'll bet once you take a ride, you'll be hooked. There's something about the feel of the openness, the wind around you, the sun on your back. It's pure freedom and adrenaline. It's so fuckin' addictive."

"You make it sound like something I'd like to try."

"You will. I'll make sure of it."

A metallic burgundy Harley with a skull hood ornament and gleaming chrome stood in a parking space. "Is this your bike?" He nodded. "It's awesome. It's so big. The motorcycles I see are way smaller than yours. This one screams power and speed."

"It's a fuckin' awesome bike, and the ride is outta this world." She swore she saw his chest puff out. "The ones you've seen have been rice burners. No bike is worth shit unless it's a Harley. They're a hundred percent American-made, and they can kick any rice burner's ass. Imports suck big-time."

She smiled, loving the way he became so animated when he spoke about his motorcycle. One day she'd have to see what the fuss was all about. Picturing herself behind him, her arms wrapped around his firm, tapered waist, his back muscles rippling under his skintight muscle shirt, definitely made her body tingle. "Here I am," she said when she got to her Impala. "Thanks for walking me to my car."

"I'll follow you home to make sure you get there okay."

"You don't have to do that. I've managed to get myself home for a long time."

"That's true, but I didn't know you before. I do now, and I wanna make sure you're good. You've had a few drinks and you're a small woman. How tall are you, anyway?"

"Five four."

"You look taller. It must be your heels. By the way, what happened between you and the dude buying your drinks all night at Balls and Holes?"

"Dave? Nothing."

"Good." He took the keys from her and opened the car door. "I'm following you home. No argument."

"Ridiculous," she grumbled as she slid into the driver seat. She switched on the ignition and he closed the door. Before taking off, she waited for him to start his Harley.

When she got to her house, she parked on the street and got out. He was already waiting on the sidewalk for her.

"Why didn't you pull into the garage?"

"It won't open. I called the management company, but Deanna wasn't too helpful. I'm not sure if it's her personality or if it's me, but it seems like she's got a real problem with me. I don't know why."

"You should've called me. I'll get the guy out on Monday morning to take a look. I'll speak to Deanna."

"Don't do that. She hates me enough already."

When they were on the porch, her stomach clenched when he looked through his key ring. *Shit! He's gonna find out I changed the locks. I'm not up for his anger when he finds out. I actually had a good time with him.*

"I must've left the tenants' keys at home. I thought I had them on this key ring." He shoved them in his vest pocket.

As she took out her key and slipped it in the lock, he stood right behind her, his hot breath on her shoulders. Moving her hair aside, she heard him inhale sharply.

"I didn't expect that. What a kickass tattoo. It looks like a painting." He softly kissed the purple rose on the back of her neck. She shivered despite the heat, and when his hands grasped her shoulders as he kissed her more ardently, a small moan slipped through her parted lips. Then she turned the lock.

"You want me to come in?" he asked thickly.

She swiveled around, her back against the door. "I don't think that'd be a good idea. I think we've both had too much to drink."

A startled look crossed his face, and as his features hardened, he stepped back. "Whatever. Just wanted to make sure you got home safely." He jumped off the porch and walked to his bike.

As he rode away she wondered if he was rushing off to see Ruby—whoever she was. Thinking about another woman enjoying his soft lips on her body made her feel empty. *You're the one who turned him away.* Her brain knew it was the right thing to do, but her body was so fucking pissed at her. It wanted more of his touch, craved his mouth against hers, his tongue licking the ache between her legs, his fingers—

Stop it! You know this would never work out.

Opening the door slowly, she smiled when she saw Sooty waiting for her, her luminous green eyes fixed on Raven's face. She shut the door and locked it, glancing outside one last time as a part of her wished he'd come back, knowing he never would. He wasn't the type to beg or chase a woman, too used to them doing that to him.

"Looks like it's just you and me again," she murmured as she picked up Sooty. She quickly changed her clothes, then came back to the living room and sank down on the couch. It was another night of staring at the TV screen, but that time, instead of thinking about jewelry designs, she thought about Muerto pleasuring a woman named Ruby. She'd wanted to ask him earlier at the restaurant who Ruby was, but she didn't want him to think she cared.

But she did care. A lot.

Chapter Nine

FROM THE LARGE tree across the street, I waited for her to come home. She'd left a few hours before and I'd thought she would've come home by now since she rarely went out. I knew. I'd been watching her for the past several days. A low rumble drew my eyes up to the inky sky, but there wasn't a cloud in sight, just winking lights surrounding an almost-full moon. The continuous deep, resonant sound came closer, and I clung to the trunk of the oak tree, wondering if a downpour would follow the thunder. Then I saw him round the corner on his Harley, the sound of his bike shattering the normalcy of the neighborhood. A breath caught in my throat. *So that's why she's late.* She got out of her car as he cut the engine, and quietness was once again restored.

They walked up to the porch, and I saw him press against her. The black-haired girl let him touch her. What a slut. A twig snapped under my foot and I held my breath. I couldn't have them see me. I didn't want her to know I was on to her. She would find out soon enough what happened when a woman whored around.

My mother had been right about not trusting women. She'd told me they were all wanton whores who'd spread their legs on command. I hadn't believed it, really. I knew she'd blamed the cunt with the overly made-up face for taking her husband—my father—away from us. I'd blamed her too. My dad had been a great guy who'd always had time for his family until he'd met her at his office. Soon, our family dinners were just Mother and me. At first he'd pretended to be working late, but later he didn't give a fuck what we thought. All he wanted was his mistress's pussy. It was like he was a slave and she was the master, commanding what he could and couldn't do. When he finally left us for her, she used him hard and, in a couple of years, she'd thrown him out when he didn't have any more money or energy to give.

He'd come back home and Mother took him in, nursing and re-minding him every day what he'd done to us. She'd tormented him until he died. I often thought he'd willed himself to die just to get away from Mother, but I never blamed her; he'd broken her heart in the worst way.

Voices murmuring drew me back to them. *Is he kissing her? Is she planning to fuck him? If she lets him in, I don't know what I'll do, but I can't lose my head. I'm not ready yet. It's too soon.*

I bet she was one of those women who liked flowers—roses—and demanded that a man give them to her. Blood red ones because it meant that the man had fallen hopelessly under her spell. And I was convinced it was a spell. There were women who knew how to make a man fall in love with them even if he didn't want to. They were seductresses, and they only wanted to show a man that they could get him. After their little game was finished, they'd chew him up and spit him out.

She was like that. I should've known that about her. I should've sensed it, but I didn't. Now I did.

Chuckling, I had to put my hand over my mouth to make sure they didn't hear me. He was leaving, and she looked so forlorn. *Good for you, bitch! Your tight ass and tits couldn't lure him in, but you'll try again. Cunts always do.*

But wait… he looks mad. I could tell by the way he sped off that he was angry with her. *Why do men keep falling for women who are such sluts?* I stepped away from the cover of the oak tree, my eyes glued to the picture window, hoping to be a voyeur of her loneliness and possible rejection. But no such luck; she closed the blinds and locked her discontent up. *Fucking bitch!* She robbed me of the pleasure of her pain, but I'd be back. I had to. I had to make sure things didn't progress between them.

As I crept down the slight slope onto the sidewalk, a thought seized me. *What if she calls him back? A man can't resist a willing slut. I'm sure he'd come right—*

"Oh, I'm sorry." The elderly woman was apologetic behind me. "I didn't mean to bump into you. I didn't see you."

She looked vaguely familiar, and I scanned her face which was partially illuminated by the moonlight. It took a few seconds for the memory to surface. That's right. She was the cashier at Bartell Drug Store, the place that still had the lunch counter in the back. I'd eaten there many times, but it'd been a while since I'd been there. *Why is she out so late? Don't freak out. She probably won't recognize me. Just stay cool....*

"No worries. I didn't see you either." *Don't engage in any conversation. Keep moving on.*

"I was concentrating on Teddy." She looked to her left and I saw a small white dog sniffing around a bush. "We were out for our walk before we retired. It's such a beautiful summer night."

Just be polite. I nodded and turned my face away from the streetlight.

With a wave, she pulled lightly on the leash and walked past me as she made her way down the block. A strangled breath came out through my chapped lips. That was too damn close. I couldn't be spotted anywhere near the slut's house. *I'll have to be more careful next time.* And there would be a next time, and another one after that until I was ready to kill the bitch. And when I did, it would be so sweet.

Shoving my hands in my pockets, I walked to my car that was parked four blocks away. Using a car would make someone think I lived away from the neighborhood in case the police ever got involved. As I opened my car door, the yellowed glow of lit homes reminded me that it was Saturday night and people were still up. The murmur of voices floated on the warm breeze.

Patricia! That's the name of the woman who bumped into me. Of course. I'm surprised she didn't recognize me. Switching on the ignition, I headed out of the neighborhood.

The next time I came out, I'd have to watch out for Patricia. If she happened to bump into me again, I'd have to show her what happened to people who weren't careful.

I clucked my tongue as I hung a right on Pine Street. *It'll be a shame, but I'm in survivor mode, and the only one left standing will be me.*

Chapter Ten

MUERTO SCREECHED TO a halt, switched off the motor, and jumped off his bike. His insides were burning as he stormed into the clubhouse and made a beeline for the bar. When he came up to it, a cold bottle of Dos Equis waited for him. As he guzzled it down, Chains and Goldie joined him.

"How'd it turn out with the dark-haired beauty?" Goldie asked as he motioned for Ruger to bring him a drink.

"What's that supposed to mean?" Muerto snarled.

"Did you fuck her or not?" Goldie picked up his beer.

"Nothing happened." Ignoring their widening eyes, he leaned over the bar. "Ruger, give me a double Jack."

"We gotta cut the music and have a minute of silence to mourn the death of your goddamn charm," Chains said as the corners of his mouth twitched.

Goldie busted out laughing. "I never thought I'd see the day when a chick turned you down. And she seemed into you. What the fuck did you do?"

Muerto stewed while his two buddies ribbed him, and when Sangre came over, he'd decided that if the brother started any shit about it, he'd punch his fucking lights out.

"What's so funny?" Sangre asked as he took a handful of *chicharró-nes*—fried pork skins—and popped a few in his mouth.

"A chick turned our brother down," Chains said as Goldie sniggered.

Sangre lifted his eyebrows, then finished chewing. "Is that true?" Muerto narrowed his eyes. "I'll take that as a yes. It seems the chick isn't interested in men." He scooped up another handful of chicharrónes.

Muerto jerked his head back. "It could be. Hell, I never thought of that. It makes a lot of sense." *That explains why she didn't want me to come in. No woman's ever turned me down before. Fuck. I definitely read her wrong.*

"Maybe you can convert her," Sangre said.

"That'd be a lot of fun." Goldie winked.

"Maybe. She's so hot that it may be worth the effort," Chains chimed in.

"She may be bi. I mean, I fuckin' know when a woman's flirting with me, and she was totally doing that with me. I bet she's bi and is more skittish with men."

"Who's bi? You?" Paco sat next to Muerto, his eyes crinkling in the corners.

The muscles in Muerto's body tensed and he bared his teeth. "Fuck no."

Chains cracked up and tried to talk, but he kept laughing. Goldie cleared his throat. "The chick Muerto has a hard-on for. The black-haired one at Alfonso's."

"You mean the one who was hustling at the pool hall?" Paco rubbed his chin with his thumb and index finger. Muerto nodded. "She's not bi. Who told you that? I've seen her at Cuervos, especially last year with some dude, and she definitely acted like she was into men only. She likes to flirt." He lightly punched Muerto's arm. "Seems like you met a woman who's just not in to you."

As the men guffawed, Muerto glared; he was fuming. "What the fuck does that mean?"

Paco shrugged. "She's just not interested. It happens."

"Not to me," he grumbled.

"Just move on to the next one. Like Ruby. She's headed our way. Fuck her until the cutie you're thinking about is out of your head. That's what the club girls are here for." Paco looked at Chains, Sangre, and Goldie. "Am I right?"

The trio nodded vigorously.

"Fuck off." Muerto turned his back to them, his nostrils flaring as he heard the men chuckling behind him.

"You look like you could use some fun," Ruby's soft voice caressed him. He shot her a sideways look and grunted. She ran her fingers down his powerful arms. "Your skin is real smooth. I can tell you work indoors." She stepped up on her tiptoes and kissed his cheek. "I've missed you."

"I'm too fuckin' pissed to think about anything. Go find another brother who loves your soft touch. I'm done for tonight." She opened her mouth to protest, but he put a finger to her lips. "Go on now."

"Okay... if that's the way you want it." She turned to the three guys behind him. "You guys wanna have some fun?"

"Like all at once?" Sangre asked, a devilish tone in his voice.

"Sure. Why not?" She looped arms with Chains and Goldie while Sangre followed behind them. They walked toward the door leading to the backyard.

"You wanna get in on a poker game? We're starting in about fifteen minutes," Paco said.

"Nah, I'm beat. I'm headed upstairs." He slammed his glass on the counter and stomped up the stairs. When he got to his room, he kicked off his boots, whipped off his T-shirt after carefully hanging up his cut, and lay down. *I know I didn't imagine her attraction to me. The woman was fuckin' comin' on to me. What the hell's her deal?*

He threw his arm over his eyes. Tomorrow was another day, and he'd just go over to *his* place and pay his pretty tenant a visit. He'd be remiss as a landlord if he didn't follow up to see if the plumbing problem was fixed. It didn't matter that Deanna had already done that. He wanted to do it himself.

And he'd give her another chance at him. *I'm sure she was just tired.*

As he thought of all the wicked things he wanted to do to her, he slowly slipped into a deep sleep.

BRILLIANT SUMMER SUNLIGHT bathed the town as the heat pushed in on him while he rode over to his duplex. On the shaded porch, he took out his key and inserted it into the lock of his rental. It didn't turn. He took it out and reinserted it. Again, it didn't turn. As he tried for the third time, the heat from the day was soon replaced by hot streaks of anger zigzagging through him. Once again, the lock didn't turn.

Wiping the sweat from his forehead, he tossed the key in the grass. *She fuckin' changed the locks!* Enraged, he pounded on the door. It groaned under his assault while the picture window shook.

Behind the door, he heard rushing footsteps and then a pause before the door flung open. "What the fuck's your problem?" Raven's eyes flashed and her brow creased.

"You changed the fuckin' lock. You can't do that." He pushed his way in, making her stumble back. "You're fuckin' out of line, and I'm not gonna put up with your bullshit." He stormed into the kitchen and opened the cupboard under the sink, inspecting the new pipe.

"I changed the locks because you seem to think you can barge in here whenever you want."

"I can. And you can't change 'em unless I give you permission, which I didn't." He stood up and faced her. The sunlight streaming into the kitchen made her black hair glisten, her lips look redder, and her big eyes shine brightly. *She's so damn gorgeous.* She had on a pair of jean shorts and a white T-shirt knotted in the middle. She wasn't wearing a bra, and from the way the sun was hitting her, he could see her pert breasts and their nipples. How he wanted to suck on one of those nipples. He'd always thought that a woman's nipple was one of nature's most eye-catching works of art. How he craved to suck on hers, drawing it into his warm mouth and then gliding his tongue over the hardened bud, giving her the erotic attention she deserved.

I gotta concentrate here. Why am I pissed?

"The lease is supposed to explicitly say that I cannot change the locks. It doesn't, so I can change them without your permission," she said.

That's right. She changed the fuckin' locks!

"You really should've hired a lawyer to draft your lease." She placed her hands on her curvy hips. "I have a friend who's a lawyer, and he said that a landlord cannot just enter a tenant's house. The landlord has to give twenty-four hours' notice before he can barge in unannounced like you did a few days ago, and were attempting to do just now."

The smug look on her face infuriated him. "Fuck you." He brushed past her. "And I need a copy of the key in case of an emergency. And that's allowed. Ask your *lawyer* friend," he said over his shoulder as he went into the living room. He heard her padded footsteps behind him.

"Why did you come over here?" she asked softly.

"I wanted to see how the plumber did."

"How'd he do?"

He knew she was right behind him, her intoxicating scent surrounding him, threatening to strangle him. He whirled around and she jumped back. "Fine." They stood facing each other, an awkward gap between them.

"You want something to drink?"

He leaned forward, his gaze still on her. He liked the way she seemed a little anxious and kept licking her lips.

"I have a bottle of Jack and a couple cans of Coors. There's always water and cranberry juice."

"Coors is fine."

She looked relieved that she had a reason to leave the room. As she went to the kitchen, he sat down on the couch. A cat jumped up and sat on the other end, its shining eyes staring at him. Muerto stared back.

"Sooty, are you trying to show our landlord who's boss?" She laughed as she handed him his beer.

"I'm the boss," he said as he brought the can to his lips.

"If it's important to you, I'll agree you're the boss since you're the landlord." She sat down and crossed her legs, her cat curling up in her lap.

"I'm the boss. Period." He jutted out his chin. He'd never met such an intriguing and exasperating woman before.

"If you want to be. Does that make you feel better?" She smiled sweetly as she stroked the cat's fur.

He grunted as he looked around. "You fuckin' painted all the walls in here."

"Do you like it?"

"It's okay, I guess." He took another gulp. He'd be damned if he admitted she'd done a great job in her color selection and made the place look more inviting. *She's full of herself enough without me telling her the place looks way better than before.* "So, are you an artist? I mean other than the jewelry making. Do you paint pictures?"

She nodded. "My medium is acrylics. My first love is painting, but the jewelry makes the money. I make jewelry out of other people's junk, and enjoy repurposing things into art creations. I'm thrilled I can make a living at it."

"That's cool. Are you sure you don't have a man?" She choked on her water and started coughing. "Are you okay?" he asked.

She nodded as she wiped her eyes. "Sorry. Your question took me by surprise. I mean, we were talking about jewelry, and then you asked me if I'm with anyone."

"I was just curious because you acted kinda funny last night."

"Funny? What do you mean?"

"I don't know. You didn't act like women I'm used to."

She guffawed and it grated on his nerves. "Because I didn't ask you to come in and fuck my brains out?"

"Forget it."

"No. Is that what you meant? I bet you're used to women throwing themselves at you."

He cocked his head to the side. "Actually, I am."

"Well, meet one who doesn't do that. I told you last night that I broke up with a guy I'd been living with about six months ago. Do you have a girl?"

"Nah. I don't go in for the girlfriend thing." He placed the empty beer can on the coffee table. "I got plenty of chicks—that's never been a problem." *Until you. But I'm gonna get you, sweetheart, and when you're good and hooked, I'll move on to the next one. I can't wait to break you.*

"I'm sure it hasn't. Sounds like you're having a good time and you've got it all figured out." Pointing at the can, she said, "Do you want another one?"

"I'm good. I gotta get going." *Your indifference doesn't fool me.* He stood and she pushed up from the couch. "You ever sell your stuff at rallies?"

"Rallies? What do you mean?"

"We put on a couple of biker rallies every year. We got a big one coming up in October. It attracts bikers from all over the region, and even from Colorado Springs and Pueblo. Anyway, we raise money for a charity dealing with child abuse. Breanna, our president's old lady, is trying to get more vendors to rent spaces at the upcoming one in a couple months. I thought you might want to get a booth. I think you'd do real well."

"I'd love to do that. I guess I'd have to buy some skull and dagger charms for the biker crowd."

"You betcha." He winked. "I'll text you Breanna's number and you can connect with her."

"Sounds great. Thanks." Her fingers skimmed over his forearm, scorching his skin.

Placing his hand on the doorknob, he looked at her. "You wanna go out for a drink sometime?"

"I'm not sure that's such a great idea. I mean, I'm not looking to get involved with anyone right now."

"I'm asking you out for a drink, not a lifelong commitment. But if you don't want to, that's cool. I'm outta here. Call if you have any other problems with the rental." He stepped on the porch and went to his Harley. He felt her watching him, and he wanted to turn around and look at her in the sunlight again, but he didn't. Instead, he jumped on his bike and pulled away from the curb without a backward glance.

As he rode to the Climax Lounge, he still couldn't believe that she'd turned him down again. He'd thought they were connecting and that she'd jump at the idea of going out for a drink. That shit stopped. Now. He'd given her a few chances to be with him and she'd thrown them back in his face, so she was out of his mind. Gone. Like she never existed.

That suits me just fine, sweetheart.

When he pulled into the parking lot of the Climax Lounge, he scanned the area looking for his brother-in-law's truck. Nothing.

Inside, the lights were dim and it seemed as though it were nighttime. Waiting until his eyes adjusted to the darkness, he stood by the bar and looked around. The club looked like one from the 1960s, with red velvet chairs, red leather booths, and heavy full-length curtains. Smoky black mirrors lined the walls and the ceiling.

His eyes adjusted to the low lights and he saw a pretty brunette writhing on stage, touching herself all over. There was a sprinkling of men, which wasn't surprising since it was midmorning on a weekday.

A man of medium height came up to him. "What's shaking, Muerto? What brings you into my establishment?"

"Hey, Jimmy. Just seeing what the competition looks like." He snorted while Jimmy laughed too loud.

Muerto didn't trust Jimmy Delarosa one iota. The slimebag always tried to ingratiate himself with the Night Rebels, and it just rubbed him the wrong way. At that moment, Delarosa was acting like they were long-lost friends. The grease was just sliding off him.

As they spoke, Muerto kept his eyes peeled for Joe. While Jimmy was telling him about the newest thing to make money on, Muerto spotted a couple in a booth at the other end of the room. It looked like one of the dancers sat on a man's lap, and he was running his hand over her curves. The rotating stage lights bounced off the customer's watch, lighting it up.

Muerto breathed out. *It's Joe. Fuck!* He recognized the watch on the guy's wrist. The previous year, Laura had begged him to find a good deal on a Rolex she knew Joe wanted really bad. She'd wanted to give it to him for his birthday, so he looked up an old contact of his who dealt in stolen goods and bought the watch. Laura never asked where he'd gotten it, and she'd insisted on paying for it.

Yeah… I definitely recognize the damn watch.

"I'll catch you later," he said to Jimmy as he walked away.

When he came over to the booth, Joe had his face buried in the stripper's cleavage. "How's it going?" he said.

Joe jerked his head up, his face falling when his gaze fell on Muerto's. "Dude…."

Muerto glanced at the woman, grasped her wrist, and gently pulled her off Joe's lap. "Your dance is over. Scram."

"What the fuck?" She looked at Joe. "You gonna allow that?"

Muerto took out a few hundred bucks and handed it to her. Her eyes grew as big as saucers and she smiled. "I like you. Next time you come back in here, ask for Joley." The stripper sashayed away.

"You want a drink, Mateo?" Joe looked nervously around the room as if trying to tag a waitress.

"It's Muerto, and this shit stops now."

"What're you talking about?"

"Are you fuckin' someone on the side? And don't even think of not telling me the truth, 'cause if you lie to me you're gonna be sorry you ever came into the family."

Joe shook his head. "I'm not cheating on Laura. I know she thinks I am, but I'm not. At least not yet. I've thought about it, but I haven't acted on it."

"And you're not fuckin' gonna. You're not gonna break my sister's heart. What the hell's going on with you two? I thought you guys were solid. Don't risk her throwing your ass out over some different pussy. Shit."

"It's just the same thing all the time. Nothing different or exciting. All we ever talk about is money and the kids. Laura's always too tired for sex."

"Then talk to her. You don't throw away eleven years of marriage on pussy and tits. I get that you wanna have more sex, so just talk to her. She's your wife, dude. Fuck."

"I love Laura a lot and I'd never leave her, but the thrill of sex with someone new is hard to fight."

"You do that shit and it'll never be the same between you. You talk to her and set this right. What you don't do is break my sister's heart. Instead of spending time here, you should be with Laura. Get outta here. Go home."

Joe nodded and slid out of the booth. "You're right. I'll talk to her." He put his baseball cap on and walked out.

With a heavy heart, Muerto watched him go. Jimmy intercepted him as he made his way to the front door. "I'm not liking what just happened."

"What're you talking about?"

"Coming in here and chasing my customers out."

"This was personal."

"Doesn't matter who it was. If a guy wants to be in here, it's none of your business to tell him otherwise."

Muerto grabbed him by the shirt and shook him. Through clenched teeth, he said, "You're teetering on a fuckin' fine line between respect and disrespect. Don't go over it. Got it? You don't tell me what the fuck to do."

As he threw back a pasty-faced Jimmy, one of the bouncers came up. Muerto's fists clenched instinctively.

"You okay, boss?" He gave Muerto the evil eye.

Smoothing down his shirt, Jimmy smiled weakly. "I'm good. The gentleman was just leaving."

Muerto locked gazes with him for several seconds, then slowly broke away and walked out of the club into the bright sunshine. As he pulled out of the lot and headed to the club, he hoped Joe and Laura could work out their problems. If Joe couldn't keep his dick in his pants, Muerto would have to beat the shit out of him for shattering Laura's heart and the kids' lives.

He really didn't want to do that.

Sighing, he veered out of town and rode down the two-lane highway as the sun beat relentlessly down on him.

Chapter Eleven

FOR THE PAST two weeks, Muerto hadn't shown up at the house, and Raven found herself listening for the roar of his bike. As much as she hated to admit it, she missed him. A big part of her craved something wild and dangerous to take her out of the mundane routine of everyday living. That something was Muerto. Even though she was fighting it like hell, she was definitely attracted to the biker, and it wasn't just for his good looks. That night at Alfonso's had shown her another side of him. He'd spoken from his heart about his mom and sisters, and when he'd told her about his dad, she heard pain in his voice. *There's still a little boy in him.* And that's what she liked.

Her phone vibrated against the table and she went over to see who was calling. *It's* him *again. Shit.* Ever since she'd encountered Brent on her porch a few weeks before, he'd been calling and texting her like crazy. Sometimes she picked up and put him on speakerphone as he rambled about how he wanted them to get back together. She'd made two pairs of earrings during one of his monologues, but mostly she ignored him. The previous week she hadn't received the requisite bombardment of calls, and she'd hoped he'd moved on. *No such luck.*

She slid her unanswered phone into her jeans pocket.

"If your plan is to drive me crazy, asshole, it's starting to work," she said aloud as she put a tube of lip gloss in her fanny pack. She grabbed her keys, scratched Sooty behind the ears, and went into the garage.

Soon she was headed over for her bi-monthly run to Junkyard Blues. Sometimes she'd find the coolest stuff, and other times it was a bust, but she'd never think of not checking it out. Inserting Hammerfall's CD into her player, she put on her sunglasses and drove to the junkyard.

Junkyard Blues was a two-block square of dead and broken parts a few miles out of town. A high cement wall enclosed it, topped with barbed wire. Inside, rusty, dented cars were piled high in precarious heaps, hubcaps were scattered around the ground like donuts in a supersized box, and stacks of tires lent to the pervasive odor of metal and rubber.

As she walked around, she picked up a couple of hubcaps, three sheets of scrap metal, and unscrewed a few hood ornaments from the dead cars. The one from an old orange Mustang caught her eye: a busty woman with long flowing hair. She'd use the woman's head and some of her hair as a pendant for a necklace, or she might use the whole ornament as part of a retro collage. At the time of purchase, she never quite knew where the pieces would end up in her repurposed art.

Turning down one of the lanes, she saw two guys standing in front of a pile of broken cars. As she began to walk down the aisle, she recognized one of the men as being the doofus who lost a wad of money to her about a month before. *What the hell was his name? Cory. Yeah, that's right.* Not wanting to have an encounter with him, she spun around and went in another direction.

Deciding that leaving was probably the best thing to do, she walked toward the office to pay for her finds when what looked like a 1930s' radio caught her eye." Fucking awesome," she said under her breath as she put her items on the ground and ran her fingers over the scratched wooden console. Turning it around, excitement coursed through her; most of the small radio tubes were intact. She'd been looking high and low for them, and the ones she'd found and bought online were pricey. To find them at the junkyard was beyond awesome. She could already picture them filled with semi-precious stones, or beads of varying colors, or colored sand to create a Native American look. *I can even put dried flowers in them, or just leave them clear. This is great.*

"Look who we have here," a gravelly voice said behind her.

Hair lifted on the nape of her neck and arms as her heartbeat raced. *Fuck!* She slowly turned around and gazed into Cory's tight face, his eyes cold and hard. "Hey," she mumbled. Darting her eyes around the area, she tried to figure out how she could get away.

"Taking a break from hustling, bitch?" Cory spit out, and the short guy next to him laughed.

With her adrenaline pumping, she pretended to be clueless. She couldn't let him see how scared she was. Bad people lived off the fear of others; if he could see she was afraid, she knew that would be her undoing.

"Just looking for some things to repurpose. They have some cool stuff here." *Be friendly but not overdone. Nonchalance is the key.*

Cory seemed taken aback for a couple of seconds, and then his face twisted in anger again. "Spending the money you steal from hard-working people?"

"Look, I don't want there to be any hard feelings. I'll give you your money back."

"I don't want it anymore, bitch. You made me look like a fucking fool."

You're already a fool, so don't blame me, asshole. She bit her inner cheek so her thought didn't accidentally slip out. Even though she was scared, she was also pissed that Cory was threatening to ruin what had started out as a good day. "I didn't mean to. Just take your money and let's put this behind us, okay?" She started to shuffle away but Cory's friend came up behind her.

"I want a piece of your ass. I admired it every time I saw you. Your ass for my money. Seems fair. What do you think, Tyler?" Cory grinned like a grotesque pumpkin on Halloween. She shuddered.

"It'd be fairer if her ass was for both of us. After all, she hustled you out of your paycheck."

What kind of an idiot bets his whole paycheck on a pool game? Fuckin' moron! As images of what could be flashed in her head, she gulped down breaths to steady herself. She couldn't lose her cool. Again she looked around, but it was as quiet as a graveyard. The only sound was the background clanking of a distant freight train as it sliced through the desert.

"Oh my God! What is that?" she yelled as she pointed behind Cory. He whipped around and his friend moved away from her, and she took off running. She knew the few seconds she'd distracted them wasn't much but she ran with all she had, dust kicking up behind her heels. Her lungs struggled to keep up with her panting, feeling as though they would burst, but she kept going.

Right before she rounded the corner to go down one of the aisles, searing pain assaulted her scalp as she was snapped back like a rubber band. "Fucking bitch!" Cory's voice boomed as his hand wrapped tighter around her long hair.

"Leave me alone!" Desperately, she tried to break away from his grip, but she was no match for his strength.

"Grab her legs," Cory said to Tyler. He complied and soon Raven was on the ground, Tyler holding her down as Cory sank to his knees. Tyler's hand muffled her screams, and both of them restrained her kicks.

"She's a fighter," Tyler said as he clamped his hand tighter over her mouth.

The bright sun beat down on them and black spots danced in front of her eyes. *What am I going to do?* Bile rose up her throat.

Cory ran his hands over her breasts and squeezed them. "You're gonna find out what happens to bitches who dupe me." Sneering, he unzipped his jeans.

She closed her eyes, swallowing the lump forming in her throat. *He's going to rape me. Oh God. No. No. No!* Her insides screamed with terror as Cory's fingers tugged at the waistband of her jeans. Tyler snickered as he hovered over her, his hand still pressed against her mouth.

A feral growl filtered into her ears as Cory's friend said, "What the fuck?" His hand slipped away from her lips. She opened her eyes and saw a looming mass of a man standing a couple feet away from her. She guessed him to be six-four, and his shaved head shone in the sunlight. He had a bushy brown beard, plugs in his earlobes, and sported two sleeves of colored tats. Licks of ink rode up his throat from under the neck of his muscle shirt.

Without warning, he yanked Cory off her in one fluid movement, his massive arms shaking him as though he were a ragdoll. Cory swung his arms aimlessly but didn't land a punch on the tatted Goliath. Tyler ran to his aid, and when he landed a fist in the tatted Goliath's side, the man threw Cory to the ground and backhanded Tyler so hard that he stumbled and fell on his ass.

"Where the fuck are you, Diablo?" a husky voice asked.

"Here," the man answered as he bent over and dragged Cory to his feet.

Coming around the corner, Raven sucked in her breath as Muerto appeared. She sat up and brought her hands to her heated cheeks as he looked at her, then at Diablo, and finally at Cory, suspended a few inches off the ground, his neck in Diablo's hand. A gasp escaped her when she spotted Tyler approaching Diablo with a steel pipe. Without a word, Muerto jumped in, kicking the pipe out of his hands and landing several hard punches to the man's face and stomach. Diablo threw Cory back on the ground and kicked him hard in the stomach.

In a matter of minutes, both men lay crumpled on the ground, blood trickling from Cory's mouth. Muerto ran over to Cory and began kicking him, but Diablo pulled him away. "Enough."

Muerto breathed heavily as he eyed the man groaning on the ground as Raven slowly rose to her feet.

"What the fuck happened here?" he asked Diablo, but his gaze was on her.

"Didn't like how they were treatin' her." Diablo spat on the ground.

"Did they hurt you?" Muerto asked her. She shook her head. "You sure?"

The last thing she wanted was a major problem. She just wanted them to stop, and the guy who Muerto called Diablo had taken care of it. All she wanted to do was buy her finds, go home, and shut the world out. She wanted to get lost in her art; it was the only thing that made her feel better when things seemed awful and out of control. Painting and creating jewelry were her therapy.

She cleared her throat. "I'm sure."

Muerto spoke in a low voice to Diablo as Tyler stood, brushed off the dust from his pants, and helped Cory up.

Cory wiped the blood from his mouth with the back of his hand and glared at her. "This isn't finished, bitch," he muttered to her. She glanced at Muerto, but he was still talking in a low voice to Diablo.

As the two men walked away, Muerto's hard voice said, "Leave her the fuck alone. Next time, I'll kill you." Without looking back, they disappeared among the junk.

Muerto came over and put his arm around her, his head dipping down toward her ear. "You sure you're good?"

Nodding, she brought her index finger to her mouth and tugged the dry skin around her cuticle.

"Is this the woman who has your dick?" Diablo asked, his face hard.

Muerto pulled his arm away from her and walked toward Diablo. "No chick's got it," he said in a low voice, but she heard him. She bit her inner cheek.

"Thanks for helping me out," she said to Diablo, extending her hand. "I'm Raven." Diablo glanced at her hand and then her face without reaction. "Uh… I dropped some things I wanted to buy back there." She pointed behind her. "I should go get them."

"What were you doing in the junkyard? It's hardly a place women like to shop at." Muerto's dark eyes were mellow and tender as he looked at her, and it gave her the warm-and-fuzzies.

"I check it out a couple times a month to get stuff for my art."

"Show us where your things are. We'll carry them for you." Muerto came next to her and she quickly walked ahead as the two men followed.

When they arrived at the place where she'd dropped everything, she bent down and began picking the items up, her hands visibly shaking. Muerto took them from her and handed them to Diablo. "Take these to Bud. We'll be there in a minute." The tall man grunted and stalked away.

"I could've taken them. He was so nice to help me out. I don't know—" Her voice cracked when the reality of what could have happened hit her.

In one tug, he had her in his embrace, the warmth from his body and his strong arms making her feel safe. Without warning, tears spilled from her eyes and she buried her head against him as all the fear seeped out of her. Muerto held her close, rubbing her back, and for a long time they stood there, the sun burning their skin, the muted wail of a train whistle echoing.

When her tears subsided, she pulled back. "Sorry. I didn't mean to lose it. Thanks."

He smiled and stroked her cheek with his fingers. "No worries. And no need for thanks. That sonofabitch's still pissed at you for hustling him."

Nodding, she blew out a long breath. "The moron bet his whole paycheck. I didn't know that at the time or I wouldn't have agreed to play for the whole amount."

"That was his decision. You tell me if he ever bothers you. Does he know your name or where you live?"

She rubbed her chin. "I don't think so, but I don't know for sure. Alina isn't that big, and I stand out with my long hair. Anyway, after what you and your friend did, I don't think he'll bother me again. What were you guys doing here?" She slipped out of his hug.

"Looking for hubcaps for the repair shop." He held her gaze.

Her mouth went dry. *What's going on with me? I'm so nervous.* "I should go now."

"Okay."

They stood staring at each other, the pull she felt to him intense. Breaking eye contact, she started walking to the office. He came up next to her and put his arm tightly around her. *I'm so attracted to this guy. I love his arm around me. Maybe I should give him a chance.* Her common sense screamed that she was crazy and emotional. Who wouldn't be? Two men had attacked her and scared the hell out of her, and Muerto and his friend had come to her rescue. Muerto was her dark knight who offered her aid and comfort.

That's all he is. Don't get all sappy and mushy over it.

He opened the door for her and she went inside, the cool air enveloping her. A smile brushed across her lips when she saw her items neatly piled on the counter. Diablo leaned against a wall inspecting a hubcap.

"How much do I owe you?" she asked the owner.

"Sixty bucks."

As she pulled out her money, Muerto came over to the counter. "She's a friend of mine. Make her a better deal, Bud."

"I gave her my lowest price."

"Bullshit. We're buying a ton of shit from you. Give her a better deal."

"You're killing me, dude. I can't go any lower."

"That's okay. Really," she said as she gave the money to Bud.

Muerto ripped it out of her hands, giving her back twenty. "Forty's enough."

"Fuck, man."

"You know I'm right."

Bud pulled out a strong box and shoved the bills inside. "Thanks for your business, lady. What's your name? I've seen you around here before."

"Raven. I try to come in a couple times a month, but usually the long-haired guy is here."

"Jake. Yeah, he's here most of the time." Bud glanced at Muerto. "You ready to settle up?"

Diablo stepped up to the counter. "We need one of the trucks to bring the hubcaps over." Bud nodded.

"Thanks again, Muerto and Diablo… for everything." She walked to the front glass doors.

"We gotta settle up here, then drop everything off at the repair shop. I'll be in touch." Muerto came over and held the door open.

"Yeah. Sure. Thanks again."

"See you." He dipped his head down and kissed her gently on the cheek. "Be careful. If you need anything, you got my number."

"Okay," she said softly. As she went to her car, she glanced over her shoulder, tenderness unfurling within her as her gaze went to his. He slouched against the doorway watching her. Turning around, tingles raced along her spine as she slid into the driver seat. Driving away, she glanced in her rearview mirror and saw that he was still watching her, his white T-shirt gleaming in the bright sunshine. For reasons she couldn't articulate, she liked that he watched her until she was out of his sight.

I really like him. Maybe he'd be an okay guy to date. Then she remembered what Ava had said about the women who lived at the clubhouse only to service the men. And there was Ruby, whoever she was.

Disappointment crushed her good feelings as realization set in that he would never be the type of man she could get involved with. She could never survive another intense relationship with a man who would break her heart. Being a hustler, she knew the odds were stacked against her. She had no doubt that he'd be an intense, wild man who'd pleasure her beyond all her expectations. But she was sure he was also the type who'd leave one woman for another.

I don't want that. One broken heart is enough for a lifetime.

Chapter Twelve

FOR THE PAST several days, Raven couldn't get Muerto out of her mind. His usually cocky attitude had been absent at the junkyard, and it made her think that they may have crossed some line in their relationship. *What type of relationship do we really have?* He was her landlord, but what they had between them was much more than a renter/owner interaction.

Why am I thinking so much about him? I'm sure I haven't crossed his mind since the junkyard. He hasn't called or dropped by. I'm definitely making more out of this than there is.

Padding onto the back porch to get her weeder and watering can, her bare feet glided over the shiny hardwood floor. Ever since she was a child, she'd preferred being barefooted whenever she could. She especially loved walking outdoors in her bare feet, her toes wiggling in the lush grass as she gardened or watered the lawn. Each time she came into her house, she'd toss her shoes off and enjoy the feel of the ground beneath her soles.

Armed with her gardening tools, she opened the front door and went out on the porch. "Ow!" she cried as a stab of pain shot through her foot. Thinking she'd stepped on a bee, she looked down. Strewn on the welcome mat were many long-stemmed red roses. "What the hell?" she muttered aloud as she bent down and carefully picked them up. Glancing around for a card or something that would tell her who left them, she found nothing.

That's weird. Maybe Muerto put them there. As she pictured the handsome biker putting the roses on her porch as she slept, butterflies fluttered in her stomach. She liked the idea that it was him, but her gut told her it wasn't. He didn't strike her as a flower type of guy. Anyway, she was pretty sure he'd want her to know he'd given them to her if he'd done it.

She considered Brent. *No, he'd want me to know it was from him too.* The way they were drooping told her that they'd been there for a while and were in desperate need of water. She went back into the house and took out a tall vase, filling it with water.

After she arranged the flowers, she went back outside to attend to her small garden. Happy that the oppressive heat from the last few days had dissipated somewhat, she adjusted her sun hat and went over to uncoil the hose. In her peripheral vision, she saw Walter walking toward her. Groaning inwardly, she turned on the water and aimed the spray nozzle at her vegetable patch.

He stood right next to her, uncomfortably close and invading her personal space. Each time she inched away from him, he filled the gap. Finally, she craned her neck and looked at him. "Do you mind? And what do you want?"

"You smell real good." He inhaled deeply, his nose sounding stuffed up.

"Thanks. Can you move back? I'm trying to water."

He took a step away from her. "I like watching your vegetables grow. I remember when you planted them in the spring. They're coming along nicely. You've got a knack for it. Like my mother. She can grow anything. In that way you're similar to my mother."

How the fuck am I supposed to reply to that? "Thanks…?"

"You've got pretty feet. I like women who paint their toes. What color are yours? They look blue, but not as bright as the sky."

Okay, this guy is really strange. Then a thought hit her and a shiver of ice stabbed her gut. *What if he put the flowers on my porch? I wouldn't put it past him. I need to talk to Muerto about him.*

"So, what color blue are they?"

"Uh… oh… turquoise. Did you put some roses on my porch this morning?" Her gaze fixed on him.

Averting his eyes, he shook his head, his hands going in and out of his pockets. "No, but I saw them when I went for my walk."

"Are you sure you didn't put them there?"

"Why would I do that?"

"What time did you go for your walk?"

"The time I always do—seven o'clock."

Not convinced, she turned away. "I don't mean to be rude, Walter, but I'm not up for talking right now. I usually like to zone out when I water and garden. It's my quiet time, you know?"

"So you don't want to talk to me?" A hard edge crept into his voice.

She rolled her shoulders; she hadn't realized how tense she was since he'd come over. "That isn't what I said. I said I want some quiet time, so for now I'd rather not talk."

He clucked his tongue and stepped forward so he was in her line of vision. "Do you like dancing?"

Sighing, she nodded. "Do you?" *I couldn't care less if he does or doesn't. I just wish he'd go away and leave me the hell alone.*

"The way people hold each other and grind into each other is just nasty. And most of the time they're strangers. The way I see it is that it's just an excuse to grope each other."

What a fuckin' nut. "Everyone is free to think what they want. Dancing has always involved touching, even as far back as the ancient civilizations."

"That doesn't mean it's not dirty. No one cares about morality. Look how God destroyed Sodom and Gomorrah and how the Roman Empire crumbled because of immorality. The world is going to find out that enough is enough."

Whoa. Just agree with him. Maybe he'll go away. "I think you have a point there." She went over and turned off the hose.

Watching her intently, he licked his lips. "I bet you're real popular with men. I also bet that you love them clamoring after you."

She laughed tightly. "I really don't. What about you? Do you have a special woman?"

An intense darkness covered his face and he glowered. "I don't trust any woman except my mother." His gaze lingered on her mouth.

When she bent down to pick up her weeder, the hairs on the back of her neck rose as she sensed his stare on her. "I have to finish a painting I've been working on. It was good chatting with you." *Not!*

"But you're not finished." He looked at the weeds.

"I'll do it later. I didn't think it'd be this hot out. The cloud covering fooled me." The man creeped her out; she had to get away from him. She'd finish gardening when he was holed up watching TV like he did every night. On the evenings when she'd take a walk, she'd see the flickering of the screen from his open window. He was always in the dark, and if she cocked her head a certain way, she could see his face illuminated by the glow of the TV. It looked like a ghastly mask, and sometimes the image of it invaded her dreams.

"I really do have to start painting. See you." Rushing past him, she heard his noisy breaths. Closing the door behind her, she locked it and leaned against it. "We got one fuckin' nutcase for a neighbor," she said to Sooty. Shaking her head, she went to the back porch and put away her tools, grabbed a large bottle of water from the fridge, and went over to her canvas. She'd placed her easel in the living room to catch the early afternoon light.

A few hours later, a knock interrupted her flow. Rolling her shoulders backward and forward several times to get the kinks out, she laid down her brush and went over to the door. Looking through the peephole, she gasped as her heartbeat raced. Slowly, with trembling hands, she opened the door.

With wide and glowing eyes, she greeted him. "Hey."

Muerto grinned. "You seem surprised to see me."

Recovering from her initial shock and anxiety at seeing him at her door, she smiled. "Just surprised you knocked."

He chuckled. "I came by to see how you're doing."

"I'm good. That incident is behind me. I've been in scrapes before and I don't let them get me down. You want a cold beer?" He nodded and she unlocked the screen door, moving aside as he entered. "I'll be back in a sec." She shuffled to the kitchen. *I can't believe he's here, and that he fuckin' knocked.* Giggles burst through her lips as she grabbed a Coors and an iced tea and went back to the living room. "Here you are." She handed him the cold can.

He took it, popped the tab, and put the tiny piece of metal in her open and waiting hand. He laughed. "You really do use anything for your jewelry." After taking a deep drink, he set the can down on the table. "It looks like you're working on something."

"Yeah. I got accepted to show a few of my paintings at an art gallery in Denver. I'm beyond excited." She drank a gulp of iced tea; her mouth was dry as dust. And the way his gaze penetrated her made her nervous as hell. "I took a couple of workshops with Elliot Caraway. He's an awesome artist and paints in my medium. Anyway, he ended up liking my work and we've kept in touch. He referred my artwork to this gallery in Denver." She swallowed. "They have a lot of folk and pop art. I need to finish before the end of next week." Another large gulp. "It's a big deal to get your work in a gallery." Pressing her lips together, she brushed away some lint from the couch.

"That's cool. Am I making you nervous?"

"No. Why?" Heat radiated from him as he moved closer to her.

"You're acting like it." Again his dark gaze bored into her.

"Just anxious excitement over finishing my painting and getting it to Denver. You want another beer?"

"A water would be cool."

She leapt from the couch and dashed to the kitchen. *You're acting like an ass. Damn. Get a grip. Why're you letting him get to you all of a sudden?* It was because she was beginning to see the layers that made him who he was. Before, he was like a bad cardboard cutout, but she was beginning to see past his persona, and liking it. It scared the hell out of her.

When she came back into the living room, he was standing in front of her painting, his face expressionless. "Do you like it?" she asked, scrutinizing what she'd created for the past several hours: bold colors depicting a nude woman kneeling on red sand with bones scattered around her. The woman had long black hair that covered her nakedness except for her perky breasts. She stared ahead as if she were looking at the person regarding the painting. A colorful umbrella in her hands shielded the bright yellow sun. The heads of three men hung from the handle of her parasol, streaks of red dripping onto the sand.

"It's interesting. Is it the desert?" Muerto asked as he cocked his head to the side.

Handing him the water bottle, she picked up a wet brush and shaped its tip with her fingers. "Yeah. The woman lives in the desert of blood, devouring men as they come upon her. Have you ever heard of *Devoradora*—the Mexican folklore?"

Slowly he nodded, a lazy smile spreading over his lips. "She seduces and deceives with her beauty, then kills every man she meets."

"Or castrates them." Her gray gaze held his.

He took a swig of water and chuckled. "Is that what you're aiming for, sweetheart? My balls?"

With her gaze still locked on his, she placed her brush in a tattered wooden box. "Maybe." She ran the tip of her tongue over her top lip and his eyes followed the movement.

In two large steps he was beside her, one arm wrapped around her small waist and the other tangled in her hair. He yanked her head back and stared deeply into her eyes. "I'm totally up for the challenge." He pressed his lips to hers, kissing her firmly.

Heat flooded her, and she twisted away. "Don't do that."

Letting her go, he stepped backward. "I'm planning to do a lot more than that." He winked at her, his crooked smirk switching to a small smile. "Glad you're good. Gotta run." He swaggered out the door.

As she watched him get on his Harley, she brought her fingers to her mouth, her lips still warm from his kiss. Her calm was shattered; it seemed that it was beginning to happen more often and more completely each time she was around him. She knew the signs: dry mouth, giggling, butterflies in the stomach, always thinking about him. She was falling for him and she didn't want to. It was like she was on a runaway freight train barreling down a hill—unstoppable until it finally crashed.

Cringing, she knew the ride would be fast, hard, and exciting, thus making the inevitable crash that much worse. And she didn't know how the hell to stop it.

Chapter Thirteen

M UERTO STOOD UNDER the awning on the back porch waiting for Deanna to pick up. He'd been meaning to talk to her about her attitude with Raven, but club business, his mother's birthday party, and running the pool hall had eaten away at his time. The constant desire he felt for his tenant hadn't helped. She was always on his mind, driving him crazy and making him shake his head in bewilderment. There was something about her that captivated him and made her irresistible. Raven fascinated and intrigued him, and he wanted to get to know her better.

"Muerto, what a pleasant surprise. How are you?" Deanna's cheery voice pissed him off.

"What do you have against Raven?"

"Who?"

"The tenant at the duplex. She said that she told you about the garage door not working a while back and you didn't do shit about it. Gave her some attitude. What the fuck, Deanna? Do you treat all my tenants like that? Dealing with problems at the rentals is supposed to be your job."

"She's lying. She's trying to turn you against me. Has anyone else complained?"

Muerto ran his hand through his damp hair. *Fuck, it's hot today.* "No."

"Then why would I just pick on her?"

"That's what I'm trying to figure out. I can't see Raven making this up. She's not the type to do shit like that."

"You know her that well? She's got the hots for you. I saw it that night at the pool hall. She knows you and I get along real well. She probably found out we used to date and is jealous of our relationship."

Muerto scrunched his face. "I don't think so. Look, she obviously rubs you the wrong way. It happens. Hell, most people rub me the wrong way. I'll tell her to call Jay if she can't get a hold of me. That should solve any future problems."

"You've never given out your number to a tenant before. We've handled all the problems. Why would you give her your number?"

"'Cause I'm the owner and can do what the fuck I want. If you have to talk to her for any reason, drop the damn attitude and be civil. Let's not make our working relationship go sour."

"Is that all we have, a 'working relationship'?"

"Yeah. You need to move on, Deanna."

A dry cackle pricked his ears. "You certainly have. You didn't even miss a fucking beat, did you?"

A deep sigh. "Just do your job. I gotta go." He set his phone on the patio table and took out a joint, lit it, and inhaled deeply. Even though he liked the drama that ensued with citizens when he switched girls, it sometimes got to be too much. He'd made a big mistake by going out with someone who worked for him. He swore he'd never mix business and pleasure again. His short-lived affair with Deanna wasn't worth the grief she kept giving him about it. Most of his brothers wouldn't dream of getting involved with a citizen even for a one-night stand because the women just didn't get it. They weren't like the club girls or hangarounds who were down for one night and nothing more. Citizens always wanted to make a couple of fuck sessions into a relationship with love and commitment.

So why the hell am I even entertaining wanting to get to know Raven better? Somehow, she'd pulled him in further than any other woman ever had. And if truth be told, he really didn't know what the hell he wanted from her. He just knew that he *wanted* her.

"You got another one of those?" Army asked as he came up to the porch. "What the hell you doing outside in this damn heat?"

Handing him a joint, Muerto pushed away from the wall. "I was using the phone. Let's go inside. It must be over a hundred right now."

The two men entered the cool clubhouse and went over to the bar to join Skull, Diablo, Goldie, Paco, and Chains. Patches had a Dos Equis on the bar when Muerto came up and a shot of Jack for Army. Neither man acknowledged the prospect as they wrapped their fingers around their drinks. Prospects did the grunt work for the club without appreciation or acknowledgement unless they screwed up; then they received the wrath of a member, or the whole brotherhood if they really fucked up. All the patched members had gone through prospecting, all receiving the same treatment. Being able to don the club's colors meant that the brother had proven himself. The Night Rebels weren't looking for those who couldn't hold their own with the utmost loyalty to the brotherhood.

"How's your woman?" Diablo asked.

Chains choked on his beer while Goldie and Skull muttered, "What the fuck?" in unison.

"You got a woman?" Paco said, jerking his head back in surprise.

"No." Muerto stared straight ahead.

"Why'd you ask that, Diablo?" Goldie placed his drink on the counter.

"'Cause he does," Diablo answered.

"I bet it's the long-haired chick with the perfect ass. Am I right, Diablo?" Chains's earnest look at the sergeant-at-arms made Muerto want to punch him.

Diablo nodded, his face stoic.

"I knew you had a boner for her." Goldie clapped his hand on Muerto's shoulder. "Have you fucked her yet?"

Shrugging off his hand, anger seethed in Muerto like a vat of boiling wax. "Watch your goddamn mouth. And it's none of you assholes' business what the hell I do. Raven and I are just friends."

Everyone but Diablo guffawed. "Raven's her name?" Chains said.

"Oh, excuse us, dude. We didn't realize you and *Raven* were just *friends*," Goldie said as he calmed down from laughing.

"With benefits," Paco added, which started another round of hearty laughs.

The shattering of glass against the wall tore through the conversation, laughs, and voices on the TV. All eyes fixed on Muerto, whose arm was poised to throw another bottle. Steel walked in just as it crashed against the wall. Muerto let go of the beer in his hand when the president's gaze bored into him.

"What the fuck's going on?" Steel asked.

"I dunno. I was just watching TV when this beer bottle zipped over my head and hit the wall," Brutus said as Cue Ball and Eagle nodded.

"Muerto?" Steel started walking toward him.

"Ask these fuckers," he fumed.

"What's going on, Diablo?" Steel asked.

The big man shrugged. "I just asked Muerto how his woman was. Maybe he didn't like me asking."

Steel turned to Muerto. "You got a woman?" The brothers who'd been ribbing him burst out laughing again.

"Fuck it!" Muerto threw his beer bottle, narrowly missing Cue Ball's head, kicked over a chair, and marched out. Before he went through the doors, he heard Steel say, "I guess he does. I'll be damned."

Dashing over to his Harley, he cursed when his phone rang. It was Laura. *Fuck. I was supposed to get a place for Ma's birthday party.* He let the call go to voice mail and then tapped in his friend Raul's number. He and Raul had been friends since high school, and he owned a hall that he rented out for weddings, *quinceañeras*, proms, and a bunch of other life events.

"Hey, Muerto, what's shaking? It's been too long, bro."

"Yeah. Been busy. I need to rent your place for my mom's birthday party. I fucked up so this is kinda last minute. I'm hoping you can help me or Laura's gonna ride my ass about this for the next twenty years."

Raul chuckled. "When's the party?"

"In a couple of weeks on a Saturday night."

"You're making this hard for me. I'm booked every Saturday 'til the end of September."

"Fuck." Muerto leaned back on the seat of his Harley. "What the hell can I do? I gotta get something."

"You can't have it in your mom's backyard?"

"No way. Laura's invited a hundred or more people."

"That many?"

"It's crazy, I know. This all started out as a party with just us, a few aunts and uncles, and my mother's closest friends. I shoulda taken over."

"You should've. You know your sister. Let me think about it. Does it have to be in Alina? I may be able to secure you a place in Firestone. It's about a thirty-minute drive but—"

"That won't work. Laura would have my head. It's gotta be in town. I guess if nothing works out, I can have it at the clubhouse."

Raul laughed deeply. "And how do you think Laura will feel about that?"

"Pissed." His phone clicked. *Laura's calling me again. Damnit!* "Can you get back to me real soon?"

"Yeah. Wait, there's also another possibility. I can get you a tent and set it up in the back of the hall. It's beautiful back there with a waterfall, trees, flowers, and all that."

"A tent? I don't know...."

Raul chuckled. "Not like the tents you're thinking of. A nice one with air conditioning, lights, floor, dance floor, the whole bit. It'll be beautiful. It'll cost you, but you'll have a great venue, and the kids can run around outdoors."

"Sounds good. I can't visualize it, but I know you won't let me down. How much are you gonna steal from me?"

"You're desperate, which is a great position for a vendor to have a buyer in, but for you I'll give you the friendship price."

Muerto groaned jokingly. "I think I'm gonna wish I had the stranger price when this is all done."

"Don't worry, bro. I'll take care of everything. It's gonna be beautiful."

"It better fuckin' be. We'll go out drinking after the party's behind us. It'll be on me. Say hi to Linda for me. How's she been?"

"Busy with the kids and telling me all the things I'm supposed to do and fix around the house."

He sniggered. "You're the one who wanted to get married."

"And I wouldn't trade it for the world. I'll tell her you said hi. I'll be in touch with you about the pricing. We gotta move fast on this."

"Later, dude." Relief washed over him as he slid the phone in his pocket. Raul was a good buddy he could always depend on, even though they didn't see each other as much as they used to. Once Raul married and started having kids, he became more preoccupied with his business and family. Muerto got it, and he was always glad that he wasn't the one saddled down with a wife and kids, but at that moment, after speaking to him, he felt a prick of restlessness.

"Hiya, handsome." Ruby walked over to his Harley. "Are you going for a ride in this heat?" She ran her long fingers over the handlebars, slightly brushing against his hand.

"Nah, I'm going over to my sister's. How've you been?"

"Horny for you. What gives? None of us girls have been with you for almost a month. You fucking someone in town? Not that that ever stopped you before." She giggled and leaned in closer to him, her plunging neckline leaving little to the imagination.

"Just been busy with work and family stuff."

"You got time for a little fun before you take off? I've missed you."

"Not today. I'm already late."

"When are you gonna take me for a ride on your bike? Skull took Kelly for a ride down Highway 36 and she said it was so fuckin' cool."

Shaking his head, he adjusted his sunglasses. "I don't take chicks on my bike. No exceptions. That's the way I roll. Now I gotta get outta here. See ya." The Harley roared to life and Ruby jumped back. With her waving enthusiastically, he rode away.

As he headed to Laura's house, he made a sharp turn on Trail Ridge

Road. It was as if the bike were directing him instead of the other way around. Before he knew it, he was in front of the duplex, his bike vibrating under him. Changing his mind, he started to pull away from the curb when he heard Raven call out, "Hey, Muerto."

He killed the engine and swung his leg over. "Hey. I was just in the neighborhood. What're you doing?"

"Working on my painting. I heard your bike. It's weird but I can tell it's you from the sound of your Harley."

"That's not weird. Different bikes have a different sound. You still painting the woman who chops off the balls of the men she desires?"

Her laughter was like the sweet tinkling of wind chimes. "Still working on it. I just stepped out for some fresh, albeit hot-as-hell, air. I have a pitcher of Arnold Palmer if you want a glass."

"What the hell is that?"

"Half lemonade and half iced tea."

"Throw a shot of Jack in mine and I'll be good." Again her soft laugh made him smile. He walked up to her porch.

"I'll be right back with that shot."

Settling on the cushion of the bamboo chair, he lifted his feet and placed them on the ottoman. His phone pinged again. Laura. Not in the mood to talk, he shot her a quick text telling her he was tied up and would get in touch with her later.

"Here you are." She placed a glass full of amber liquid on the side table next to him.

Her long hair was up in a messy bun, showing off the graceful curve of her neck. He wanted to reach out and tug her to his lap so he could kiss her creamy white skin. *Maybe even put a nice love bite on it to give her some color.*

"I love lazy summer afternoons," she said as she sat in the chair next to his. "The hours just drift like they're small pieces of eternity dropped into our hands. I'm always sad when the summer ends. It feels like the end of carefree days and easy living. I guess it's because the heat doesn't make you want to do anything. When it's cold out, I always feel so much more productive and invigorated." Shifting her gaze from the street to him, she smiled.

I'm so into this woman. She intrigues the hell outta me. "When it's hot as hell, I always want the cold and when it's cold as fuck, I wish it was hot." He shrugged. "I like fall the best. It's awesome to ride your bike over the small roads around the mountains and see the trees lit up in red and yellow with the desert below."

"That sounds gorgeous. I'd love to see that sometime. I haven't explored much of the countryside."

"I can take you when it cools down. Riding with the wind hugging you is the best."

"I may take you up on the offer." She sipped her Arnold Palmer.

Did I just ask her to ride on my bike? What's going on with me?

"You look pretty with your hair up," a gravelly voice said. Muerto craned his neck and saw Walter. "Oh… Muerto. I didn't see you with Ms. Raven."

Huh? "Hey."

"Are you and Ms. Raven imbibing in some cool refreshments? It's certainly a hot day."

Muerto noticed the man's gaze fixed on Raven, and she fidgeted around in her seat. "Yeah, we're shooting the shit and having a couple of drinks." He chuckled when Walter's nose crinkled. "Did you want anything?"

"No. I just came back from the store and stopped to say hello to Ms. Raven." With his head bent down, he slinked away.

"What the fuck's up with him? I know he's weird, but he was stranger than usual."

Wringing her hands, she looked at him and said in a low voice, "He creeps me out. He's always skulking around, popping up when I start to garden or coming up to me whenever I'm outside. At this rate, my vegetables are going to die because he watches me the whole time I'm weeding and watering them. It makes me very uncomfortable, so I just go back in the house."

"Really? How long has this been going on?"

"Since I moved in."

"You should've told me about it. You've got every right to garden and be outside as he does. He shouldn't be intimidating you."

Grasping the back of her neck, she said, "It's not like he's intimidating me. I mean, I can garden if I want to, of course. It's just that he unnerves me. I don't know how to explain it. I guess you have to be a woman to get what I'm trying to say."

"I get it. I'll have a talk with him and this shit will stop. I'll take care of it."

"No, don't do that. I don't want him to think I'm against him. I'm not sure what he's capable of."

"What does that mean? Has he done something besides staring at you?"

"I'm not sure. A few days ago, I stepped on a rose that had been left on my porch. As a matter of fact, there were a dozen roses laying on my front door mat. It was the oddest thing. And there wasn't a note."

"You think Walter put them there?"

She shrugged. "I don't know what I think. It was the strangest thing, and no one has fessed up to it as of yet."

"Maybe some teen in the neighborhood has a crush on you. You're a very striking woman."

Smiling, she looked up at him demurely. "Thank you. And maybe you're right. There're a couple of high school guys who are always smiling, waving, and offering to help me with my groceries. I forgot about that. I bet you're right."

"I'm sure I am. You're a teen boy's perfect wet dream with your long hair, cute ass, and sexy curves. Hell, you're a *man's* wet dream." Leaning over, he picked up his glass. "Did I embarrass you? Your cheeks are as red as your paints." He chuckled when her hands flew to her face.

"You don't have any filters when you speak, do you? I'm not used to men speaking so bluntly. But thanks for your... unconventional compliment."

"I just tell it like it is. I find you attractive and alluring. I have from the first day I saw you. That's all." Finishing his drink, he wiped his hands on his jeans, then stood up. "I gotta get going. I have to see my sister. We're planning a birthday party for our mom."

"How nice. Sounds like it's going to be a surprise party."

He nodded. "It is, and Laura's making a huge deal out of it." She chuckled. "I better go before she freaks out. She's already called several times. Thanks for the drink."

"I'll walk you to your bike."

After walking in silence, he leaned against the bike and fixed his gaze on her lovely face. "Come here," he said in a low voice, his arm stretched out to her. She took a small tentative step toward him. "I'm not gonna bite you unless you want me to." He winked.

Shaking her head, she said, "You'd like that, wouldn't you?" She took a few more steps forward, placing her small hand in his large one.

Yanking her to him, he breathed her seductive scent in deeply, the one that was causing his dick to wake up. "I wanna ask you something." She tilted her head back, her full lips slightly parted. "You wanna go with me to my mom's birthday party? It's gonna be in two weeks." A chortle escaped from her parted lips and he wanted to swallow it.

"I wasn't expecting that. I thought you were going to ask me something cru—uh… yes, I'd love to go to your mother's birthday party."

Fuck yeah! Cupping her chin in his hand, he dipped his head down and kissed her gently. "Awesome." His phone pinged. *Give me a fuckin' break, Laura.* "I really gotta go. I'll be in touch."

"Okay. Thanks for the invite. Ride safely." She stood back as he jumped on his bike and peeled away from the curb.

As he turned at the corner, he looked back and saw her shimmering in the sunlight. Turning back to the street, he rode to Laura's house.

Chapter Fourteen

SILVERADO WAS A town about an hour away from Alina. The brothers liked going there to hang out with the guys in the Fallen Slayers MC. The two clubs had been friendly with each other for several years, and they met up every two months or so to play pool, party, shoot the breeze, and ride together. They usually took turns between coming to Alina and Silverado. The last time the Night Rebels saw the Fallen Slayers was when the Silverado club came to Alina for one of their no-holds-barred parties. Since then, the Fallen Slayers had been bugging the brothers to come to their neck of the woods to shoot some pool at a new place, the Trick Shot, that one of their buddies had opened a few months back.

Since it was Monday night and Balls and Holes was closed, Crow and Muerto thought it would be a nice gesture if they asked Brandy and Jaime to go to Silverado and check out the new place. The women had worked their asses off over the weekend, and a night spent in another town with a new group of men provided them with a much-needed distraction. They'd readily agreed, and since neither Crow nor Muerto wanted to have the women on the back of their bikes, Crow volunteered to take the four of them in his SUV.

Several Night Rebels rode up on their Harleys to meet up with their Silverado buddies. Fallen Slayers MC was a smaller club with only ten members. Roughneck, the president, had met Steel at a biker rally several years before. They hit it off, and when Steel invited Roughneck and his brothers to one of the Night Rebels parties, a bond had been formed. The revenue for the Fallen Slayers club came mostly from receiving and selling weed and stolen property—usually bike and car parts. Since they didn't have a license for selling pot, their transactions were illegal. Every once in a while, they'd enlist the help of the Night Rebels in an arms trade with another club or a low-level gangster from the bigger towns.

"Hey, Roughneck, what's up?" Steel said as he entered the pool hall with his brothers.

"Not much." He raised his eyebrows when he saw Brandy and Jaime. "You brought women? I thought you had a woman."

"I do. They came with Crow and Muerto. They work for us at Balls and Holes. They're not club girls or hang-arounds. You got my drift?" Steel pulled out a chair with his boot.

"Too fuckin' bad. They're real lookers. I gotta tell my men. I see the hunger in their eyes already." Roughneck went over to a group of guys hanging around the bar.

Muerto noticed all the Fallen Slayers were there: Skeet, Buzz, Tequila, Tats, Griller, Knuckles, Ironclad, Patriot, and Brick. Knuckles was the sergeant-at-arms and was always on the lookout for a good fight. Muerto had jumped in on many a barroom brawl with him, Buzz, Griller, and Brick. He held his fist in the air and they returned the gesture.

"It's really nice in here," Jaime said as she sat down on one of the barstools.

"It looks like an upscale bar." Brandy scanned the place while pulling her spandex top down a bit more.

Muerto saw the look a couple of the Fallen Slayers gave her and knew if she laid it on too thick, he'd be knocking their heads before the night was over. *I'm gonna have to play babysitter to her and Jaime. Fuck.* They probably shouldn't have asked them to come; he hadn't thought it through. A light tap on his arm made him turn around.

"Thanks for bringing us here," Jaime said, her eyes shining. "I don't get out much, and when I do, I always end up at the same places. Alina isn't that big. It's fun being in a different place. I've never been to Silverado."

"No problem. Order yourself a drink. Tonight's on the club."

Paco came over to Muerto, a skinny girl hanging onto his arm. "You in for a game of pool? Knuckles and Brick are asking."

"You work fast," he said as he nodded to the girl. "I'll pass on the game. Maybe later." He leaned closer to Paco. "I gotta keep an eye out for Brandy and Jaime. I don't want any shit to come down on them. You playing?"

Paco smiled and pressed the woman closer to him. "Yeah, but not pool."

Muerto laughed and shook his head as he watched the vice president walk away. Looking around the place, he spotted Goldie, Chains, and Skull by the pool tables in the back. The pool hall was one of the modern ones: top-of-the-line pool tables, wooden tables and red leather chairs, a dance floor, and a menu for sandwiches and appetizers. It was the total opposite of Balls and Holes, and Muerto wasn't crazy about it. It looked like some of the modern places he'd seen in Durango and Pueblo. It didn't have the feel of the game about it.

"You look real handsome tonight," Brandy said to Muerto as she outlined the rim of her glass with her green-tipped fingernail. Muerto smiled and picked up his beer bottle.

"What about me? I took hours to get ready. You're always going on about Muerto." Crow winked at his buddy.

Brandy laughed. "And you look damn good too. You're always coming on to me and Jaime. You're too easy. But Muerto?" She glanced at him and cocked her head to the side. "You're a different story. You act so aloof, but I know you've fucked half of Alina. What's the secret to riding you?"

"Don't work with him," Crow said. "We got a policy of no fuckin' the help."

"Didn't stop you from making out with me and Jaime when we first got onboard. You remember that, don't you?" She looked at Jaime and then Muerto. Jaime smiled tightly.

"We were all so damned drunk and I didn't think either of you would last more than a week. Anyway, making out and screwing are two different things." Muerto took a long pull on his beer. "You sayin' you never made out with Crow?"

"Don't drag me into this, brother. I follow the policy." Crow leaned back against the bar.

"Muerto does too. It was just that one night, and I'm just giving him a hard time." She leaned against him. "And you've been a perfect gentleman ever since, hasn't he, Jaime?"

Nodding, Jaime stared at her drink.

"Lay off, Brandy. You're embarrassing her." Muerto put his arm lightly around Jaime. "Don't pay any attention to her. She's tipsy. Remember, she had a few shots on the way up and a couple since we got here. Just have a good time." He pulled away and raised his fist to Army, Jigger, and Sangre as they walked in.

As the brothers talked, played pool, and flirted with Brandy, Jaime, and a few other women, Muerto found his thoughts drifting to Raven. He still couldn't believe he'd asked her to his mother's birthday party, but he wanted to share that part of him with her. For the first time in his life, he wanted a woman to meet his mother and sisters.

A buxom blonde stared at him from a booth against the wall, smiling broadly when he looked at her. If he was into it, he figured it'd take him maybe twenty minutes and a couple of drinks before she'd spread for him in one of the back rooms. Shifting his gaze away, he reached for his beer. *I haven't fucked in almost a month. Damn! How the hell did that happen?* He'd been so busy with the pool hall, bike repair shop, and running his rental properties that he hadn't been interested in anything else. Actually, he hadn't really been that involved with his properties except for one of the duplexes, the one the black-haired vixen rented.

I don't know how she's doing it, but she's got a hold of my dick and it doesn't want to go anywhere else but in her. No woman had ever had such an impact on him, and he wasn't quite sure how to handle it. The more he tried to forget her, the more he thought of her. And then he went and asked her to his mother's party. *I don't know what the hell is—*

His thoughts were interrupted by some ruckus in the back where the pool tables were. Before he could figure out what was going on, Roughneck, jaw tight and scowling, came over with one of his brothers, Tequila. Slamming his fist on the counter, he yelled, "Fuck that shit!"

A muscular, broad-shouldered man in his late thirties came over. "What's got you so pissed off?"

"You got a fuckin' pool shark hustling my brothers, Mac. Since when do you let that shit go on in your hall?"

As the owner and the biker president spoke, apprehension and anger knotted inside Muerto. He glanced at Crow, who stared back at him. As Muerto opened his mouth to say something, Brick came over, cussing up a storm.

"I fuckin' lost my balls to a bitch who hustled me. I been playing the game for the last couple of hours and she acted like she was a dumb fuck. Turns out she's a damn good player. Like a fuckin' pro."

"I'm not gonna have that shit in my place." Red splotches flared up over Mac's frowning face. "I'll take care of this."

Crow cleared his throat and pointed to Muerto, then himself. "We may know who you're talkin' about."

Army pushed himself into the conversation. "I heard the bitch tried the same shit at our pool hall." He glanced at Crow and Muerto. "You guys know her, right?"

"Does she have long black hair?" Muerto asked as dread wrapped around him.

"Down to her rounded ass that I'm planning to fuck hard. I'll show the cunt what happens when she fucks over a biker. Get rid of the citizens, Mac. You're closing shop. We're pulling a train on the bitch. I'm gonna make sure I rough up all her holes."

In biker vernacular, "pulling a train" meant all members had sex with a woman any way they wanted. In many of the outlaw clubs, it was the way to initiate a club girl. Being a club girl meant that the woman wore the MC's "Property Of" patch. A woman who wanted to be a club girl knew the initiation process and agreed to be part of it. In some clubs, pulling a train was used as punishment for a woman who disrespected the brotherhood.

Muerto stood up. "I got this, dude. I know her. I'll make it right."

By that time, several more Fallen Slayers had come over to see why Brick was so riled up. Knuckles pounded one of his fists into the palm of his hand. "The cunt has to pay for disrespecting a brother. No one makes a fuckin' fool out of a Fallen Slayer. And we don't give a damn if it's a bitch or a dude—they're going down if they mess with us."

"Knuckles, Brick, I got this." Muerto started to go but Brandy grabbed his arm, stopping him.

"Let the bitch fend for herself," she said in a low voice. "You've warned her about doing this shit, so why break up a fun time over her?"

"Brandy's right. She knows the consequence of doing this sort of thing. I wouldn't get involved in it," Jaime said softly.

"It sounds like this cunt has been warned, so this is probably the lesson she needs," Knuckles said while Tequila, Griller, and Skeet nodded.

"We'll take care of this. No reason to pull a train without the chick wanting it," Army said.

"That's the way we teach bitches a lesson when they disrespect the club," Brick gritted, the vein in his temple pulsing. "You guys gonna stop us?" Several of the Fallen Slayers came over, their faces taut, their fists clenched.

"We're just saying no one's doing shit to anyone until we see what's going on. And as long as we're here, no one's pulling a train unless the woman wants it," Steel said as he walked over. "You got a problem with this, Roughneck?"

A strained silence fell between the two clubs, then Roughneck cleared his throat. "Make this right or we will."

Tension squeezed every nerve in Muerto's body as the battle between loyalty to the brotherhood waged with his feelings for Raven. *I can't have anything happen to her.* Pulling his arm out of Brandy's grasp, he said loudly, "I said I'd fuckin' take care of this." Turning his back to the group, he made his way to the pool tables.

Before he got to the area, he saw her bent over the table taking a shot. She looked so sexy in her jeans and crop top, her black hair cascading down her back. It looked like Indian ink as it shined under the brass light fixture. As he approached, her signature scent tantalized him. Right before she made the shot, he coughed loudly.

Jumping, she missed the ball. "What the fuck?" She whirled around angrily, her eyes glistening brightly, cold and metallic. Then when her gaze landed on his, she stopped dead in her tracks. "You made me miss that shot," she said softly.

"And it's a damn good thing I did. These guys are ready to strip your hide. Come on." He grabbed her arm and yanked her away from the table.

"I haven't finished the game yet."

"Yeah you have." He dragged her to the other side of the room, ignoring the jeers and glares. As she tried to break away from him, he tightened his grip.

Finally he stopped. "How much money did you win?" She shrugged. "Raven, I don't have time for this bullshit. Where's the money?" She crossed her arms and looked away. "Woman, even if I have to take all your clothes off to find it, I will. Now hand it over."

Tossing her head, she said, "I keep my winnings in my bra, and I'm not going to give them to you."

"Yeah you are, or I'm gonna take it. You got two seconds to make your choice."

"You wouldn't dare." She raised her chin.

"Really? Sweetheart, I've been wanting to touch your tits for a while now, so this is as good a time as any." His hand skimmed her top.

"Wait! I'll give it to you." In one movement she retrieved the dough. "What're you going to do with it?"

"Give it back. Do you realize you were playing against bikers? From the look on your face, I'll take that as a no. Biker lesson one: When dudes wear leather vests with the name of an MC on the back and the guys are covered in tats, they're bikers. And we don't fuckin' like being hustled. They're ready to teach you a lesson you'd be lucky to survive. Why the fuck are you hustling? Do you wanna get yourself killed?"

"What do you care? I'm nothing to you."

"What the fuck are you saying? If you didn't mean something to me, I wouldn't be explaining all this shit to you, and I wouldn't have asked you to my mom's goddamn birthday party. You're the most infuriating woman." He counted out the money. "How much did Brick lose?"

"Who?"

"The dude with the shaved head built like a brick house. Looks like he lives in the gym."

"Oh. Him. A couple thousand. Why?"

"'Cause you're giving it back. You're giving all the money back to everyone you hustled."

"And why would I do that?"

He shrugged. "I don't know. Maybe it's because you wanna live, or you don't want your pussy and asshole ripped to shreds?" When her face blanched, he knew he'd made his point. "Don't move. Wait here."

He walked over to the table where Brick and a couple of the other guys who lost money to Raven sat. "Here," he said as he handed each of the men their bills.

"You hot for the bitch?" Brick asked as he shoved the money in his pocket.

"Not exactly." Goldie, Crow, Chains, and Skull sniggered. Muerto threw them a dirty look. "She's one of my tenants. I need the rent."

Brick clapped Muerto's shoulder and let out a loud laugh. "Don't want you to go hungry, brother. And I don't blame you for wanting to keep her pussy safe. She's a looker, but she better never hustle in this county again. You tell her she got a freebie on account of you."

"Yeah. We're gonna take off."

"What do you mean?" Jaime asked.

"You don't need to go. You girls can stay with the others, but you should leave when the Night Rebels do. I'm gonna make sure Raven gets home okay." He bumped fists with his brothers and the Fallen Slayer members, then went over to Raven. "We're outta here. Consider yourself lucky as hell."

"Thank you." Her gray orbs gazed deeply at him, bewitching him, and then she smiled and an irresistible urge to kiss her seized him. Slipping her hand into his, she whispered, "Let's go."

For a split second he couldn't move; he'd thought for sure she'd fight him, but she acted like she wanted to be with him. Nodding, he squeezed her hand and led her outside.

"Give me your keys." Again, without argument, she handed them over. After closing her door, he slipped into the driver seat, and soon they were on the freeway heading back to Alina.

"I was surprised to see you tonight," she said, breaking the silence.

"Likewise. Why the hell did you do that shit tonight? Do you need money?" He glanced at her sideways and saw her turn her head to look out the window. Miles of rocky sand and sagebrush blurred by. Not prodding her, he waited for her to speak as he counted the mile markers on the side of the road, lighting up when the headlights shone on them.

After a long while, she said in a voice he could barely hear, "I needed the money to get to Denver to deliver my paintings. Things are a little tight right now, and I didn't want to lose the opportunity."

"Why didn't you come to me? I would've loaned you the money."

She stared straight ahead. "All my life I've never asked anyone for anything. My dad and I fended for ourselves. It never occurred to me to ask you or anyone else for help. It's just not my way."

"Sometimes you have to. Is your business slow?"

"No. It's just that I have a lot of expenses, and I send money home to my dad."

He looked at her. "I thought he was doing okay."

"He is, but sometimes he spends all of his allowance and hates asking Wanda for more, so I send him something to tie him over until the next month. I don't do it all the time."

"Next time, just ask me and I'll loan it to you. What you're doing is fuckin' dangerous and stupid, and it's going to wind up getting you seriously hurt or killed. If I hadn't been there tonight, you'd have found yourself in a real fucked-up situation. Promise me you'll stop hustling." He glanced at her, her gaze now on him. "I don't want anything to happen to you." Grasping her hand, he squeezed it.

"You know, I didn't know you cared. It makes me feel weird in a good way that I have someone who cares and is looking out for me. My dad took care of me the best way he knew how, but sometimes I felt like I was crimping his style, holding him back from the kind of life that he really wanted to lead. I don't know. With you, I feel something. I'm drawn to you, and I think you are to me too." Her voice was soft like velvet as it covered him with tenderness.

Not thinking, he pulled over to the shoulder of the freeway and tugged her to him. A surprised yelp slipped from her throat before he pressed his lips to hers, devouring their softness. His tongue dove into the sweet depths of her mouth, her enticing scent flooding his senses.

Clasping her hands on either side of his face, she pulled him closer until there was no space left between them. In that moment, as she kissed him back, his brain lit on fire and heat roared through him. He was addicted.

Pulling back, a small smile danced on her wet lips as her silvery orbs glimmered. "We should probably get back on the road."

Nodding, he merged back onto the freeway. After he tuned the radio to the only station he could find—country—he clasped her hand in his and looked up at the carpet of blinking stars. *I'm fuckin' hooked on her and I haven't even fucked her. I've never felt like this before.* Clutching her hand, he glanced at her and smiled when she grinned devilishly. His foot pressed the accelerator to the floor; he couldn't get back to Alina soon enough.

Chapter Fifteen

A S RAVEN SLIPPED the key into her door, she glanced over her shoulder and looked up at him. "Do you want to come in?"

"You gonna cut off my balls?" he asked as he nipped the side of her neck, then peppered it with small kisses.

Electric tingles skated along her skin and she shivered. "I'm planning to do a lot more than that." The door swung open and they were bathed in the soft light from the living room. Sooty rubbed against her, purring while her big eyes fixed warily on Muerto. When Raven bent over to pick up Sooty, her behind brushed against Muerto's legs, his sharp intake of breath telling her that he was going to stay.

Since he'd asked her to go with him to his mother's birthday party, her stomach would clench and twist each time she thought of him. And the way he'd swooped in and taken her out of the arms of danger earlier in the night made her hope that he felt something more than lust for her. Lust was there for her as well, but she also *liked* this rough-and-tumble kind of man. Excitement and unpredictable went hand in hand with what she knew of his personality and lifestyle, pulling her tighter into his net of sexiness, power, and desire.

"Get comfortable and have a seat. I'll get us some drinks. Whiskey or tequila?" she asked as she walked to the kitchen, Sooty padding behind her.

"Whiskey." The deepness of his voice stroked her. While she took out the bottle of Jack Daniels, she heard two loud thuds coming from the living room. "You okay?" Stretching up, she grabbed two glasses.

"Yeah. Just kicked off my boots."

I love that he's comfortable with me. And fuck, can he kiss. Quivers danced in her stomach when she recalled the heated kiss he gave her on the side of the freeway. She couldn't believe how intense it was. She had never known a man as blunt, spontaneous, or confident as Muerto. *Brent would never have pulled over like that. He'd have worried that someone might hit the car.* When he'd first pulled to the side of the road, she thought there'd been a problem with the car, but when he drew her into his arms and kissed her, her body went into overdrive. The more heated his kiss became, the faster she melted. *It was incredible.*

"Need some help?" his voice cut in on her thoughts.

"I got it. Thanks. Coming." After replenishing Sooty's dish with more food, she went into the living room and placed the bottle and glasses on the table.

When she sat down, his arm immediately moved around her shoulders, nudging her closer to him. Leaning into him, she breathed in his leather and soap scent, the one she had determined was one of her favorites. Light strokes brushed away her hair from her neck, and she looked at him, her heart skipping a beat when his gaze fell to the creamy expanse of her neck. Bending down, his lips pressed against her skin and shivers danced through her.

"You have such soft skin. It fuckin' drives me crazy, woman." His breath was hot on her neck, and as the kisses became more passionate, tiny whimpers escaped from her parted lips. Moving his mouth near her ear, his lips grazed her earlobe. "You have me wanting to do nasty things to you."

His words landed right between her legs, and she clenched them together to relieve some of the aching. Muerto's knowing chuckle only made it worse. "I think we should cool off a bit with a drink," she murmured against his lips as she pushed back slightly. Picking up the bottle of Jack, she opened it, poured them a drink, and leaned back against the couch. "Cheers." She clinked her glass against his.

"To a fun night." He winked at her as he brought the glass to his lips.

As they sat next to each other, drinking whiskey, all she could think about was the hot-as-sin biker beside her. The heat from his desire radiated from him, making her senses spin. His fingers brushed her midriff right under the hem of her crop top. With her pulse pounding in her ears, she held her breath in anticipation but his hand merely rested on her ribs, scorching her skin, teasing her.

"When do you have to send your paintings to the gallery in Denver?" he asked casually.

"Next week." She was too aware of his hand on her exposed skin.

"You gonna drive or mail them?"

"Not sure now that I don't have the money. I'd prefer to mail them."

"When you're done, give 'em to me. I'll take care of it." Two of his fingers slipped under the hem of her top. Sucking in her breath, she nodded. "Did you think about getting a vendor booth at the upcoming rally?"

"Yeah." His fingers singed her skin as they crept very slowly upward underneath her top.

"Did you ever call Breanna?" He took another gulp of his drink.

"Not yet," she answered tightly. *He's right under my boob. How the fuck can he be sitting here talking like nothing's happening? I'm dying here.*

"Make sure you do. She's really nice." He stroked the underside of her breast and she moaned. "You like that?" he asked thickly.

"Yeah."

When his index finger flicked against her hardening nipple, she squirmed in her seat, the jolt of pleasure hitting her right in her wet pussy. She was a hot mess and all she wanted was for him to fuck her. Hard. Deep. Rough. In one fluid motion, she turned so that she was astride him, her hands raking through his thick hair. Without missing a beat, he lifted her top and brought his mouth to her tits, tasting, biting, and sucking them. Arching her back, she pushed them into his face, loving the feel of his tongue as it teased her buds to reddened points.

"That feels awesome," she sighed. Underneath her butt, she could feel his hardness; she wanted to touch it, suck it, taste him. "Let's go to the bedroom," she rasped. She stood and a startled cry rang out when he picked her up in his arms and carried her to the bedroom.

The minute he put her on her feet, he yanked her to him, kissing her passionately, his tongue delving in deep as his hands trailed down her back and tried to dip inside her jeans. "These are too fuckin' tight," he growled as he fumbled in the front until he found the zipper. "And take this off. I want to see your tits, sweetheart."

She flung the top over her head and it landed halfway off the bed. Bothered by his bold and frank stare at her breasts, she instinctively covered them with her arms.

"Why're you covering your tits? They're gorgeous." He untangled her arms and whistled softly. "So beautiful, and they're mine." Cupping the underside of each breast, he pushed them up and bent down to lick their creamy tops. Running his tongue over them, he gently sucked in each nipple, nipping them with his teeth.

As he played with her breasts, his hands dipped inside her jeans, cupping her buttocks and squeezing them hard. "You've got such a luscious ass," he said against her tits.

Groaning, she tugged his head up and brought his face closer to hers. Her tongue tangled with his as she humped his denim-clad leg. He shoved her jeans down and they puddled at her feet.

"You're so damn beautiful," he said as he fisted her hair. "I wanna see all of you." Taking a couple of steps back, his gaze swept over her. "Take off your panties," he ordered.

With excitement bubbling inside her, she slipped off her plain cotton bikini undies, wishing she'd had on something sexier. But from the lust in his look, she didn't think he cared all that much if her panties were cotton or silk.

"I knew you'd be curvy, but damn, woman, you're fuckin' hot." In one step, he had her in his arms, his hands roaming over her skin as his lips consumed hers. Fiery. Passionate. Demanding. In that moment, her senses had been seduced, and she gave herself over to him wholeheartedly.

Lying on the bed, she watched his muscles ripple as he pulled his T-shirt over his head and shook off his jeans and boxers. His dick jutted out, hard and thick. Bathed in the light from the lamp, she could see the vein pulsing and the crown glistening with pre-come. An urge to taste him overcame her and she sat up and crawled to him, her fingers itching to grasp him.

When she licked the top of his dick, a guttural moan rose from deep in his chest. She looked up and caught his smoldering gaze before slowly taking him in her mouth, her eyes never leaving his.

"Fuck," he exhaled as she pushed him farther into her mouth.

When she cupped his balls and gently stroked them, she smiled inwardly at the thought of the painting and their private joke.

He must've been thinking the same thing because he chuckled and stroked her hair. "Be careful with those, sweetheart. Remember *Devoradora* is just folklore."

Raven winked at him and kept sucking him deep and slow. As she kicked up the pace, he gently pulled away and eased her down on her back. He reached behind him, took out a packet, and then tossed his jeans to the floor. "When I'm ready," he breathed before he hovered over her and kissed her deeply.

Breaking away, he leaned back on his knees, his eyes running over her. He spread her legs wide, opening her glistening mound. "Fuck, you have the most beautiful pussy I've seen," he said as he ran his fingers up from her ankles to her inner thighs. Goose bumps peppered her skin and she shivered under his touch as a small moan slipped through her lips.

Holding her breath, she watched as he lowered himself between her legs, trembling when he lightly nipped and kissed her lower belly and inner thighs. Then he dipped in and flicked his tongue against her clit. Fire burned through her at the contact and she thrust her hips toward his face. She lifted her head slightly off the pillow to watch him pleasure her, loving how his gaze engulfed hers.

When he raised his head, his slick face was covered in her juices. Looking at his shiny chin and lips turned her on and she reached for him. Hanging his head down, his mouth covered hers and she tasted herself on his tongue while he plunged a finger into her heated wetness. A jolt of white-hot gratification arced through her body.

"You're so fuckin' wet and ready for me. You wanna feel me inside you?"

"Yeah. I need you."

He tore open the packet with his teeth and rolled on the condom. Picking up her legs, he rested them on his shoulders, then looked down at her sex. Burying his finger between her folds, he rubbed her special spot and she writhed under his touch. "Does that feel good?"

"Yeah," she panted.

She watched him rub his stiff cock against her clit, then felt his hardness probing her wet slit. He winked at her and plunged into her slippery pussy. Her walls clamped around him and he groaned as he began to move in and out of her.

"I'm gonna make you come until you beg me to stop," he said thickly.

She watched him lose himself in his need, in her warm, wet pussy. Every so often he would bend over and kiss her lips, her throat, her tits, and then he'd start pounding her hard and fast. His kisses melted her heart while his fucking melted her pussy.

"I love watching you when I fuck you. You're so tight and wet. Damn, you feel good around my cock."

Harder and harder he slammed into her, his balls smacking against her ass. And when he slipped his finger between them, his fingertip steadily rubbing against her hard nub, tendrils of wicked pleasure tore through her sex. "Oh fuck!" she cried.

He pushed her knees closer to her face and pummeled her while a whirlwind of rapture still spun inside her. When she heard him grunt and stiffen, she knew he was climaxing, and she ran her nails up and down his arms.

"Fuck. Fuck!" he grunted.

Then he collapsed on her, panting and shuddering. She stroked his damp hair while her body began to calm down. *That was the most intense orgasm I've ever had.* Her mind was still reeling when he kissed her before he pulled out. He lay on his back, tugging her close and kissing her head and face. She inhaled deeply. She loved his scent—the scent of them. She rested her head on him, tracing the tattoos on his chest with her fingertip.

"That was fuckin' awesome." He clutched her tightly.

"It was incredible." She dusted soft kisses on his chest.

Cupping her chin, he tilted her head back and kissed her deeply. "I'm not gonna lie to you. I've never come that hard. I didn't expect that."

"It was a first for me too. I mean coming that intensely. Wow. I don't know what to say."

He kissed the tip of her nose. "We're good together." And when he smiled tenderly, her insides lit up like a firework display.

Nuzzling her face into his chest, she closed her eyes. She was full, spent, and exhausted. As he stroked, sleep came quickly.

THE FOLLOWING MORNING, Raven woke to Muerto's breathing. At first she was disoriented since she'd grown accustomed to sleeping alone, but when the memories of the previous night flooded her mind, she rolled over and watched as he slept. Strands of dark hair clung to his forehead and neck, and his usual smartass demeanor was gone in sleep. *He's beautiful.* She lightly brushed the tendrils from his face, then softly kissed his lips. His eyes fluttered open.

"I'm sorry. I didn't mean to wake you. Go back to sleep," she whispered as she stroked his cheek.

Smiling widely, he snagged her waist with his arm and drew her closer. "You look beautiful in the morning." He kissed her eyelids, then her lips. "You're so fuckin' awesome," he murmured against her skin as his kisses trailed down past her chin to the soft flesh of her neck. "So sexy," he breathed as his strong hands began to caress her along with his mouth, lips, and tongue.

So gentle and enticing. Shivers swept across her skin, and she felt her nipples rise. Slow, heated strokes singed her as he moved down her body. She let go, feeling nothing but the delicious sensations his sensual ministrations lavished on her until she was nothing but her body. His tongue, like soft velvet, dipped into her aching folds and a sweet spasm went through her. It was intense and its quickness startled her. Then ripples of pleasure washed over her as each nerve, cell, and muscle responded to her orgasm. His panting drew her attention to him, and she grinned as she yanked him hard against her.

Soon the small room was filled with the sounds of their ecstasy and scent of their arousal as they gave each other what they craved.

A couple hours later, Raven sat at the kitchen table sketching a new idea she had for a painting when Muerto walked in, the scent of soap and freshness lingering on him.

"Do you want me to make you a breakfast burrito? Eggs, cheese, serrano peppers, green chiles, potatoes, onions, and red peppers?"

He came behind her and draped his arms over her shoulders. She tilted her head back and looked up at him as he planted a big kiss on her mouth. "Sounds delicious." After giving her breasts a squeeze, he went over to a kitchen chair and sat down.

"Coffee, orange juice, cranberry juice, all of the above, or none of the above?" she asked as she bent down to take out a frying pan.

He laughed. "You like choices. Coffee and orange juice are good."

While they ate, they chatted about her paintings, the upcoming rally, the child abuse charity the club supported, and his mother's birthday party.

"Do you think your sister's going to be mad about the tent?"

"Probably. She's one of those who isn't happy unless she's pissed about something."

"I went to a wedding once where the reception was in a huge tent and it had AC, chandeliers, lights everywhere, fancy table settings, and so much more. It was just like I was in a fancy hotel in one of the ballrooms. I was blown away. If the tent your friend's getting for the party is anything like that, it'll totally rock." She cleared the dishes from the table.

Muerto nodded. "I trust Raul, so I know it's gonna be kickass." He stood up. "I gotta get going. I've got a ton of stuff I have to do before I head over to the pool hall. You wanna come by tonight?"

"Sure. Around nine or ten? I'm going to work the rest of the day on my painting. I'm almost done."

"Cool." Throwing her a hard stare, he rubbed his hand over his five o'clock shadow. "No hustling, okay?"

"Yeah, sure. I wasn't planning on it."

Catching her around the waist when she came by to wipe off the table, he kissed her deeply. "I wish I could spend the day with you. I can't wait for tonight. You do something to me."

"Tonight seems like it won't came fast enough. I'll drop you at the clubhouse." She kissed him back, then stepped away.

"No worries, sweetie. I texted Goldie to pick me up and he just said that he's out front. I gotta go."

She followed him outside and he kissed her quickly before he opened the car door. "See you tonight," he whispered in her ear, the feel of his lips against her earlobe lighting up her sensory circuits. Sliding inside the car, he winked at her and then closed the door.

She watched until the vehicle was out of sight, then turned around to head back inside. Humming, she was on cloud nine. Her whole body buzzed and a rush of warm excitement spread through her. *I'm so damn happy!* But she had to pull back on the reins because she didn't want to get hurt. *He gets major kudos for being sweet as shit this morning and making a date with me for tonight, but I don't want to lose myself yet.*

As she ambled up the walkway, she felt someone watching her. She spun around and met Walter's glaring eyes. His face had red splotches and was bloated with anger.

"Hey," she said in a small voice. There was no answer, only rage emanating from him. Quickly turning around, she dashed to her porch, went inside, and locked the door. *What the fuck's his problem?* Deciding that he wasn't going to ruin the good mood she was in, she picked up her paintbrush and began working. As she painted, Muerto and their time together flitted through her mind, and she worked feverishly with a big smile on her face.

Chapter Sixteen

MUERTO STARED PLACIDLY at Laura, who sat across from him knitting her brows. He'd expected much worse when he'd told her about the tent for the party. From the time they were kids, her way of punishing him was to make him feel guilty. Giving him the *mal de ojo*—the evil eye—seemed to be a new tactic, and it was just as ineffective on him as her old tactic used to be.

After several minutes of silence, Laura sighed deeply and placed her hand over her heart. Muerto glanced at the wall clock, then back at her. "Cut the fuckin' dramatics. I get that you're pissed about the tent, but Raul promised me it'll be awesome. I thought it would be great for the kids too 'cause they can run around outside and let the adults have some peace."

"I knew I should have handled the place. I wanted a proper venue for Ma. This is a milestone—fifty years old." She sighed again.

"It'll be nice. You want me to get the band?"

"Are you sure? I thought having ranchera and mariachi music would be nice. We could have mariachi earlier in the evening and ranchera for dancing after dinner."

"Sounds good. I can get both bands. I think that's about it." He glanced at the clock again and then, against his better judgment, said, "I'm bringing someone to the party."

Her eyes widened. "A girl?"

"Of course."

A big smile spread across her face. "She must be someone you really like if you're bringing her to Ma's party. What's her name?"

"Raven, and I do like her."

Laura clapped her hands. "Finally! Ma will be thrilled, and I'm so happy. It's about time you settled down. You're at the age where you have to think about your future."

"Will you calm the fuck down? I asked her to the party, not to marry me. Don't make this out to be more than it is."

"You don't fool me. I know you, and you've never brought a woman to meet Ma. She's got you, and I love it." She laughed loudly.

Scowling, he stood up and went into the kitchen to get another beer. Even in high school, he didn't bring his dates home. Back then, he'd never been the type to date just one woman at a time. He'd preferred messing around with the fast girls because they'd loved the thrill of a quickie romance and weren't looking to date exclusively. *Raven's exactly the type of woman I want Mom to meet. She fuckin' grounds me. How the hell does she do that?*

"Can you bring me a Pepsi?" Laura asked, crashing in on his thoughts.

He opened the fridge again and grabbed a can. As he walked into the family room, his niece and nephews came rushing in. "Hey, Uncle M!" they cried out in unison. They grabbed his legs and slid as he dragged them across the wooden floor on his march to the couch. When he got there, he handed Laura her cola and his beer, bent over, and then started tickling the kids until they let go, rolling away in laughter, their small hands on their bellies.

"They love it when you come by," Laura said as she popped open her can.

"I can see that." He winked at the kids and held his hand out to Laura. "Raven makes jewelry outta pop tabs and caps. Give me yours so I can pass it on to her."

She placed the tab in his palm, her eyes sparkling. "You really *do* like her." She hummed "Here Comes the Bride" as she brought the can to her lips.

"Asking for your pop tab hardly means that I'm ready to propose. Give it a break, will you?"

"Do you wanna play a game with us, Uncle M?" Carlos asked.

"I'd love to, but I gotta get to work. I'm down for it the next time I come over, so you better be ready for me. I'm a mean gamer."

Javier and Carlos snickered. "Can we have a popsicle, Mom?" Javier asked, as Lorena nodded in agreement.

"Just one for each of you. If you take more than one, there'll be trouble." The last part of her sentence was drowned out by gleeful cries as the three kids raced into the kitchen. She laughed. "Remember when a popsicle was all it took to make us happy?" Placing her elbow on her bended knee, she rested her chin on her hand.

"How's it going with you and Joe?" Muerto asked quietly.

She shrugged. "I'm not sure. Did you find anything out?"

He nodded. "He's not cheating on you. There may be some money spent on strippers, but he's not crossed the line."

"I guess that's good. Sometimes I think our marriage isn't worth fighting for. It seems like we don't really talk anymore or go out. It's become so humdrum. I don't know…."

"If you're looking for advice, you're asking the wrong fuckin' person. I don't know shit about this kind of thing, but I know you both made three wonderful kids and they're worth fighting for. Why don't you guys see a marriage counselor? Sometimes it takes someone from the outside to help and point out what's the problem. And before you tell me you don't have the money, it's on me. I want to help you guys work this out. Enough said." He stood up. "I better head out."

When he got to the front door, Laura's hand on his shoulders stopped him from opening the screen. He turned around and she threw her arms around his neck, kissing his cheek. "Thank you for everything. You're the best brother. And the tent will be fucking awesome. Now go." Reaching around, she unlatched the screen door and pushed it open.

Ruffling her hair, he flashed her a smile, then walked out the door and to his Harley.

BY THE TIME Raven entered the pool hall, only the faintest of light shone through the leaves on the ash trees lining the sidewalk. A rush of adrenaline shot through him when she tilted her head and threw him *that* smile, the one that pulled him in like a magnet, as always.

With an effortless saunter, she approached the bar, her heels clicking against the rhythm of a soft jazz melody playing overhead. Several men turned to look at her, making Muerto's blood boil, and then she was at the counter, leaning over enough that he could see her firm tits and smell her sexy-as-fuck fragrance. She placed her hands on each side of his face and pulled it closer to hers as sexual tension crackled in the air. Pressing her lips on his, she kissed him eagerly, drawing his tongue into her mouth. *Fuck!*

"Hey," she breathed as she broke away.

"I love the way you greet your man. When I get a break here, I'll take you in the back and show you how I reciprocate." He nipped her soft lips, then licked them.

"You promised me food and drinks. I'm starving and thirsty." She hoisted herself on the barstool.

"Is that the only reason you came tonight?" he asked as he set a glass of Jack in front of her.

"An artist never passes up a free meal and drink," she answered, her eyes dancing with merriment as she brought the amber liquid to her lips.

"Stick with me and I'll keep you well fed." He laughed and handed her a one-page menu. "What're you in the mood for?"

"Besides you?" She dipped her finger into her glass and took out an ice cube. Popping it in her mouth, she crunched down on it.

Pulling her to him, he took hungry possession of her mouth, the coolness of the ice wrapping around his hot tongue. "Fuck, babe. You're making me all kinds of crazy. I'm craving you something fierce right now."

"Is it time for your break yet?" She licked his bottom lip and he seized her pink tongue with his teeth, pulling it into his mouth and sucking it. "Mmm…," she moaned, and the sound made him hard with desire.

"Are you tending bar or what?" Brandy's voice broke through his lust.

Pulling away, he wiped his mouth with the back of his hand. "What do you need?"

"I'll be right back. I want to freshen up," Raven said as she slid off the stool.

Watching her perfect ass and hips move so delectably didn't help his dick any.

"Are you dating *her*?" Irritation laced Brandy's voice.

"Who's dating who?" Jaime asked as she tied a short apron around her waist.

Brandy pointed to Muerto as he mixed the drinks for her order. "This one's going out with the pool shark. Must've been a hell of a ride back from Silverado."

"Really? Is that true?" Jaime looked at Muerto as she picked up her tray.

"How is what I do any of your fuckin' business?" He placed the drinks on Brandy's tray.

"We're just surprised. I didn't think you were the type to hook up with someone who's not in your club." Brandy lifted her tray.

"I've gone out with a lot of citizens. And again, none of your fuckin' business. You're here to work, not worry about what I do." He clenched his jaw.

"Whatever. It probably won't last past tonight, or the weekend at the latest," he heard her say to Jaime as the women dispersed into the crowd.

"Fuck them," he said under his breath as he stacked the glasses to the side. What he had with Raven was something he couldn't put into words because he didn't understand it himself. She made him feel things he'd never felt about a woman, and he had no clue how she did that. All he knew was that he felt real good when he was with her, and it wasn't all about sex. Yeah, his dick got hard whenever she was around or he thought about her, and the way she felt underneath him as he banged her was all kinds of fantastic, but he liked *her*. He liked the way she laughed, her artistic talent, her freestyle attitude, her wit, her intelligence, her—

"You look like you're really concentrating on stacking those glasses," Raven said.

"Yeah. No. I don't know."

Laughing, she settled down on the barstool again. "Well, what is it?"

"Fuck, woman. You got me all mixed up." With his finger, he gestured for her to come closer to him. When she leaned in, he kissed her lips, then swept her hair to the side and kissed her slender neck. "And I fuckin' love it." Brandy coughed loudly. "I gotta get this, sweetie. Tell me what you want to eat."

"Nachos without meat but a ton of cheese. Oh, and a big dollop of guac. And another shot of Jack," she said at his retreating back.

"Okay. Got it," he said over his shoulder as he bent down and pulled out five bottles of beer.

A half hour later, Raven was munching on the nachos and Muerto was rushing around behind the bar. "Don't you have any help? I thought Crow was supposed to come in."

"He can't. He's got some drama goin' on with his family. Zach said he'd be here over an hour ago. I need to fire his ass." Muerto slammed the top of the ice machine.

"You say that every time he screws up and he's still here," Brandy chirped as she sat on one of the stools, took off her high heel, and rubbed her foot.

"'Cause it's a pain in the ass to find a good bartender," Muerto growled. *Why the fuck's Brandy giving me such an attitude? She better watch her mouth or I may fire* her *ass.* Ignoring her, he went over to Raven and smiled. "You look like you're liking the nachos."

"They're super good. Who made them? I didn't know you had a cook."

"We don't. I order it and it gets delivered. We have some frozen shit we nuke in order to comply with the fuckin' state law, but no one really orders that shit except for Diablo." Muerto laughed as he thought about Diablo looking forward to the soggy jalapeño poppers he ordered whenever he came in.

"State law? You have to have food in a pool hall?"

"If you serve booze you do. Just sandwiches and snacks, so it's not that big of a deal. Like I said, we got a freezer full of shitty food."

"Thanks for giving me the gourmet menu." She bit down on a chip. "You know, I really don't feel comfortable with you paying to send my artwork to the gallery." She lifted her hand in front of her face. "I don't want to see your pissed-off face or hear your arguments. Just listen to me. I thought I could play some pool and win the money *fair and square.*"

Shaking his head, he gripped one of her hands, brought it up to his mouth, and kissed it. "Sweetie, I can't have you play in here even if you're on the level. Steel would kick my ass and I'd deserve it. This is the club's business, not just mine alone."

"I know. I don't want to play here."

"Then where? You can't go back to Silverado."

"At your clubhouse." She crunched on another chip.

What the fuck did she say? The Night Rebels' clubhouse? "Are you fuckin' insane?"

"Why not? It'd be a fair game. I mean, if one of your club members didn't want to play me, then that's fine. I'd be taking a chance too, because I'm sure you got some guys who play a mean pool game."

He scrubbed his hands down over his face. "I could talk to them. I've seen you and you're damn good. But it'd be fuckin' classic watching the brothers lose to a chick." He guffawed as the idea took hold in his head. Nodding, he said, "Okay, yeah. Let me talk to 'em and I'll let you know."

"Perfect." She lifted her glass in a mock toast, brought it to her mouth, and threw it back.

As the crowd dwindled to just a few guys around a serious game of pool, Muerto told the waitresses that one of them could go home. He heard them going back and forth about it, and finally Brandy took Jaime up on her offer to stay until closing. She kicked off her shoes and padded barefoot to the back room to get her belongings.

The next hour dragged. All Muerto could think about was holding Raven in his arms, kissing her, and then peeling off her clothing, one piece at a time. She stood around the pool game, her eyes intent, her fingers twitching, and he knew she wished she was in the game. *Pool's in her blood. Just like her old man.* For a split second, he hoped he could meet her dad someday. *It'd be so cool to ride to Vegas with her on the back of my Harley. What the fuck's come over me. This chick's in my blood.*

After the place was locked up, he followed Raven home. The crickets were out in full force, their music competing with his bike's cams. The silver glow of the moon lit up squares of green in front of the houses that flashed by as he rode against the wind. At the stoplight, he looked up at the specks of light filling the inky night sky while a soft summer breeze swept over him.

Pulling in the driveway, he shut off the engine and got off his bike. Raven came over to him, her eyes sparkling. "Look at all the fireflies. They're so beautiful. They look like tiny glimmers of light electrifying the darkness. This is so cool. When I get in I have to put it down on my sketch pad."

He wrapped his arms around her and led her into the house. As she sketched, he watched her, trying to imagine what it was about some sparking bugs that enthralled her. He doubted he could, but he loved watching how fast her pencil flew on the paper while her face scrunched in concentration.

When she placed the pencil down and stretched her arms above her head, he got up and went over to her, bending down and kissing her neck. Soon the kissing was coupled with touching as he slipped his hand inside her bra, delight spreading through him when he felt her rigid nipples. "Is your pussy wet too?" He slid his hand down her pants and glided his finger under her panties and between her slick folds. "Oh yeah," he said against her neck.

Twisting around, she pulled him down farther and kissed him hard. Then she stood up, took his hand and led him into the bedroom. In less than five minutes he had her stripped down and lying on the bed. Moonbeams streamed through the space in the curtains, making her skin glow. Naked and erect, he kneeled on the bed and came over to her, smiling when she opened her legs for him. Propped on one elbow, he touched her cheek, then let his hand glide down her satiny skin, fondling her breasts as it made its way downward.

She moaned in pleasure when he touched her smooth sex. "So beautiful," he whispered, loving the way her soft skin became a field of goose bumps as his breath slipped over her. He moved his finger in small circles on her clit, a throaty moan falling from her lips.

"The sounds you make get to me," he rasped in her ear, tracing the tip of his tongue across her collarbone as he sank his forefinger into her pussy.

As she squirmed and moaned under his touch, his desire grew and his pulse quickened. He pushed up and hovered over her, his stiff dick hitting her wetness. Sliding up a bit, he kissed her gently while his finger pumped in and out of her heat like a piston, withdrawing before she got too close; he had all night to tease and pleasure her, and he was just warming up.

As they kissed, the moonlight danced on their bodies.

Chapter Seventeen

FOR A LONG time I was stationed behind a cluster of trees, kitty-corner to the small duplex on Vrain Street. I knew they were together because his motorcycle was parked in the driveway. Since the night before, he'd never stayed more than two hours with her, but now Raven Harris had seduced him. What a fitting name for a predator who stalked her prey, sinking her nails into them, seizing them, and then destroying them. After their ruination, she feasted on their decaying spirit and soul. Like the bird, Raven Harris should be feared.

It was late, and blackness filled the windows of the other houses in the neighborhood. From my vantage point, I could see her window and the curtains billowing in the night's breeze. As I stood there watching and listening, low guttural sounds mingled with the crickets' chirping and drifted on the wind around me. At first I wasn't sure what I was hearing, but then realization set in and my stomach soured and twisted as the moans of their fucking assaulted me. It sounded like pigs. Dirty, filthy pigs.

Even though I was sure there were some couples engaged in sexual intercourse behind the darkened windows of some of the other houses in the vicinity, all my focus was on the front house of the duplex. The house *she* lived in. And I blamed her entirely for the disgusting things they were doing. How could I not? How could any man resist such a temptress? He couldn't; he was powerless to her bewitching charms. And the clothes she wore would entice any man.

No, she was the evil one.

As I worked myself up over her evil ways, I saw her at the window looking out. The streetlight on the corner illuminated her face as the wind caught her disheveled hair, blowing it in toward the darkness behind her. I had to admit that, at that moment, she was striking and sexy. But that didn't mean she wasn't a whore who deserved to die.

"Enjoy the little time you have left," I said, my voice louder than I'd wanted. *All I need is for someone who's taking their damn dog out for a walk to hear me.* The thought was a poignant reminder of how much time had passed since I'd seen Mother. "I love hearing you speak your mind," I said in a near perfect imitation of Mother's voice. She used to say that to me all the time when she'd walk in on me having a perfectly sane conversation with myself. The remembrance made me smile; I hadn't thought of it in a long time.

If I had to be utterly honest, I preferred talking to myself because I was always guaranteed an attentive audience. I laughed when I remembered how I'd been chatting away in the elevator of my apartment building when I'd lived in South Dakota. The door had opened and an unpleasant old woman stepped in. When she saw the elevator was empty except for me, the surprised look on her face had been priceless and I started laughing. She'd turned to me and said, in a very rude tone, "If you keep doing that, people are going to think you're lonely or mentally ill. I've seen you talking to yourself many times. I think you're a nut." The last sentence was spewed out with such venom and contempt that I knew I'd have to make her see how hurtful words could be.

And I'd done that, two weeks later, on a cold winter night. I'd been lucky that her apartment was across from mine so I could watch her comings and goings through the peephole. That night, she'd stepped out of her apartment with her mangy dog on a leash and went down to the wooded area behind the building. I'd followed her and reminded her how horribly she'd spoken to me. The old woman had looked confused for a split second before the steel pipe crushed her skull. Of course, she didn't argue with me since she was lying in a pool of her own blood, but had I spared her, I'm almost sure she would've understood how hurt I'd been by her cruel words.

"There's nothing crazy about talking to yourself," I said, glancing around to make sure I was still the only one at the corner of Vrain and Utica.

Glancing back at the window, I noticed it was closed and she was gone. I'd gotten caught up with my thoughts and memories and hadn't even seen her shut it.

I strained my ears to pick up any sound, but there was nothing but silence. "Are they still fucking? The bitch closed the window, so I have no way of knowing for sure." I was getting madder as the minutes passed, and when I looked at my watch and saw I'd been there for four hours, I knew. He was spending the night with the cunt.

"Noooo!" My howls shattered the quiet of the neighborhood. "Nooooo!"

A few lights flickered on, their glow on the lawns like yellow patches. I pulled back and ducked down low as a couple of blinds opened and faceless people looked out into the darkness. My heart was racing, my pulse pounding. *I have to get out of here!* But I didn't move a muscle. I just waited... waited until the lights turned off intermittently, until the smudged figures moved away from the windows, until silence descended on the area once again.

Then I gulped in the night air, filling my lungs deeply. I walked to my car and drove off. And when I was several miles away, I pounded the dashboard, cursing so loudly I feared my vocal chords would break.

The bitch has to go... soon.

Chapter Eighteen

M UERTO THREW HIS phone across the table then pushed his chair back. *Why the fuck isn't she answering my calls?* He racked his brain, trying to remember if he did something that pissed her off, but all he could remember was how wonderful it was between them. It'd been two days since he'd seen Raven. She'd answered his texts with brief replies, and she didn't return his phone calls. He didn't have a clue what the hell was going on with her.

"What's up?" Skull asked as he sat down. He placed a sandwich in front of Muerto then took a large bite out of his.

"What the fuck is this?" Muerto looked at the plate.

"Ham and cheese. Lena's making them. Thought you might want one." He took another bite of his sandwich.

With a clenched jaw, Muerto shoved the plate away from him. "You thought wrong. I didn't ask you to bring me one, so why the fuck are you getting into my business?"

Skull jerked his head up and stared at him. "What the hell's your problem, dude? If you don't want it then don't fuckin' eat it. No big deal."

Muerto scowled, clenching his fists as he forced himself not to punch Skull in the face. As Skull chomped noisily on his food, hot rage burned in Muerto's veins.

"Want a ham sandwich?" Skull asked Army when he came up to the table.

Army looked at Muerto. "You don't want it?"

Muerto jumped up from his chair and slammed his fist down on the plate. Pieces of blue stoneware bounced across the table. "I don't fuckin' want it!"

Army's eyes narrowed and Skull pushed away from the table. "What the hell's your problem, asshole?" Army clenched his fists.

"Fuck all of you." Muerto grabbed his phone and stormed out, electricity shooting up his spine. He jumped on his Harley and sped out of the parking lot. As he made his way to the backroads that crisscrossed the desert, anger consumed him. The landscape surrounded him as he increased his speed on the deserted roads. Soon he and his bike became one, and exhilaration overtook the anger. As he rode past sagebrush, rock formations, and miles of open expanse, all thoughts went out of his mind. He felt alive and free.

After several hours of riding, Muerto entered Alina and headed over to Raven's place. He was going to find out what the hell was going on with her. His Harley had helped in calming the rage that had been coursing through him, so when he pulled up in front of the duplex, he smiled when he saw her watering her garden. She looked over her shoulder and nodded at him.

"Hey," he said as he came up to her. "How've you been?"

"Real busy. You?" She averted her eyes.

"Good. You've been dissing me. Why?"

"Not really. I've just been busy." He went over to the valve and shut off the hose. She turned toward him. "What're you doing? I wasn't finished watering."

"You are for now. I wanna know what's going on in that pretty head of yours. And I'm not buying your 'too busy' shit." A tense silence filled the space between them. "Did I piss you off about something?"

She chewed on her cuticles while she shook her head no.

"Then what?" He came close to her and grabbed her hand.

"Let's go in," she said softly.

Once inside, he sat on the couch and watched her as she tucked the stray tendrils into her bun. Not wanting to push her, he waited for her to start the conversation. She didn't.

"What's going on?" he asked in a low voice.

"Nothing. Why?"

"You've got a faraway look in your eyes. It's like something's going on inside you that's taking you away from us."

"Isn't an 'us' too soon? I mean, we don't know each other very well." She tucked her legs under her.

"What the hell does that mean? Some people are together for a long time and they don't know shit about each other. It's the way people connect that's important. And I've never been so drawn to a woman as I am to you. Let's face it, we tried to pretend this strong attraction we have didn't exist, but we couldn't pull it off." He reached out and grasped her hands into his. "Talk to me," he said in a low voice. "I can see something's battling inside you." His dark gaze drew hers to his.

She exhaled. "I'm scared. There I said it."

His head flinched back. "Scared? Of me?"

Shaking her head vigorously, she squeezed his hand. "Not at all. I'm scared of me. I'm afraid I'll lose who I am." As his eyebrows squished together, she let go of his hand and swept her fingers over his forehead. "I guess I have some crap still left over from my relationship with Brent. I fell so hard and fast for him, that I let it consume me. It was like we lived in la-la land. Then when reality rang our doorbell, my cocoon split open, and I was shattered."

"Your world fell apart because you had an asshole in it. He lied and betrayed you. I'm not him. I live it straight. What you see is what you get. I don't bullshit. You should know that about me." He leaned back against the cushion.

She smiled softly. "I do. You're the only man I've ever met that tells it like it is and lives his life without any excuses. Actually, I really like that about you."

"And I fuckin' love the way you hold your own. You've made a life for yourself. You're a survivor, and I admire the hell out of you. No way would I hurt you, babe. No. Fucking. Way."

"I know that. I guess I'm freaking out because I've never felt such a pull to any man before. When I'd first met Brent, I was attracted to him, but it was nothing compared to what I feel with you." She pulled out the elastic tie and her hair spilled past her shoulders. "Maybe that's what scares the hell out of me. I'm terrified of losing myself to you. You probably don't understand what I'm saying."

He laughed dryly. "I totally get what you're sayin'. I never expected to want to spend time with a woman until I met you. I figured we'd have a short fling and I'd be on my way, but it's not turning out that way. So the fuck what? I'm not asking you to give yourself up. We're having a good time and we like each other. I'm just going with that. I thought you were too."

The sun streamed through the picture window, coloring the living room in a bright white glow, and, at that moment, he'd never cared for a woman as much as he did for her. It took him by surprise, but he wanted to spend more time with her and see where this thing they had took them. He leaned over and brushed her lips with his. "You were hurt by a fuckin' jerk. Are you gonna let that keep you from living?"

With glistening eyes, she flung her arms around him and nuzzled her face in his neck. "I've been so happy that it scared me. I do want to take a chance on you. I just freaked out. I needed some time to think."

He kissed the top of her head. "Next time that happens, don't shut me out. I may not like what you say, but you gotta tell me when shit's bothering you."

"I know. I'm used to dealing with stuff on my own."

"Now you've got me."

She nodded. "I'm working on opening up more. You'll have to be patient with me."

He embraced her tightly. "I'll be as patient as you need me to be. You're so worth it, babe."

They held each for a long while, then Muerto's stomach gurgling made her snicker and pull back. "Are you hungry? Do you want me to make you a sandwich?"

He chuckled. "Not in a mood for one. Let's go out and grab a bite."

"I'd rather stay home with you. We can order pizza and I can make a salad." She kissed him softly on his lips then pulled away. "Sound good?"

"Sounds great. Just so you know, I'm a triple pepperoni type of guy."

She laughed. "I guess I better order another one for me. Anyway, leftover pizza's the best." She whipped out her phone.

Before she tapped in the number, he grasped her wrist. "Are we good now?"

A wide smile broke over her face. "We're very good."

As she placed their order, warmth spread through him. He was so taken with her that it blew his mind.

Placing the phone down, she looked at him. "Beer or whiskey?"

"You first then I'll take a beer." He lunged for her, pushing her down on the couch and tickling her sides.

Between gasps for air, she blurted, "Stop." Laughing she pushed against him, and he replaced the tickles with kisses on her face and neck.

"When did they say the pizza would be here?" he whispered as he flicked her earlobe with his tongue.

"Forty minutes," she breathed.

"I'm gonna give you the best forty minute fuck you've ever had, sweetie."

He kicked off his boots then turned his attention to her, his hands roaming over her curves as his mouth crashed down on hers.

Chapter Nineteen

A FEW DAYS later, Muerto checked his phone just as Steel pounded the gavel on the wooden block. Looking up, he saw the sour look on the president's face. *Some shit's not good.* Muerto put his phone down and gave his full attention to the front of the room.

"It's been confirmed that underage girls are working at the Climax Lounge," Steel said between gritted teeth. "What fucking sucks more than that is I know one of them. She's a nice girl from the reservation. Her sister and Chenoa were friends. This girl is only sixteen." He slammed his fist on the table. "We're closing that fucking club down."

The members yelled their support, some of them cussing and pounding the tables with their fists. Brutus stood up, his face red from fury. "I know one of the girls stripping over there and she told me that the club's actively recruiting younger girls so they can fuckin' rip them off. They get paid half of what the regular women make. They're using the girls in every way they can. Who owns this place?"

Steel turned to Chains. "Did you find anything out?"

Nodding, Chains stood up. "Satan's Pistons are definitely involved. They—"

Crow leapt up so fast his chair fell over, clanking on the linoleum floor. "I knew those fuckers were behind it. They're such pieces of shit. I want to kick their asses so bad. We gotta get them outta our county. They're like a goddamn disease, and they'll keep spreading."

"I gotcha, but let Chains finish. I'm just as pissed as you are, but we need to get to the bottom of this so we can come up with a workable plan."

"Killing their asses works for me," Crow fumed as he set the chair right and then sat down.

Other members started yelling, "Death to Satan's Pistons!" over and over until Steel had to slam the gavel down again.

"Everyone shut the fuck up! We're never going to get anything done." Pausing while the brothers calmed down, he nodded at Chains. "Go on."

"Okay, so the Pistons are acting like they're not a hundred percent involved. They have a strawman on all the paperwork, a gang from Pueblo called the—" He glanced down at a piece of paper he had in front of him. "—39th Street Gang. A bunch of wannabe gangsters. They basically extort from businesses in their area and do some loan sharking. They're listed as the owners of the strip bar, but we know that's a load of crap."

Muerto pushed his chair back from the table. "Sounds like they want to attach themselves to the Pistons to elevate their pathetic standing in the criminal world. Is Delarosa in on this, or is he just a dumb pawn?"

"A dumb pawn. This dude has stupid written all over him." Chains chuckled.

"Seems like these 39th Street fucks want to kick their operations up a notch. They're four hundred miles from here, and they don't know what the hell's going on," Army said.

"Satan's Pistons are using their puny asses. They'll get rid of them as soon as they don't need them anymore. The Pistons have been wanting to control the Four Corners for a long time. They already got Arizona and Utah. Assholes." Crow twisted the cap off his bottled water.

"No way the Deadly Demons are gonna let the Pistons take that part of New Mexico. And I doubt that Banger's gonna be on board with it," Paco said. "I know we're not letting them into our county."

"Fuck no!" Diablo yelled, and then the other brothers began talking, yelling, and cussing up a storm.

Muerto's phone pinged. He glanced down and smiled. A text from Raven always made him smile.

Raven: *Whatcha doing?*

Muerto: *Church. U?*

Raven: *Thinking bout how I want ur soft lips on mine. Mmmm....*

Muerto sucked in his breath. All around him the brothers were still talking about what they were going to do to Satan's Pistons.

Muerto: *Send me a pic of u. Surprise me.*

"We gotta make sure the Pistons know we mean business. Have you told Banger 'bout the fuckers setting up a business without Insurgents permission?" Muerto asked.

"I'm going to, and I'm sure we'll hear his response all the way from Pinewood Springs." Steel chuckled.

A ping. Putting the phone under the table, Muerto opened the message, his mouth going dry when he saw her delicate hand and her index finger extended. On the end of her finger was a tiny, lacey pair of red panties. *Fuck.* He couldn't move his eyes away. Another ping. Hurriedly, he opened it. A matching red bra with a tiny pink bow strewn over the bed made him adjust his jeans as he moved around in his seat. *Double fuck.* There was something about this woman that made his body respond like wildfire.

As he started to reply, another ping.

Raven: *Wish u were here.*

Muerto: *Me 2. Ur driving me crazy, baby.*

Raven: *Don't mean 2.*

Muerto: *BS, but I love it. Can't wait 2 see u.*

Raven: *We'll have some fun. ;)*

"Is church interfering with your phone time?" Steel's hard voice broke through the lustful haze Muerto was in since he'd started texting.

Muerto: *Gotta go. Later.*

Slipping his phone in his pocket, he looked at the president. "Sorry.

I got something going here." *That's ambiguous enough.*

"Like sexting your latest squeeze?" Goldie wiggled his eyebrows and the brothers roared. Eagle, Army, and Cue Ball made kissing noises while Brutus and Skull simulated hard fucking sounds.

Muerto glared until Steel hit the gavel for the third time, a smile on his face. "Keep your private time outta church." Picking up a 7-Up, he drank deeply, then scanned the members. "We're gonna shut these fuckers down. No MC puts a business in our territory, and no strip bar on our turf hires underage strippers."

"I say we blow their fuckin' club up," Army said. Several members voiced their agreement.

"I was leaning in that direction," Steel replied.

"We gotta do it soon," Paco said.

"Are the badges gonna leave us be?" Skull asked.

"Wexler practically gave us carte blanche," Muerto said. "We need to teach Satan's Pistons that they can't mess with us. The fuckers knew exactly what they were doing, and having a phony group of wannabe gangsters on all the paperwork is such a crock of shit that it's insulting." He shook his head. "I vote we torch the place."

Paco put up his hands as the brothers excitedly agreed with Muerto. "I think we know how this is going, but we gotta take a vote. All in favor of blowing up the damn bar say 'Aye.'"

A thunderous boom of "Ayes" filled the meeting room.

"All opposed say 'Nay.'" Paco waited for a couple of seconds. "It's unanimous. We're gonna torch the damn place."

Amid the applause, Steel pounded the gavel many times until some quiet was had. "We move fast on this. Army, I'm putting you in charge of the operation. Pick a few brothers to be on your team. Any questions?" Army shook his head. "Good. That wraps it up. Go relax and have a few beers. We've got a hellish week coming up." Steel hit the gavel on the block, adjourning church.

In the main room, Muerto ambled to the bar, grateful for the double shot of Jack that waited for him. The cool liquid went down real smooth, lighting his throat with the type of fire that warmed a person all over.

"You've been gone the past several nights," Goldie said as he sidled up to a barstool.

Muerto shrugged and took another gulp of whiskey.

"Where you been stayin'?" Skull asked as he grabbed the beer the prospect handed to him.

"How's this your fuckin' business?" Muerto growled. He wanted to look at the pictures Raven had sent him again, but he didn't dare chance it. The brothers would have a heyday with that, and he didn't want them to disrespect Raven that way.

"He likes the woman. I'm with Muerto on this," Diablo's deep voice fell over them.

Muerto jerked his chin at him, surprised the sergeant-at-arms threw in his two cents. Normally, Diablo minded his own business and didn't get involved in any drama about the women the brothers fucked. Muerto rarely saw him with any of the club girls, and never with a hang-around. He rarely shared any information about himself; all Muerto knew for a fact was that the big guy was from Salt Lake City.

"He likes a lot of women," Chains said, and the brothers around him laughed.

"Don't we all?" Crow chuckled.

"Yeah, but our brother here"—Chains lightly tapped Muerto's shoulder—"isn't the type of guy who goes out with a chick for more than a night or two. And he never stays the night."

"Is she teaching you some pool tips? Are you in training to be a hustler?" Eagle had come over and joined in on the ribbing.

"I'm hangin' with her. What's the big deal? Can't you losers get anyone but the club girls?" He motioned for another whiskey.

"I could beat her ass any day in a pool game," Army said as he leaned against the bar.

Crow shook his head. "I don't think you could. I've seen her play and she's damn good."

"Bullshit." Army looked at Muerto. "Tell her that I challenge her to a game. She may be too scared, but the challenge is on the table."

"I'm with Crow on this one. Raven's a badass player. I don't want any shit when you lose."

"No worries, bro, 'cause I'm not planning to lose. I can beat her hands-down. She's a bitch, for fuck's sake."

Before Muerto could respond, Paco came over. "I overheard about the pool game. I'm cool with it, but it can't be at Balls and Holes. You know we don't mix business with personal shit. If you want to play against Muerto's chick, don't do it at the pool hall."

"We could do it here," Goldie said.

Muerto smiled inwardly. *This is exactly what she wanted.* "I'll ask her if she wants to do it, but no problems when you lose."

"I'm not going to lose." Army guzzled the rest of his beer.

"Who wants to place bets on the pool game between Muerto's pool shark and Army?" Goldie announced in a loud voice. The rest of the brothers came over and started placing their bets. "Call her. See if she wants to accept the challenge. If so, the game is tonight at eight."

"Okay." Muerto took out his phone and sent a text to Raven.

Muerto: *R u a witch? Army's challenging u to a game. Just what u wanted.*

Raven: *Yessss! I've been called a bitch but never a witch. Ur funny. :)*

Muerto: *Well... u cast a spell over me, & now the game....*

Raven: *;) When's the game?*

Muerto: *Tonight if ur good.*

Raven: *Oh yea. Tell him to bring it on. Time?*

Muerto: *8 good? Come over. Want 2 see u. I can pick u up.*

Raven: *U just want 2 see my bra & panties.*

Muerto: *True... & what's inside them.*

Raven: *hehe. I'll come on my own. See u at 7ish. Gives us time 2* *talk b4 the game.* ♥

Staring at the heart, a funny feeling rode up his spine. Raven did something to him, made him feel things he'd never experienced before. Touchy-feely shit that women loved to talk about. And he didn't feel like a pussy; it was just good. Real fucking good.

"So, is she in?" Army's voice brought him back to the clubhouse.

"Yeah."

"The game'll be at eight. Hope she can cover the loss." Army grabbed a handful of pretzels from a bowl on the bar.

"If she can't, Muerto will, right, dude?" Crow asked.

"Yeah."

"Did you tell her she can't bring her own cue stick or cue ball?" Army said while chewing.

"She knows. She's a pro, dude." Muerto drained his shot glass.

"We'll see." Army looked over Jigger's head. "Hey, Kelly, get your ass over here. I need some good fucking before the game. Bring Fina with you. I'm feeling real lucky tonight." He laughed and swung his arm around Kelly when she came over. "Let's go to my room," he said as Kelly giggled. They walked off and Fina joined them, hooking her arm around his waist as the trio disappeared from the room.

"I almost wish Raven would beat his ass tonight. It'd bring the cocky bastard down a few notches," Crow said in a low voice. Muerto nodded, hoping the same thing.

A LITTLE BEFORE six, Muerto sat on a barstool, munching on spicy chips—potato chips coated in chili powder—adrenaline surging through him. He couldn't wait to see Raven. Even though he'd seen her that morning, he missed her and wanted to wrap her in his arms and breathe her heady scent.

When she walked in, he almost jumped out of his skin. Her skinny jeans looked like she'd painted them on, and the scoop-neck top revealed some serious cleavage that made him want to dip his tongue down into it and taste her salty skin. Four-inch heels—*how the hell does she walk in those?*—long, flowing hair, and some kickass, sexy makeup made his dick wake way the hell up.

He jumped off the barstool and made his way to her. The room was quiet except for the drone of voices on the TV. All eyes were on her, and from the way she curled a strand of hair around her finger, he knew she was nervous. Looking around, he noticed the only one smiling at her was Crow, all the other brothers either stone-faced or slightly perturbed. The club women crinkled their noses as they checked her out.

"Hey, sweetie," he said as he brushed his lips across hers. "Let's have a drink." The tension in her face slacked a bit as she grabbed his hand and followed him to the bar. He picked her up and plopped her on a barstool, ordering a whiskey sour from the prospect.

"So, this is where you live and party. I'm finally given a glimpse into your life."

"You look gorgeous," he breathed in her ear as he slinked his arm around her small waist. "How do you like the clubhouse?"

Picking up her drink, she said, "Not sure. I'll have to give it a bit more time before I decide. It's a lot neater and smells way nicer than I thought."

"What'd you think it was going to smell like?"

"I don't know. A men's locker room, something like that."

"The club girls keep it nice and sweet-smelling. They're in charge of taking care of us."

She glanced behind him to where a group of scantily clothed women sat. "Are those the club girls?"

"Yeah."

"They're pretty." She took another sip of whiskey.

"You're prettier, and way-the-fuck sexier." He kissed her lips, slipping his tongue inside her cool mouth. She tasted of mint and whiskey.

"Have you fucked every one of them?" Licking her lips, she shook her glass around, causing the ice cubes to clink.

"What difference does it make?"

"So that's a yes? I'm not going to get mad. I just want to know."

He nodded. "That's the way it is. The women like it and choose to be here. It's just fucking, nothing more."

"It must be nice to have a woman available twenty-four seven." She pushed her head back and tapped the bottom of her glass to dislodge the ice.

Leaning in, he kissed the soft skin on her throat. "You're the only one for me. Yeah, it was fun having a woman whenever the urge hit you, but it also got boring. I mean, the challenge wasn't there, and I like a challenge. Like you. You're the opposite of easy and boring." He kissed her again.

"The blonde is staring a hole right through me," Raven said as he continued peppering her neck with soft kisses.

"That's Ruby. The girls are suspicious of citizens. They're not too crazy about hang-arounds, but citizens just piss them off." He laughed.

"Ruby? Didn't you have something with her?"

"How do you know her?"

"I don't. I just remember the guys mentioning her name to you that night we bumped into each other at Alfonso's."

"That night you made me crazy with lust and then shooed me away?" Nuzzling her neck, he loved how soft her skin felt.

"Is she your girlfriend?" She pushed him away.

"Girlfriend? She's a club woman, I told you that. And she's not my anything now. I'm with you."

"You don't sleep with anyone else?"

Scowling, he asked, "Do you?"

Shaking her head, she picked up her empty glass. "No. I just thought that maybe…. I mean, you have all these women here. You know what I mean."

He motioned to Ruger for another whiskey sour for her, then took her hands in his. "I'm not some fuckin' douchebag. Just because the women are here doesn't mean I'm constantly having sex with them. And besides, I'm going out with you." Kissing her gently, he said in a low voice, "I'm right where I wanna be. You got that?" She nodded. "Good. Now let's get some food."

Lena, the cook for the club, had just finished putting out the last platter of ribs when they came up to the buffet table. Muerto piled his plate with pork ribs, green chile, fried potatoes, coleslaw, corn and black beans, and a big wedge of cornbread. When he saw Raven's plate, she had a dollop of coleslaw, a spoonful of potatoes, and a small amount of green chile.

"That's all you're eating? Don't you want any ribs?"

"I'm not that hungry." She placed her hand on her stomach. "Nervous tension. And I'm not a big meat eater."

Pulling her chair out, she sat down and asked him to bring her a Diet Coke. After he came back to the table, Crow joined them.

"You're not at the pool hall tonight?" Muerto asked as he shoveled a good portion of fried potatoes in his mouth.

"I arranged for a relief bartender to help out Zach. I wouldn't miss this game for the world. I think we're going to score big tonight, bro. Almost all the brothers placed bets on Army."

"This is a betting game?" Raven asked as she picked at her food.

"Yeah. We always bet on the games. It's no biggie. Don't let it throw you," Muerto said.

"It doesn't," she said coolly. "I need the cash, so it's good to know that I'll get it."

Muerto and Crow laughed. "That's my girl. Full of confidence." He squeezed her hand.

Soon Army came by and chatted with Muerto and Crow, his eyes darting to her every few seconds or so. As the time neared eight o'clock, the brothers turned off the TV and overhead music, and the club girls scrambled to clear off the tables.

"It's time for me to win some money," Army said while looking at Raven.

Muerto smiled when she stood up, looked Army straight in the eyes, and said, "Agreed. I could use some cash. Where's the pool table?"

Clasping her hand in his, Muerto walked with Raven to the back of the room. Under a brass fixture stood the table. Several of the brothers flocked to the stools that had been set up against the wall. Muerto bent down and kissed her. "Kick his ass," he whispered, loving the way her whole face lit up when she grinned. Taking his seat on one of the stools, he scooted a bit to the left when Crow sat on the one next to him. Except for Steel, all the brothers were there, and the club girls flocked around them. Kelly and Fina blew kisses at Army, who winked at them.

The air crackled with anticipation and tension. Raven went over and picked up several cue sticks, examining them until she settled on one. Army smirked and grabbed one for himself. Taking out a quarter from his jeans pocket, he looked at Raven. "You choose what breaks, heads or tails."

"Heads."

He handed the coin to Muerto. "Toss it."

Muerto threw it up in the air, caught it, then flipped it on his hands. He looked at it. *Shit.* "Tails."

Army grinned and sniggers circled the area.

The game was on.

Chapter Twenty

R AVEN TURNED TO the brothers. "After this game, I'll play a couple more with whoever wants to."

Brutus clucked his tongue. "You're pretty cocky."

"I'd characterize it as confident." Turning to Army, she said, "Take your shot." Army broke up the balls, a solid one landing in the far left corner of the table. "Solids are yours, stripes mine. Stripes are lucky for me."

"Be prepared for me to change that." Army leaned over, studied his shot, then hit the cue ball again. Another ball landed in the pocket. Cheers rose up from the brothers. Raven watched, a cool smile gracing her lips.

Ball. Pocket. Ball. Pocket. Army kept hitting and pocketing the solids. "This is too fuckin' easy," he said as he aimed once more. He missed. The brothers groaned; they'd thought it was going to be a sweep.

Raven picked up the chalk cube and brushed it over the tip of the cue stick. To Muerto, it looked like she was using a paintbrush, the strokes that light and airy. She went to the table, assumed her stance, and studied the positions of the ball. Then in one beautiful, fluid stroke, her precise aim scattered the balls, pocketing three stripes at once. She didn't bat an eye, just went for the chalk cube and repeated her motions.

Muerto saw a light sheen around Army's hairline, and he knew his brother was beginning to worry. Since a brother was playing against a citizen, and a woman to boot, Muerto was expected to watch the game stoically, but inside he was rooting for Raven. He loved watching her play. And every once in a while she'd glance up at him before making her shot, tossing him the smile that woke up his dick before her face would grow stern in concentration. *Clack.* She made the shot again.

Army scrubbed his face and Muerto knew that meant he was getting pissed. When she missed a shot, he practically pushed her out of the way in his eagerness to show her up. But emotions and pool didn't mix, and Muerto knew Army wasn't concentrating. He missed the shot. Instead of gloating, Raven picked up the chalk cube, ran it over the tip of her stick, and studied the balls.

Her concentration was spot-on, and even when some of the brothers tried to throw her off by knocking down stools, coughing loudly, and yelling out, she bagged all the balls. *She's a real pro.* Pride spread through him, lighting him up, and when she hit the winning shot of the final game with Army, he couldn't help but jump off his stool and go to her.

A dead silence descended on the room for a few seconds as the reality that a woman with impossibly high heels had just taken down Army. He was the brother who usually cleared up the pool tables at club parties. Army, who was the Night Rebels' best player, won most games at the Insurgents' and Fallen Slayers' MC parties, had lost to a citizen woman. It was incomprehensible.

Consoling him, the club girls handed him his favorite drinks, hung onto him, kissed him, and tried to wipe away the humiliation Muerto knew he was feeling as he handed over his money to Raven. She nodded and said, "Good game. You're a great player," as she shoved the bills into her tight-as-sin jeans.

"I fuckin' challenge you," Cue Ball said, his voice laced with anger.

"Okay. What's your name?"

"Cue Ball." He grinned.

Raven's eyes widened, and Muerto knew she thought his brother got the road name from being a pool pro. He didn't. Ten years before, he'd been at a pool hall in Durango when a guy came over and started some shit with him. He'd accused Cue Ball of giving his woman the eye. Cue Ball didn't deny it, and he'd pointed out that "his woman" had been flirting with him since the biker had first come in. That had pissed the man way off, and he got into Cue Ball's face. Cue Ball told him to back off, and the guy had asked, "What are you gonna do about it? Hit me with a cue ball?" And he did, after he'd sucker punched him. Then he beat the guy senseless until he heard sirens wailing in the distance. He'd done seven years in the pen and earned the road name Cue Ball.

"You scared?" Cue Ball smirked and the brothers guffawed.

"No. How much do you want to bet?"

"Everything you just got from Army."

Again her eyes widened and she glanced at Muerto. He wanted to go over and hold her tight, tell her she didn't need to prove shit to him, but he just locked eyes with her. In his world, the men ruled and women knew their place. Brother showed loyalty to brother first, then to the women in their lives. Raven was definitely upsetting their outlaw world, and Muerto fucking admired her for that. It was her toughness, her sass, and her independence from caring what others thought that attracted her to him. And the way she was commanding the room and pissing off his brothers was turning him on way more than he wanted his brothers to see. He draped his cut over his crotch.

Once again, Raven commanded the table, and he heard Ruby say in a low voice to Angel, "It's not natural for a woman to play pool."

Muerto turned to her. "Shut the fuck up."

Hurt crossed Ruby's face, but he didn't want the girls dissing his woman. And as she played the game with coolness and grace, he realized that she was his woman. He'd never claimed a woman, had never wanted to, and he didn't pretend to understand what the fuck was going on with her. Being with her was like he'd stepped on a high-tension wire and his dick was always magnetized.

Raven made another shot, and another, and another. As the brothers drank more, their grumbling got louder and angrier, and he knew he had to put a stop to it. After she collected Cue Ball's money, Brutus challenged her. She looked at him calmly; she hadn't even broken a sweat.

Muerto came over, taking the cue stick out of her hands. "She's done. That's it."

"I'm good," she whispered in his ear.

"You look tired. I want you full of energy, baby." He kissed her jaw.

"You're shutting down the game just when a brother who can win steps forward. Where the fuck does your loyalty lie, asshole?"

Brutus's words ran through Muerto like a hot poker, and without answering, he pulled away from Raven and punched him in the face. Brutus recovered quickly, and soon the two men were punching and swearing until Paco came over. "What the fuck is going on?"

Wiping his mouth, Brutus pointed at Muerto, "This sonofabitch is way fucked-up."

Muerto lunged, but Crow and Goldie held him back. "Don't you tell me about loyalty, asshole!"

"Enough!" Paco boomed. "I knew this was going to happen." He turned and glared at the brothers. "I've been watching the games. Raven played a fair game and she won the money fair and square." He fixed his gaze on her. "You're a good player, but you're done for the night."

Grumbling, the brothers dispersed and someone turned on the music. Hard rock beats reverberated around the room. Muerto wiped the blood from his nose and gripped her hand, pulling her along with him, going to the bar and grabbing a bottle of Jack and two glasses. Holding onto her, he led her upstairs, leaving the cacophony behind them.

Chapter Twenty-One

A DOUBLE BED, neatly made, stood in the middle of a nice-sized room. A nightstand on each side of the bed, two chrome lamps with gray shades, and a tall dresser where sunglasses and a stack of rolling papers sat on top of it. There were so many posters of motorcycles, bands, and Day of the Dead vignettes on the walls that Raven wasn't too sure of the paint color behind them. In the corner stood a black and gray upholstered armchair that had a leather jacket and a couple pairs of jeans draped over it.

Her gaze gravitated back to the paintings and she smiled. Being in his room gave her a glimpse into his passion and his soul. "I didn't know you liked paintings. I love your collection of Day of the Dead reproductions. Diego Rivera is one of my favorite artists, and his oil paintings of the Mexican holiday are awesome. I'd kill to own an original."

"It's actually my favorite holiday after Halloween." He grinned. "If there're skulls, ghouls, and demons, I'm in." He pulled off his boots.

"Is that where your name comes from?"

"In a way. When I first started as a prospect, I'd told them that the one day I couldn't hang was November first because my family and I went to the cemetery to decorate and bring food to our ancestors. So it was that, coupled with a few altercations I had with assholes who like messing with bikers, that gave me my road name." When he walked by her, he stopped, kissed her briefly on the lips, and then went over to his computer on a small table next to the armchair. "It's cool you're into it."

In a matter of minutes, the beats of a Hammerfall song curled around her, and she laughed. "I can't fucking believe this. Hammerfall is one of my favorite bands. I saw them in Denver last year and it was one of the best concerts I've been to. This is totally lit as fuck."

"Seems like we have some good shit in common. I like that." He stripped down to his jeans and then poured her a drink. "Get comfortable," he said as he put her drink on the nightstand.

She kicked off her heels and sat on the bed cross-legged. After taking a sip, she held the glass in her hands and looked at him. "I think your club hates me." She grimaced.

Laughing, he shook his head. "They'll get over it. They were the ones who wanted to play. I warned them that you were a badass player." He took a gulp of whiskey.

"Sometimes it's good for a man to have his ego taken down a few notches by a woman." Smiling, she brought the glass to her mouth.

"*Devoradora*," he said softly. He finished his drink and, with the bottle of Jack in his hand, went over to her. The mattress sagged when he sat down. After taking a swig from the bottle, he put it on the nightstand and turned to her. "Baby, you got a hold of my cock like no other woman ever has." His finger running up her arm made her skin pebble. "I loved watching you play tonight, and it made my dick so fuckin' hard." Tugging her to him, he kissed her firmly on the lips.

He tasted smoky and she grasped his face, drew him closer to her and kissed him deeply. Pulling back, she smiled and licked her lips. "You taste good." Standing up, she buried her hand in her pockets and took out the money she'd won. A few of the bills ripped and she giggled.

"I'm surprised you could put anything in those jeans. Woman, the way you wear clothes and move makes me all kinds of crazy. Now take off those tight-ass jeans so I can touch your skin."

When she walked over to the dresser to put her money on top, she exaggerated her moves, swaying her hips even more. Behind her, Muerto whistled under his breath. With her back to him, she unzipped her jeans and slowly slid them down, bending over to peel them off each leg. She'd worn a thong, and when she heard him inhale sharply, she felt a flush of heat rise in her.

"If you're trying to make me hard, it's working," he said thickly.

"Get your hot little ass over here."

Before she went to him, she took her time, counting her winnings, finger-combing her hair, and looking out the window at the quarter moon and blinking stars.

"Sweetie… I'm dying here," he said, and she knew he was loving the game. With deliberately slow movements, she turned around and took small steps. When she was finally within arm's reach, he grabbed her and yanked hard. Yelping, she toppled over, landing on his firm chest and hard-as-stone cock.

Before she could chastise him, he silenced her by devouring her mouth. As he kissed her, he rubbed his hands firmly up and down her back. Soon her sexual hunger began to build, and she grabbed his hair and tangled it around her fingers, tugging it harder as her desire grew. His hands were touching her shoulders, back, and sides as he alternated his kisses between her lips, neck, and earlobes. Raspy whispers of "You're so fuckin' sexy" and "I can't get enough of you, babe" scorched her senses, sending her arousal to an all-time high. And each long stroke of his tongue sent another shiver of pleasure through her body.

In one movement, she was on her back and he was hovering over her, his palm grazing her exposed breasts. A guttural moan rose from deep in her throat when he sucked her nipples, gently at first but then with a ferocity that both titillated and frightened her. Kisses, licks, and bites covered her neck, shoulders, throat, tits, and belly, and as he colored her pale skin with shades of red, her pussy flooded with heat. Her body wanted everything he could give it and much more.

Clasping her wrists firmly, he raised them above her head and held them there while he tormented her body with hot, fervid kisses. "You like that?" he said against her skin.

Panting, she breathed, "Yeah." Looking at her, he swallowed her pants as his free hand tickled her taut skin lightly. The way he touched and looked at her left her pussy tingling and throbbing.

Dragging his mouth down her throat, he said, "Leave your hands above your head." He brought his down to her flesh, tweaking, pinching, and scratching their way down to her aching, sopping sex. When he slowly pulled her thong down with his teeth, the anticipation of what was to come was agony for her. He kissed his way up from her feet to her inner thighs. Heat pulsed between her legs.

When he slid his finger into her wet, engorged folds, lightning bolted up her spine. "Muerto," she gasped as she clawed at the headboard. She was already on the edge.

His day-old scruff scratched her as he moved his face close to her sex. Inhaling deeply, his gaze, heated by lust, captured hers. "I can't get enough of your smell."

Desire tore through her and she pushed his face into her aching pussy. His chuckle vibrated against the sensitive folds, fueling the fire of passion even more. At first, his tongue teased her softly, slowly, but then he picked up the pace, licking her like he was possessed.

"Oh... fuck!" she cried out. Each moan, each cry seemed to drive him faster, reaching a frenzied state, until her insides lit up as if emblazoned with glitter paint and streaks of color floated deep in her. Closing her eyes, the sheet stuffed in her fist, she rode the waves of neon green, yellow, and purple. And as the spasms and colors mixed together and became a rainbow, her body rose higher, ethereal in its ascent.

Before she came back down, he was kissing her, mixing her salty sweetness with his smokiness, his tongue and hers tangling in a seductive dance.

"That was unbelievable," she said as she dug her fingers into his hard flesh.

"Watching you come is what's unbelievable." He stroked her cheek and kissed her again, more gently.

"Let me take care of you," she said softly as she inched her hand down toward his hardness.

Without a word, he leaned back and guided her to her knees, her back to him. Rubbing her creamy, tight butt cheeks, he whispered in her ear, "You've got one hell of an ass, sweetie. Has anyone ever fucked it?"

Stiffening, she shook her head. "Never."

"'Never because you didn't want it, or because no one ever asked?"

He kept massaging her ass, his fingers sinking into her flesh.

"I don't know. I guess because no one ever asked." She swallowed. "Are you asking?"

"Yeah. I like the idea of me being your first."

"I've always wondered about it. I don't know if I want to do it now."

"I have to prepare you, so another time. I just wanted to know if you wanted it." A smack on her ass made her jump. "And I'm glad you do." Another smack. Then another. The more he spanked her cheeks, the wetter she got. Then when the sting was on the cusp of being painful, he licked the redness with his cool tongue. She couldn't believe how turned on she was.

Muerto pushed her legs further apart and slid under her, his fingers digging into her hips, coaxing her downward. She felt his warm breath on her swollen, throbbing pussy, and the slow swipe of his velvet tongue made her shiver and wiggle in delight. His tongue bathed her fevered flesh, tasting and teasing it, bringing her to the brink of orgasm and then pulling back. Each time she was ready to go over, he moved away, making her a quivering mess of desire and lust.

Then he slipped from under her and spread her juices over her ass. "So tempting," he said as he squeezed her cheeks, pulling them apart. Placing his finger on her puckered opening, he pressed hard against it, and a zap of electric heat ripped through her. Looking behind her shoulder, she loved seeing the way he watched his finger dip slightly into her tightest hole. Glancing at her, he leaned over and kissed her lower back.

He opened the nightstand drawer and took out a packet.

"I want to feel your rawness inside me. Are you clean?" she asked over her shoulder.

"Yeah. Are you on the pill?"

She nodded and smiled when he put the packet back in the drawer and closed it. The nudge of his cock against her slick opening had her pussy clenching in anticipation. His lips on her back made her tingle, and she gasped when he grabbed her hair and pulled, her back arching and her ass high in the air. Then he drilled into her with such ferocity that she screamed from the sheer force of it.

While he rode her, he smacked her ass, tugged on her swinging tits, and stroked her hard, sweet nub. His frenzied thrusts made her senses reel and her body explode. "I love the way your ass bounces when I fuck you hard," he breathed as he clenched one of her ass cheeks. "My cock has been craving your tight pussy since you first walked in the bar." More pounding. Her moans mingled with Muerto's feral grunts.

Harder. Faster. Rougher. The pressure was building. So tight. So damn good.

"I'm gonna fuck you so hard that you won't be able to get out of my bed," he said. At that, the tension in her exploded and she soared while euphoria filled every cell in her body.

"Muerto!" she screamed over and over again.

He growled low and deep. "Fuck. Raven. *Fuck*." His hands rubbed along her damp back. Her knees couldn't support her anymore, so she collapsed on the bed. He lay next to her and pulled her closer so her ass was pressed against him, and he kissed her shoulder. "Amazing," he said, his voice thick with exhaustion.

Clasping her hands over his, she wiggled her butt against him. His heavy breathing told her he'd fallen asleep, so she slipped out of his grasp and went to the bathroom. When she came back, she switched off the lamp. The dim light from the moon fell across him, and she decided that she loved him in moonlight. She was so enamored of him. Racking her brain, she couldn't remember ever having felt so excited or connected to a man. *Muerto blows Brent out of the water by a long shot.* And to think she'd thought Brent was the only man for her—her soul mate.

Since meeting Muerto, her senses had been in overdrive. He seemed to understand her art, passions, and longings—in short, *her*. At that point, as she tiptoed over and snuggled back in bed with him, she didn't care if she ended up brokenhearted. She wouldn't trade him for the world.

He was real, dangerous, exciting, and sensitive, and he was hers. At least for the moment. And she fully intended to make the most of it.

Chapter Twenty-Two

A FEW DAYS after she beat Army and Cue Ball at pool—something she secretly gloated about many times—Raven fed Sooty, checked all the windows and doors, and took off to do her weekly antique store and garage sale runs. Sometimes she'd find treasures amongst all the junk while other times her ventures were a bust.

Her five-hour outing proved to be a mixture of some great finds and some real duds. Driving home, she was already visualizing the jewelry designs, excitement building inside her. She pulled into the garage and, with packages in hand, opened the back door and stepped into her kitchen.

She froze. *Someone's been in here.*

Fear settled uncomfortably in her chest. A strangeness permeated the air, and she knew an intruder had been there. *Or is* still *here.* The hair on the nape of her neck rose as a cold shiver tangled around her nerves. Sooty meowed and rubbed against her legs. Placing her bags on the floor, she picked the cat up and nuzzled her face against Sooty's as she purred.

"You wouldn't be purring if someone was in here, would you, girl?" She walked slowly out of the kitchen and down her short hallway. As she made her way to the bedroom, she flung open closet doors and checked her studio. Nothing amiss. No one around. "Maybe I've been watching too many true crime documentaries on television," she whispered aloud.

As she entered her bedroom, she heard a click behind her in the living room. She stopped. Her muscles tensed. She held her breath. *What is that?* She strained to hear. Nothing. Rooted to the floor, silence engulfed her. Slowly, she let out her breath, her muscles relaxing a bit.

Then another click. Her ears pounded. *It sounds like someone's turning the doorknob on the front door. Did I lock it? I can't fucking remember.* She ran her fingers over her clammy skin. Willing herself to move, she turned around and crept into the living room, the front door looming before her.

Nothing.

Inhaling deeply, she tiptoed to the window and peeked out the blinds. There were two brown boxes on the front porch. Looking at the street, she saw the delivery truck. Feeling giddy, she grabbed the window sill to steady herself. Sooty meowed and she looked down. "See what a crazy woman I am? I'm imagining all kinds of crap." After several deep gulps of air, she opened the front door and picked up the boxes. They were the art supplies she'd ordered a couple weeks before.

After placing the boxes on the coffee table, she went to her bedroom. When she walked into the room, she gasped. On top of the small desk laid a wilted red rose in a puddle of liquid. *What the hell?* Taking small, tentative steps, she inched closer to the desk. Dabbing her finger into the liquid, she clutched her throat, gasping for air.

"Shit!" she cried out, her head spinning. The dying rose was drowning in a pool of blood that glistened in the sunlight. Whirling around, she stumbled on her feet and tripped, Sooty screeching as they both hit the wood floor. Sensing Raven's fear, the cat scampered away.

"Sooty! Come here. Sooty." Her voice echoed in the small house, but Sooty stayed obstinately hidden.

Raven rushed out on the front porch and called Muerto. *Please pick up. Please... plea—*

"Hey, babe. Good to hear from you." His deep voice comforted her immediately.

"Someone broke into my house," she blurted.

"What the fuck? Are you in the house?"

"On the front porch. Whoever it was left a wilted rose in a puddle of... blood." She grimaced when she said the word.

"Get off the porch. Stand on the sidewalk. I'm on my way."

She opened the screen door and called in a soft, soothing voice, "Sooty. Come on over here, pretty girl." A ball of fur padded over to her and she scooped up her pet, then went over to stand on the sidewalk in front of the house.

Who would do something like that? And why me? People are so fuckin' weird. Annnd speaking of weird.... She gazed at the picture window in the back house and saw Walter staring at her. He didn't wave, smile, smirk, or acknowledge her in any way other than his piercing stare that drilled right into her.

And then she heard the rumble of Muerto's bike. *Now I'm safe. I can breathe.* Shifting her gaze from Walter to the corner, warmth radiated throughout her body when she saw him. Waving, she rushed over to the curb when he pulled up. He came over to her and crushed her in his arms. Sooty hissed loudly, so Muerto stepped back and laughed.

"You stay out here. I'll make sure the place is clear," he said.

"I already looked everywhere but the bedroom closet and bath. I think if someone was in there, they'd be long gone by now."

"Just stay out here until I clear the place. Don't argue." He went into the house.

After what seemed like forever, he finally returned and gestured her to come in. Inside, she asked, "Did you see it? The rose?"

"Yeah. Is anyone mad at you?"

Her eyes widened. "I don't think so. No, wait.... Brent's pissed at me. I mean, he acted madder than hell when I told him I wasn't interested in him anymore." She shook her head. "There's no way it was Brent though. I know him. He wouldn't even think of doing something like this."

"You never know what people are capable of. Everyone has a dark side that no one knows about."

"It didn't look like whoever did it broke in."

"Locks are still good. No broken windows. Did you leave a window open?"

She shook her head. "No, I always close and lock all the windows and doors when I leave. It's a ritual for me, has been for years. I know I didn't leave any open."

Muerto tried the windows in the living room, kitchen, studio, and bathroom while Raven tagged along. When they got to her bedroom, he went over to the large window and pulled on it. It flew open. "Seems like you forgot to lock this one. That's probably how the guy got in."

Shaking her head, she muttered, "No. There's no way that window was open. I distinctly remember double-checking to make sure all windows were locked and secured. I absolutely did not leave that window unlocked. Who else has a key to my place besides you?"

His smile told her he was placating her. "Only the management company. They have a key to all my places. They have to in case of an emergency and I'm not around."

With her arms crossed, she looked pointedly at him. "I'm telling you that I *did not* leave a window unlocked. Someone came in here with a key."

Muerto came over and hugged her. "Okay."

Shrugging him off, she shook her head, her face muscles tense. "Don't patronize me. I know what I did. Can someone get in here without a key?"

"I'm not patronizing you. I'm only saying that sometimes we make mistakes. And yeah, someone can get in here without a key, but the lock isn't pried open and you said the deadbolt was set. A bump key can open most locks, but I doubt someone would use it to come in and leave you a rose. Has anything been stolen?"

"No. Have any of your other tenants had a similar problem?"

"Nope."

"Do you think Walter would do something like this?"

"Walter? I don't think so. Anyway, I talked to him after you told me that he was bothering you. He didn't realize he was giving you the creeps. Has he kept away from you lately?"

"So that's why I've been able to garden in peace. I just thought he'd gotten a job or something. It's been nice. But he was staring at me while

I was waiting for you. He had a real odd look on his face. I couldn't figure out what he was thinking." She shivered.

"He obviously finds you attractive. I'm sure you've had your share of creepy guys staring at you. To be honest, he looks like he's out of shape. If he came in through that window, you'd see it. I bet it was the same teenagers who left the roses on your mat a few weeks ago. They're just trying to mess with you. I'll see what punks are living around here and have a talk with them."

"We never established that the first incident with the roses was the work of the teenagers. You're just assuming it is," she said softly.

"You gotta admit it's a pretty lame thing to do. This shit has 'punks' written all over it. You want me to put in an alarm?"

Rubbing the back of her neck, she sighed. "No. I'm mostly here, and now that you're spending the night with me, I feel safe."

A few hours later, as they sat on the small patio in the backyard watching the sun set, she took a gulp of red wine while Muerto finished the last morsel of the steak he'd grilled. As he talked about motorcycles, her mind drifted back to the wilted rose in the puddle of blood. *I know I locked the bedroom window.* A dark sense of foreboding grabbed hold of her and choked her until she dropped the wineglass on the cement, the shattering glass mimicking her nerves.

"I'm sorry. Let me get the broom." She leapt up and retrieved a dustpan and broom from the closet off the kitchen. While she swept, Muerto received a call from one of his brothers. He excused himself and went inside. As she threw the last glass shards into the trash, goose bumps pricked her skin despite the warmth of the evening air. *What did the rose in blood mean? Is it a warning?* For the past couple of weeks, a suspicion had niggled at the back of Raven's mind that someone had been watching her. She hadn't seen anyone, but she *felt* it like a frosty breath on the back of her neck.

"Did you get all the glass?" Muerto asked as he came out with another glass of red wine in his hand.

"Pretty much. Everything okay at the clubhouse?"

He laughed. "Yeah. Brutus wanted to know if you were up to playing a game of pool with him. I told him that shit was a one-nighter only." He shook his head, laughter in his chest.

"I think it's best if I retire my cue stick." She forced a smile.

"Come here, babe." He stretched out his arm and she took his hand as he got up from the chair. He yanked her to him, settling her down on his lap and pressing her head on his shoulder. Stroking her hair, he said in a low voice, "Don't let what happened today get you down. I'm with you, and I'm sure as fuck not going to let anything happen to you. You're special to me." He kissed the top of her head.

They held each other until the mosquitoes started feasting too much on her exposed arms. Laughing, she jumped up and pretended to help him to his feet. Carrying the dishes inside, she felt closer to Muerto than she had to any man.

After loading the dishwasher, they settled on the couch and watched a thriller. It wasn't exactly the best choice, but her man was with her, so she felt invincible for the moment. She was exhausted, so after she checked all the doors—Muerto followed behind her double-checking—they went into the bedroom. Soon they were tangled in the sheets, Raven grinding her rounded ass against his chest and his belly. Then she mounted him and rocked back and forth until they both fell back, exhausted and sated.

A sound woke her up. She looked over at Muerto, but he slept peacefully. *If it was something to worry about, surely his instincts would wake him up. After all, he's tuned in for danger.*

But then there it was again, like a light rustling coming from across the street. She'd opened the window after their amazing lovemaking to cool them down and they'd fallen asleep. Again.

There isn't a wind tonight.

She rolled out of Muerto's embrace and crept to the window. Looking out, she stared at the trees across the street. *Wait. What's that? Is that a person? Oh fuck!* Her eyes flew to Muerto. He still slept. Rubbing her eyes, she focused her attention back to the window.

Is there something... someone out there? Can he see me? She jumped away and plastered herself against the wall next to the window. Furtively, she peeked out. In the night, the trees looked like men crouching down and staring at her. The minutes ticked into an hour. *This is insane. I'm letting my imagination get the best of me. I must be seeing things.* She shut the window and closed the curtain, then headed back to bed. Snuggling against Muerto, she closed her eyes and tried to sleep, his arm wrapped around her, cocooning her in his warmth and protection. As she began to drift to sleep, a car engine pierced the quiet. Before her foggy brain could make sense of it, sleep finally came.

Chapter Twenty-Three

O N A DARK and moonless night, at three thirty in the morning, a black pickup truck pulled behind the Climax Lounge. In the cab was a small container of commercial fertilizer—ammonium nitrate—and diesel oil that had been mixed earlier at the clubhouse.

Army, Eagle, Chains, and Goldie had stolen the fertilizer from a storage area on the Granby Farm about forty miles from Alina the night before. The lack of security and the pathetically small padlock on the storage room door made the theft almost too easy.

Army was adept at making bombs. He'd been an Explosive Ordnance Disposal—EOD—technician while he'd been in the military. During his eight-year stint, he'd served both in Afghanistan and Iraq, handling bombs built in factories as well as those built by individuals. When he'd come back from the war, bitter and used up, he found solace in the Night Rebels MC. The men there understood his pain, his hardness, his hatred. They shared a common bond of insurgency against authority, and Army's forte in bomb making was an asset the club welcomed.

Muerto drove the black pickup on the quiet streets. On a weeknight, the town normally rolled up at about ten o'clock, making covert operations much easier to pull off. The plan was simple: disengage the security system if there was one, break into the club, place the bomb inside, and detonate it from a safe distance. Army had used a blasting cap and detonation cord, with a coffee maker timer. He'd attached the speaker of a cell phone to a relay that applied the current needed for the detonation cord. When the cell phone rang, the current to the speaker would actuate the relay, which would then energize the cord. The spark would set off the bomb, and the strip bar would be destroyed.

Not wanting to damage other businesses in the area, the container used had enough power to shake down some walls, but it was the fire it would start that would burn the place down to the ground. And if Sheriff Wexler acted the way the Night Rebels suspected he would, he'd delay putting out the fire until the building was irreparably damaged.

Jigger and Brutus had been scouting the place all night to make sure no one was in the building; the goal was to destroy it, not kill anyone. If Satan's Pistons retaliated, however, all bets were off and war between the rival MCs would ensue.

Pulling over to the curb on the backside of the building, Muerto killed the engine. He and Skull got out of the truck and made their way to Brutus and Jigger, who stood in the shadows of the bar.

"You figure out how to disengage the security cameras?" Muerto asked as his eyes darted from the various ones in the parking lot.

"The cheap fucks don't have them connected," Jigger said.

"What a bunch of losers," Muerto said. "Makes our job a helluva lot easier."

Army and Eagle came over. "We good with the security system?" Eagle said.

"Lazy, cheap fucks only have the cameras for show," Brutus said. The men chuckled.

"We ready to move?" Army asked as he glanced around the dark streets. The men nodded, then quietly went back to their respective posts.

Muerto moved the pickup into the parking lot, right up against the back doors, and jumped out of the truck. In less than ten minutes the back doors swung open, and he motioned for his brothers to bring the container into the building. Without talking, they moved quickly and stealthily, and in less than fifteen minutes, they were out of the building and driving away. As they turned down a dirt road, Muerto heard the blast. It wasn't a thunderous, showy boom, just a small rumble echoing in the darkness. The brothers made their way to the clubhouse where they would burn their gloves. Diablo would take the truck to Junkyard Blues and have it crushed the following day.

And life would go on.

THE HEADLINES IN the *Alina Daily Journal* read "Massive Blast Destroys Strip Bar," and a picture in full color showed the Climax Lounge burning, plumes of black smoke billowing out of the windows and roof.

Muerto drank his coffee and scarfed down his eggs and bacon as he read the article. "It says that 'Wexler and the fire department have concluded that a gas pipe broke, causing the blast. We're fortunate no other businesses sustained any damages in the area. And it's also lucky that the explosion occurred after the bar had closed so no one was hurt. From the looks of it, the club is severely damaged.' Fuckin' right it is. When we do shit, we do it right." Muerto shoveled in another forkful of food.

Sangre and Skull, sitting with Muerto, laughed. "We can always count on good ol' Wexler as long as we're doing his work," Sangre said as he tugged the paper away from Muerto.

Muerto pushed his chair back from the table. "I keep telling Steel we need to charge the badge when we clean up shit on his watch."

"There's no way Wexler's paying us a visit after saying that 'gas pipe broke' shit. But the important thing is that the Satan's Pistons will know this was a message from us to stay the fuck out of our territory. And if they don't like it, they can come for us," Skull said. Several members in the large room agreed and chanted, "Death to Satan's Pistons."

Muerto nodded. "Those fuckers better stay in Arizona. I gotta get to the pool hall." He jerked his chin at his brothers and went out into the bright August sun.

When he entered Balls and Holes, Brandy, Jaime, and Zach were all talking about the explosion at the Climax Lounge. Several patrons had moseyed up to the bar and joined in on the discussion.

"I don't believe the gas pipe breaking story for one minute," Brandy said.

"Why not?" Muerto asked her.

"The place was a dive. I'll bet anything that after they do a full investigation, they'll find out it was arson. The owners probably wanted the insurance money." Brandy beamed when several people agreed with her.

"Don't you think the sheriff would've not said anything if they suspected arson? I mean, I would think a broken gas pipe is pretty easy to spot," Jaime said, and the same people who agreed with Brandy agreed with Jaime.

"It was a dive anyway, so it's no big deal," one of the customers said. "It was nothing like Lust."

"What do you think, Muerto?" Jaime asked.

He shrugged. "I didn't think much about it. And the way the government is, they may have blown it up and are just covering their tracks."

"A true conspiracy theorist." Brandy laughed.

"Just the way I see it." Muerto went over to a box of liquor bottles and starting pulling them out.

After half an hour or so of rehashing the destruction of the strip bar, Brandy turned to Muerto, who'd been feigning concentration in getting the bar stocked and the receipts counted. "Are you still going out with the famous pool shark?"

He bristled. "Her name's Raven, and yeah, I am."

"That's a record for you, isn't it?" Brandy winked at Jaime, who blushed.

"You tell me. You seem to be the one keeping track." Muerto crossed his arms.

"I'm just joking with you. I think it's great you have a girlfriend."

"She's your girlfriend?" Jaime asked.

Muerto shook his head. "Why the fuck is this any of your business?" he questioned as he looked at each woman. "I don't give a fuck who you date, so don't get involved with my personal life."

"We're just joking, honest. Aren't we, Jaime?" Brandy looked at her, then Muerto. Jaime nodded.

"That's enough," Muerto said, dismissing them. When he crouched down to pull out some supplies from a cupboard, he heard Brandy say, "He's got it bad for this one. I've never seen him act this way. I wonder what she has that we don't."

He snorted. *A fuckin' brain.*

"You want these tequila and Johnnie Walker bottles unpacked?" Zach asked Muerto.

"Nah. Take them to the back."

"What does a girl have to do to get a drink around here?" Raven's soft voice wrapped around him, and he spun around.

"Hey, sweetie. What brings you to the pool hall so early?" He leaned over and kissed her. "You want a shot?"

She laughed. "Not this early. How about some coffee with cream? I came into town to do a few errands. I heard that Henny's was having a huge sale on all their fabrics, buttons, and lace, so I had to check it out. I got some good stuff." She accepted the mug he handed her and took a sip. "Good coffee." She smiled at him.

"I didn't expect to see you this early. What a delicious surprise." He leaned over and kissed her again, his hand on the back of her head, tugging her closer to his face. He wanted to take her in the back and fuck her good and hard.

"Nice. I missed you last night," she whispered against his lips.

"Me too, babe." He kissed her again.

"When I heard the explosion, it scared the crap out of me. I didn't know what the hell was going on. Did you hear it?"

"Not really. The clubhouse is a ways from the town. I read about it in the paper."

"Yeah. I guess it was a strip bar that burned down. I never heard of it."

"It was a dump. No real loss."

For the rest of the morning, they chatted as he worked. When Cory and his buddy came in, they just glared at Raven, but they played a few games, had a couple of beers, and left without incident. As the afternoon hit, Raven stood up and stretched. "I think I'll take in a yoga class before I head home. It'll be a nice break before I spend the rest of the day making jewelry like a madwoman. I have that upcoming show in Cortez, so I have to bulk up my inventory."

"I'll be over after my shift. Crow's on tonight. I'll grill a couple of steaks and we'll have a good dinner before I show you how much I missed you."

"Sounds like a great plan. I'll stop by the grocery store after yoga." She turned toward the door and then stopped, her body rigid, her eyes wide.

Muerto looked at the door and saw a muscular guy with short light brown hair just inside the doorway. The man's eyes were locked on Raven. "Who the fuck is that?"

Before she answered, the man walked over to her. "Hi, Raven." His gaze swept over her. "You're looking good."

"Thanks." She took a step backward.

"Lucky for me that I came in here for a drink."

"You don't fool me for a second, Brent. Are you stalking me or something?"

Brent. That name. Wait... that's her fuckin' ex. Sonofabitch is outta here. "You need to stop bothering her." Muerto's voice had an edge in it.

"It's okay. I can handle this," she said to him.

"This is between me and Raven. You're not involved." Brent glanced back at Raven.

Licks of anger whipped over Muerto. "The fuck I'm not involved. She's my woman." As he spoke, he walked out from behind the bar and came close to her.

Jerking his head back, Brent looked from Muerto to Raven. "You're dating this guy?"

Raven leaned against Muerto's arm. "That's right."

"Get the fuck outta here. Now." Muerto clenched his fist.

"You can't throw me out. I haven't done anything wrong. You don't own this place."

"Actually, he does," she said in a soft voice.

"You're outta here." With one quick blow, Muerto's fist landed on Brent's jaw.

Brent's eyes widened in genuine shock. As Muerto went in for another blow, he stepped back, his head shaking. "I don't want any trouble. I just came in to say hi to an old friend, that's all." He walked out, but as he passed the window, he stopped for a few seconds and glared at Raven before moving on.

"The guy's a pussy," Muerto snarled.

"You know, I could've handled it. You can't just go around punching every guy who talks to me."

"Why not? I knew the fucker was gonna give you some shit, so I stopped it before it happened."

She wrapped her arms around his waist. "I know, but sometimes you have to trust me to take care of myself."

"Not gonna happen. If I'm around and someone's bugging you, I'm punching his fuckin' lights out. I don't see the problem."

Smiling, she brushed her lips against his. "You're the best. I'll see you tonight."

He walked her to her car and had her promise to call him when she got home after her yoga class. As she drove away, he felt a strange sense of emptiness. Being with her made him happy. He'd never really hung with a woman beyond their moments of carnal pleasure; wanting to hang out with Raven was a new sensation for him. And the feelings he had for her were real and steady.

He walked back inside knowing the time would drag until they were together again. For the first time, a woman occupied his mind. He was addicted to her voice, her laugh, her scent, her sexiness, and he thought she was the most wonderful, perfect person he'd ever met. And the thing that blew his mind was that he loved feeling that way. She lit up his life like a fireball.

I'm definitely falling for her.

Chapter Twenty-Four

THE FOLLOWING MORNING, Muerto kissed Raven deeply, then went out to his Harley. Looking back before he turned the corner, he saw her standing behind the screen door watching him ride away. Knowing that she didn't just close the door and start her day when he left gave him a warm glow.

Pulling up to the curb in front of the pool hall, he killed the engine and walked up to the front door. Before he turned the key, he could see the mess inside the place. *What the fuck?* He rushed in. The room was a disaster: broken glasses and bottles strewn all over the bar and floor, sliced-up pool tables, graffiti everywhere. He stood frozen for a few seconds surveying the mess. Red paint sprayed on all the walls read "You're dead."

Adrenaline rushed through his body, and a deep urge for vengeance consumed him. Picking up a chair from the floor, he hurled it across the room. "Fuck!" He whipped out his phone and called Steel.

"The pool hall's been trashed. It's a goddamn mess."

"Did you set the alarm last night?" Steel asked.

"Crow closed up, but I'm sure he did."

"Crow had an emergency, so he left early. Who closed?"

"I don't know, but whoever did would've set the alarm." A low thud came from the hallway. "Hang on. I hear something," Muerto said as he reached in his cut and took out his Glock 9mm. Walking with deliberate steps, he quietly entered the hallway. When he passed the utility closet, he heard low moans and soft knocking.

"Someone's in here. I gotta go," he said to Steel.

"Take care. The brothers are on their way."

Muerto put the phone in his pocket and slowly turned the door-knob. It was locked. More moaning, then sobbing. *A woman's in there.* He put the key in the lock and turned it, opening the door. Jaime was on the floor and she looked up at him, wild-eyed. Her hair was disheveled, her blouse was torn, blood and tears streaked her face, and her nails were broken.

"What the fuck happened, Jaime?" Muerto bent down and the broken woman clung to him, sobbing, relief etched on her face. He pulled her up from the floor and, with his arm wrapped around her, led her to the main room. He picked up a chair and set it straight, then helped her into it.

"I'm so glad you came," she said haltingly.

Coming back from the bar with a bottle of water, he sighed. "What happened here?"

She took the water and drank in large gulps. Staring vacantly, she said in a monotone, "It was horrible. Just horrible."

"What was?" He sat in a chair next to hers. "Just tell me about it. No one can hurt you. I'm here."

Another few gulps of water, and color began to come back on her face. "I was the one who ended up closing last night. Zach was supposed to, but his girlfriend had another one of her meltdowns, so he left at eleven thirty. No one was in the place and I was kinda spooked to be there alone, so I decided to close early." She finished her water. "Can I have another one, please?"

"Of course." He went over to the bar. *Zach's ass is fired for sure. He knows not to leave Brandy or Jaime alone at night. Fuck him.* "Here you go."

She took the opened bottle and drank deeply. "Anyway, as I went to lock the door, two men with bandanas over their faces pushed in. One of them was real tall, and he hit me across the face and asked for money. I told him all the money had been taken to the bank, but he called me a liar. The shorter guy pushed me and told me I better show him some money or he'd kill me." Tears welled in her eyes. "Then he took a gun out. I was so scared." She hung her head down and Muerto put his hand on hers. She looked up. "I gave it to him. There was about five hundred dollars in the drawer. Crow had taken most of the money when he left at ten. I'm sorry, but I thought they were going to kill me."

"No worries about the money. I'm just glad they didn't kill you. Were they wearing leather jackets or vests?"

She shook her head. "T-shirts and jeans."

"Any tats?"

"They both had a lot of them on what I could see of their arms."

"Anything that said Piston or Satan?"

"I'm sorry. I really don't remember. I was so terrified that all I could think about was how to get out alive."

He patted her hand, then looked at the door when he heard Goldie's voice. "Goddamn, it's a mess."

"No shit," said Skull.

Crow rushed over to Jaime. "Are you okay? Who the fuck did this?"

"I'm okay now. It was awful. They acted like they were only after the money."

"Then why the fuck did they spray-paint 'You're dead'? Seems personal," Chains said, eyes fixed on the walls.

"Did they mess with you?" Muerto asked in a low voice.

"They tried to. They seemed really mad that the amount of money was so low. They started groping and hitting me. I pleaded with them not to hurt me. The taller guy kept telling the shorter one that they should go. They dragged me down the hall, tried the door on the utility closet, and when it opened, they threw me inside. They told me that if I left, they'd kill me. The door locked and I couldn't get out." Pressing her steepled fingers against her forehead, she muttered, "It was just so awful. I've never had anything like that happen to me before."

"They obviously didn't know they were stealing from an outlaw MC. When we find their asses, they'll know. And if they live, they'll never forget." Chains slammed his hand against the wall.

When Steel walked in his face turned dark. He jerked his chin at

Jaime. "Does she know who did this?"

Muerto shook his head. "She gave a bit of a description, but nothing to really go on. She's had a bad time of it. She should go home."

"It's the fuckin' Satan's Pistons!" Army yelled while Eagle, Jigger, and Cue Ball agreed.

"Why doesn't someone take the woman home? We got some shit we need to discuss," Steel said.

Jigger volunteered and soon he had Jaime on the back of his bike, his cams roaring as he blasted down the street.

"It's not Satan's Pistons. It's not their MO," Crow said.

"It looks like it's personal, like maybe it's someone against me or Crow, or both of us. We get a lot of pissed-off dudes around here. It could be someone we threw out, or who lost big money, or whatever else." Muerto glanced again at the threat graffitied all over the walls.

"I'm with Crow on this. Paco and I were talking about it on the way over. This isn't their style. This reeks of some punks who wanted to rob the place. Probably don't know it's a Night Rebels business," Steel said as he took out his phone. "I'll get some people in here to fix it up. We don't want to lose too much revenue over this."

"Maybe they did know it was ours and that's what the thrill was. Like kicking us in the ass," Goldie said.

"They're gonna be fuckin' sorry about that stupid mistake," Paco replied.

"Could be the punks in Pueblo. What the fuck was their name? You know, the fuckers who were kissing the Pistons' asses." Cue Ball rubbed his head.

"The 39th Street Gang? Could be. That makes sense. It's retaliation for us torching the strip bar." Goldie leaned against the bar.

"Or the fuckers Muerto and I beat down at the junkyard," Diablo said.

"We'll find out who they were. Let's get this place cleaned up." Steel started picking up chairs.

As the brothers worked, Muerto's gut worked overtime, and darkness filled him. He didn't think the theft and vandalism had anything to do with the Night Rebels. A disquieting suspicion pulled at him, and he called Raven. Even though she assured him all was good, he knew it wasn't.

Something isn't right.

Chapter Twenty-Five

PICTURES FILLED THE wall, so many of them that they took on the appearance of wallpaper. I loved looking at them. I was glad Mother had bought me a camera for my thirteenth birthday. I can honestly say that it was at that moment, when I first held the silver camera in my hands, that I knew I'd never stop taking pictures of life and of people who interested and angered me. My pictures were like a journal of sorts for me; I could remember where I was, what I was doing, and on which date. Every detail was there in the photographs.

I went over my new pictures I'd just printed out at the print shop. My quandary was where I was going to put them. I stood back for a long time, the scent of the red roses on the table behind me so fragrant. And then I saw the perfect spot for my new pictures. Right between the photograph of Muerto and Raven on the front porch drinking lemon-ade—it'd been so hot that day—and the other photograph of them kissing on the sidewalk before he rode away on his macho-man Harley.

I picked up two pictures of the pool hall: one of the wonderfully graffitied walls, the other showing the smashed glass. They were perfect. And I must admit that I did a beautiful job on the walls. The letters were all spray-painted to perfection, same height and thickness. I was sure whoever saw them appreciated the effort I'd put into the whole thing.

I had to do it. I had to punish him for being so stupid to take up with such a wanton slut. Picking up a black marker, I glanced at the wall of photographs of *them*. I took off the cap and carefully placed an X over his face in most of the photographs, and then I neatly wrote "slut" and "whore" over her face in red marker. It'd taken me a little more than an hour to do it, and I had to drag out the ladder from the back, hoping no one would see me.

But it'd been worth the effort. I stood back and admired my handiwork, feeling a bit smug with myself. He'd allowed her to lead him astray. I'd given him some leeway, but now I knew he enjoyed fornicating. They both deserved to be punished.

A smile played on my lips as I remembered one of Mother's favorite quotes from the Bible, Isaiah 13:11. "And I will punish the world for their evil, and the wicked for their iniquity; and I will cause the arrogance of the proud to cease, and will lay low the haughtiness of the terrible."

And that's exactly what I'd planned to do—punish the wicked.

Chapter Twenty-Six

O N SATURDAY NIGHT, Muerto arrived at his mother's birthday party with Raven in tow. He'd wanted to ride over on his Harley with her pressed close to him, but she refused to meet his mother and sisters with windblown hair and dust on her face. When he relented, he knew she had his heart in addition to his dick.

"How beautiful," Raven exclaimed when they walked into the backyard for the party. Strings of colorful lanterns lined the fences and hung from the trees. High above on a tightrope, a bull made of papier-mâché and tissue paper in bold colors of blue, yellow, red, and purple dangled, waiting to be suspended at the appropriate time. "The *piñata's* filled with candy, right?" she asked, her head tilted back.

"And small toys. It's for the kids. I used to love it when it was my birthday and I got first swing at it. I'd beat the shit out of it."

She quirked her lips. "I'm sure you did. You were a little hoodlum in the making. And I bet you had all the little girls cheering you on." She squeezed his hand.

"Actually, I did." He kissed her softly on the lips. "If you were one of them in your cute party dress, I would've given my candy to you, handsdown."

"Uncle M!" Carlos said as he ran toward Muerto.

"Hey, buddy." Muerto let go of Raven's hand and gave the boy a bear hug. "You eyeing the *piñata*?"

The boy's eyes rolled up. "Uh-huh. It's a real big one. I bet there's lots of good stuff inside it."

Muerto laughed. "I want you to meet Raven." He gripped her wrist and moved her next to him. "This derelict is Carlos. He's my sister

Laura's kid."

"Are you Uncle M's girlfriend?" Carlos squinted at her.

A light pink colored her cheeks. "I'm… uh…."

"Yeah, she is," Muerto said, winking at her as her eyes widened.

"Hi, Mateo," Laura said as she came over, her gaze drifting over to Raven.

"Hey. I want you to meet Raven." The two women sized each other up, and Muerto knew Raven was in for a long night with all his relatives. He gripped her hand. "Where's Ma?"

"She's in the tent. You did good. Everything is so beautiful."

He nodded. "I'll catch you later. We're going to get a drink."

As he walked past her, she grabbed his arm and whispered, "She's beautiful, and you look so happy. I love it." He flashed her a quick smile, then walked toward the tent.

Inside, a burst of color welcomed them. The decorations, place settings, and lighting lent a festive air. Strings of tiny white lights twinkled everywhere, and wrought iron chandeliers with colored crystals hung around the room, creating an elegant ambiance. On white tablecloths, brightly colored dinner plates in green, yellow, red, and purple gleamed under the tiny lights.

"This is stunning. I love all the colors and textures used in the decorations. Simply lovely." Raven clutched his bicep. "Thank you for sharing this with me."

"I'm glad you're with me. Let's go meet my mom and then get a drink."

"I have a feeling I'm going to need several drinks before the night's over. I didn't know you had such a big family."

Muerto laughed. "Yeah. Tons of uncles, aunts, and cousins. Don't worry about remembering everyone's name. I can't remember half of my cousins' names," he joked as he steered her toward a big table.

A woman with dark brown hair pulled up in a chignon stood talking with a tall man who had salt-and-pepper hair. She craned her neck and her dark eyes sparkled, the lines around them crinkled. "*Mijo.*" She pulled Muerto into a loving embrace. "It's too long since I've seen you." She pretended to be upset, but her eyes shone like frost in the moonlight. "Is this the woman Laura told me about?" Her gaze shifted to Raven.

"This is Raven," he said.

"Very pleased to meet you, Mrs. Ruiz," she said, extending her hand.

Shaking her head, she said, "Call me Cecilia." Brushing Raven's hand aside, she gathered her in a strong embrace. "You don't know how happy I am to meet you."

"It's nice meeting you. Muerto speaks very fondly about you."

Cecilia glanced at Muerto and smiled. "That's good to know. Do you know how to cook?"

"Ma," he chided.

"What? I was just wondering that's all."

Raven leaned against him. "It's okay. I love to cook. I find it very creative and relaxing. I don't know much about Mexican cooking, so if you have some great recipes you'd like to share I'd love to have them."

Catching his eye, she said, "She's a keeper *mijo*." Turning her gaze back to Raven, she grasped her hand. "I'd love to have you come over sometime and go over the recipes with me. I have stacks of them. The dishes Mateo loves the most are in here." She tapped her finger against her temple. "I'll have Mateo bring you over and I can show you how to make a proper green chile."

"I'd love that."

"Don't give me that face, *mijo*." Cecilia swatted his arm playfully.

"I think I'm going to regret this somehow." He pretended to be sullen, but the glint in his eye gave him away.

After talking with his mother for a while longer, he and Raven headed to the bar where he ordered a double shot of tequila with lime and salt and a margarita for her. As she sipped her margarita, he maneuvered her to a corner in the yard away from everyone. "I thought you'd like a breather," he said. The melodic strains from the mariachis floated on the slight breeze.

"Thanks. It must've been great having such a big family when you were growing up. You're lucky."

"It has its perks, but it also means you have four times as many people butting their noses into your life."

"True. I didn't think about that. The whole time I was growing up, it was just me and my dad. I didn't know any of my cousins since my dad was estranged from his brothers and sisters. My mom's side faded away after she died." Raven licked the salt with the tip of her tongue. "Your mom and sister seemed real excited to meet me. They act like I'm the first girl you've ever brought. It's sweet."

"You are the only woman I've ever brought over."

She moved her drink away from her mouth. "Are you serious? Then why did you ask me to come?"

"Because I'm fuckin' crazy about you. Don't you know that?"

She stared deeply into his eyes. "I wasn't a hundred percent sure, but I'm glad because I'm hooked on you. Like totally, big-time hooked."

"That's good." He looped his arm around her waist and tugged her to him. "All I do is think about you, sweetie." Then he crushed his mouth to hers with such intensity that he was sure she'd have bruises the following morning. He figured they could join all the other love bites he made sure were always on her body. When it came to her, he couldn't help himself. She was like a drug that kept enticing him, and each time he indulged, he wasn't satisfied because he wanted more. He didn't think he'd ever get enough of her.

The night was a collage of food, drink, conversation, dancing, laughter, and family. Muerto had never wanted to share his family or his heritage with anyone before Raven. Watching her sway her hips to the *cumbia*, engage his family in conversation, eat heartily, and play with his niece and nephews touched him in ways he couldn't articulate. All he knew was that he wanted her to be a part of his life. He didn't know if it was the double shots of tequila, how her rounded ass looked in her white skirt, or the way the tiny lights sparkled in the tent, but the night was magical.

And when Carlos broke open the *piñata* and all the kids squealed, rushing to pick up the candy and toys on the ground, Raven jumped up and down, cheering them on, her face shining under the colored lanterns.

It was at that moment he knew he loved her.

Later that night, when they laid together, a cool breeze caressing their naked bodies, he held her close. Their lovemaking had been sensuous, slow, and tender as he strived to control the raging beast inside him that wanted to pummel her good and hard. He didn't want to fuck her; he wanted to make sweet love to her, to make her come harder than she ever had from his touches. And she had.

"Tonight was just perfect. The party, making love…everything," she whispered against his chest.

Raking his fingers through her hair, he bent down and kissed the top of her head. "I wanna tell you something I've never told any other woman."

Tilting her head up, she caught his gaze. "You're not going to tell me you're a mass murderer or something, are you?"

He chuckled. "No." Stroking her cheek, he held her gaze. "I love you."

A huge smile spread across her face. "I love you too. So damn much. You totally make my world rock." She shimmied closer to his face and planted her lips on his. They kissed passionately.

When she nestled her face in his neck, he asked, "If I was a mass murderer, would you still love me?"

"Probably… why?"

"Just checking."

She giggled and wiggled beside him, the side of her tit soft and nice on his skin.

Then his cock was hard again and he rolled her onto her back. Hovering over her, he brought his mouth to hers, strands of her black hair catching between their lips as they kissed. He could feel her hard nipples against his chest, and he knew that time around he'd fuck her.

The nighttime breeze did little to cool his fire.

Chapter Twenty-Seven

R AVEN WAS STILL walking on air since Muerto's proclamation of love the previous week. She couldn't believe he'd told her he loved her. Muerto. The tough outlaw biker. It was too wonderful. And she loved him too. Even though it seemed like the last several weeks with him were like being on a roller coaster, she loved every minute of it. She never thought she could fall in love so hard and so fast, but she did and it shocked the hell out of her. The guy she thought was the biggest, arrogant asshole in Alina was the love of her life. *But that was before I got to know him. I'm so happy I gave him a chance. When I was with Brent I thought love was supposed to be comfortable, routine, easy, but since I've been with Muerto, I know how much I was missing out on.* She now thought of her time with Brent as the dress rehearsal and her life with Muerto as the main performance.

Humming under her breath, she went outside to pick some vegetables for the evening's dinner. As she plucked red and green peppers, she saw a shadow behind her. Twisting around, she saw Walter's taut face. "Hi, Walter," she said.

"Why did you lie to Muerto about me?"

"I don't know what you're talking about." She shielded her eyes from the afternoon sun.

"You told him I was bothering you. You lied to him."

Racking her brain, she tried to remember if she'd said anything to Muerto about Walter. Then she remembered. *But that was a while ago. Why's he bringing it up to me now? He's such a fuckin' weirdo.* "I just mentioned that you made me uncomfortable when you'd stare at me while I tried to garden. That was a couple of months ago."

"You think you can seduce all men, don't you? Well, you didn't seduce me. You think you're so hot. And just because you're fucking the owner doesn't mean you have to lie about me. Were you mad because you couldn't snare me in your web?" His face mottled with anger, he kicked over her watering can. "You're a fucking slut!"

Raven had never seen Walter like that; his anger was over the top. *I need to get out of here.* She slowly inched over to the porch.

"You really think you're something. The pretty ones are always the worst. I wish a man would turn them down. Just reject them so they can know how it feels to be below average."

"I hear my phone ringing. I have to go." She made a mad dash up the porch stairs and went into the house, closing and locking the door behind her. Sooty's luminous eyes stared at her. "We're fuckin' out of here," she told Sooty, who just sat at Raven's feet.

She watched Walter out of the peephole as he stood glaring at her porch, talking to himself. It seemed to her that the more he talked, the madder he became until he was cussing, screaming, and waving his fist at her closed door.

She plugged in Muerto's phone number. "Walter's really gone off the deep end," she said to her attentive cat as she waited for Muerto to answer. When her call went to his voice mail, disappointment weaved through her. She then plugged in the management company's phone number.

"JB Management," a female voice said.

"Deanna?"

"No, this is Taylor. Deanna no longer works here."

"Can I speak with Jay?" She tapped her fingers against her thigh as she waited for him. Sneaking peeks outside, Walter still stood in front of her porch, his arms crossed.

"Hello?"

"Hi, Jay. This is Raven. I'm trying to get a hold of Muerto, but he isn't picking up. The tenant in the back, Walter, is sorta freaking out and I don't know what to do about it."

"Muerto's at a meeting and told me he couldn't be disturbed. Maybe you should call the police."

"Yeah… maybe." She glanced out again. Walter seemed to be growing tired of his psychotic game and moved onto the sidewalk. "I think he's calming down a bit. It was like totally weird and scary. Something's majorly wrong with that guy."

"I've noted it. I'll make sure Muerto knows about it. I don't know the guy very well, but he always seems okay on the phone."

"Well, he isn't okay. He's a freakin' nutcase."

"It's noted. Is there anything else?"

"I was surprised Deanna didn't answer the phone. The new girl told me she doesn't work there anymore."

A small exhalation of breath. "She just up and quit the day before yesterday. I worked with her for over eight years and never would've expected she'd do something like that. It's left me in a real bind. Are you looking for a job?"

She laughed. "Not yet, but if my paintings don't sell, I may be calling you. What about Taylor?"

"She's from a temp agency. If you have any more problems with Walter, let me know."

She went into the kitchen and took out an iced tea from the refrigerator. *Walter obviously has a problem with women. And he doesn't like women he finds attractive.* It was like Walter was punishing her because he was attracted to her. "He probably has some crazy mother complex," she said to Sooty, who'd jumped into her lap.

Frazzled, she couldn't concentrate on her work, so she just sat in the kitchen, stroking Sooty's thick fur. When her phone buzzed, she leapt and Sooty meowed, jumped down, and scurried away. Looking down, her heart raced when she saw it was Muerto. She knew over time that reaction would lessen, but she was enjoying it immensely.

"I see you called. What's up, sweetie?"

He sounded so cheerful that she didn't want to ruin his demeanor. Deciding she'd tell him later that night, she chuckled. "I just wanted to hear your voice. What time are you coming home?"

"Real soon. And get ready 'cause I'm taking you on a ride."

"Where to?"

"Dolores River Canyon. It's awesome. I've been wanting to take you there before the weather changes. In the mountains, the weather can turn real fast in the fall."

"I've been wanting to play at being a biker chick. This should be fun. Should I wear anything special?"

"Jeans and boots. Bring a jacket, a head scarf if you want to keep your hair from blowing all around, and sunglasses."

"I'll be ready when you get here."

Suddenly all the tension and fear she'd felt earlier disappeared. She couldn't wait to get on his Harley and find out what all the fuss was about.

LOCATED AT THE southern edge of the San Juan Mountains, Dolores River Canyon was a natural wonder that shared its primitive pathways with the Pueblo tribe for several centuries. Raven was in awe of the noble walls carved by nature that flanked the river below. Looking down, the river was like a silver ribbon framed by trees and sagebrush. "It's beautiful up here. So majestic and peaceful. It has a spiritual feel to it."

He came up behind her and hooked his arm around her waist. "That's because parts of the area, especially Chaco Canyon, have spiritual meaning for the Pueblo tribe."

"Isn't the president of your MC Native American?"

"Yeah, but he's Navajo. The Pueblos still have festivals and other celebrations over in Chaco Canyon. It's pretty cool to see."

"I just can't get over how breathtaking it is."

"If you're up for it, we can hike to the top and you'll see the most spectacular view ever. It's not a bad hike, about a quarter of a mile."

"I'd love to. Is your Harley safe?"

"Yeah. People rarely come to this part of the canyon. Let me grab a blanket."

The hike up was an invigorating walk through the different levels of the canyon's birth. Off to the side, Raven saw ruins from a Pueblo life long gone by. It made her shiver to think of the thousands of people who lived and thrived a thousand years ago on the very ground she was walking.

When they reached the top, she gasped. They were on top of one of the highest peaks in the area and she could see all around her. There was a beauty to the eclectic landscape: raw and barren, lush evergreens, and jagged white peaks. "I've never seen anything so beautiful in my life."

He pointed to the far left. "And that's New Mexico. This place is kickass. I come here to reboot when shit gets to be too much."

Turning around to face him, she held his face between her hands. "You are the yin to my yang. I love you."

"Not sure what the hell the yang thing is, but I love you too, babe."

They clung to each other, kissing and living in the moment amid the surrounding beauty. And when Muerto spread out the blanket and eased her down, she was ready to make wild, passionate love to the man who captured her essence. She let her hands travel over his shoulders and arms, enjoying the sensation of his body.

Then he looked at her deeply and she saw the fire smoldering in his dark orbs. At that point, she turned off her mind and gave in to passion.

Chapter Twenty-Eight

I WAS IN the kitchen, ready to leave her house, when I heard the rumble of a motorcycle pull into the driveway. Panicked, I glanced at the door leading into the garage and decided it was too risky for me to leave by the back door. I rushed to the living room intending to go out the front door, but from the window I spotted Patricia and her white dog. Raven went over to her and they began chatting.

The motor stopped, and I knew it was only a matter of minutes until he came into the kitchen. He didn't strike me as the type who would go over and engage in inane conversation with the neighbor. For a heart-stopping moment, my mind shut down. I had no idea how I was going to get out of the jam I found myself in. But when I heard the kitchen door squeak open, adrenaline and stress took over.

I dashed into the bedroom and went to the window, unlocking it. Without even a backward glance, I lifted it up, popped out the screen, and thanked God when I heard her call out to Muerto. She wanted him to help her bring the kitty litter and bottled water that had been in her trunk since the day before. I'd bought some much-needed time.

I scrambled out of the window and carefully closed it, putting the screen back. I scurried across the backyard. Hiding behind a large lilac bush, I was trying to catch my breath when she came out of the house, a bag of charcoals in her hand. She placed it by the grill then glanced my way for a long moment as I held my breath. Thinking she'd seen me, my mind hastily concocted stories for me being there, but she turned around and went back into the house. I exhaled slowly, wondering if she'd seen me and was telling him that I was behind the bush.

For a few tense minutes I waited. No one came out. I slowly

emerged from my hiding place then dashed to the gate leading to the alley. As I walked away, I realized that it had been too close of a call. When they'd ridden away on the motorcycle, I'd lost track of the time. I'd grown carelessly bold. I couldn't risk taking any more chances. I was too close to executing my plan.

I resolved to not go into the bitch's house again until I was ready to kill her.

And that time was looming very near.

Chapter Twenty-Nine

"WORD IS THAT the Satan's Pistons aren't too happy their club was torched. Too fuckin' bad for the bastards," Crow said as he watched the TV screen.

"Yeah. Hawk told me that they know it was us who did it," Steel said as he came over to the table to join Muerto, Crow, and Goldie.

"Next time they won't hide behind brick and mortar, the damn pussies," Goldie said, looking at Steel's plate. "Is Lena making burritos?"

"Yeah." Steel took a bite. "They're damn good."

Goldie got up and walked toward the kitchen.

"I heard that the punks in the 39th Street Gang are threatening to kick our asses." Chains laughed. "I say bring it on. It's been a while since we had a good fight."

"Punks like them are the worst. Remember the shit the Skull Crushers pulled until we had to really beat their asses? They're trying to be men and they just end up being fuckin' pussies." Diablo sat at the table next to Muerto, a plate with two steaming burritos in hand.

"We gotta keep on top of it. The punks are the worst to deal with because they don't get the rules or have respect." Steel took another bite of his burrito.

"Is Delarosa still hiding out?" Chains asked.

Steel nodded. "Seems that way."

"Running scared. He's a yellow-bellied motherfucker." Diablo scowled as the brothers agreed with him.

"Hey, how's the chick who got worked over by the fuckers at the pool hall?" Eagle asked.

"Jaime?" Muerto shrugged. "She said she's good. She's been talking to Brandy about it."

"It's a good thing Brandy wasn't the one who was there that night. She wouldn't have handled it as well as Jaime is." Crow stood up. "I'm gonna get some food. You want a burrito, Muerto?"

He shook his head. "I'm good. I still don't think it has anything to do with the fuckin' Pistons or the punk gang."

"I agree with you," Steel said. "I think it was a random act. A couple of other businesses have been robbed in the last couple of weeks. Probably the same guys. The description Jaime gave us fits with the other robberies. We'll get 'em."

"We're doing the badges' work for them *again*?" Army plopped down at Diablo's table.

"Seems like we're always doing it. Lazy sonsofbitches," Diablo said. The brothers laughed.

"Muerto, you up for a pool game? I have to win my money back," said Army.

"What makes you think you're going to win?" Muerto answered as some of the brothers guffawed.

"Yeah, dude. You better be careful 'cause he's probably getting late-night pool lessons," Eagle said. The room roared and Muerto smiled.

"So what the hell are you doing with the chick? You should've moved on by now." Army stretched out his long legs.

"I'm dating her." Muerto braced himself. Sniggers, lewd noises, and whistles bounced off the clubhouse walls.

"*Dating* her? What the fuck does that mean?" Goldie asked as he cut into his burrito.

"You don't know what *dating* means? I didn't think you were such a stupid fuck." Muerto crossed his arms.

Several brothers chuckled and Chains added, "Yeah. We know you think a chick's for fucking, but sometimes it's fun to go out for dinner or something before you fuck."

"Why would I wanna do that?" Goldie countered.

"I'm with Goldie on this one," Paco said as he sat down. "Chicks are for having a helluva good time when they're naked. Not clothed."

"Having a woman in your life is something you don't know you want until you meet the right one. That's how it was with Breanna. I fucking fought it all the way, but it didn't help. I was hooked. I suspect that's the way it is with you, Muerto," Steel said.

Muerto nodded.

"Is this for real, dude?" Goldie looked at him in disbelief.

Another nod. "I'm in love with her." *Why the fuck am I telling my brothers? I'm acting like a club girl who talks about her feelings.*

All the brothers but Steel stared at him in disbelief. Muerto knew they were uncomfortable about what he said. They didn't talk about women in that way. And they didn't talk about sappy feelings, only tough ones that dealt with kicking someone's ass or annihilating a rival club. A brother voicing that he loved a woman was outside their realm.

"Fuck it," he grumbled. He pushed his chair back and walked out. *What the hell made me blurt* that *out?* The truth was he was over the moon about Raven and he'd never experienced such intense feelings about anyone other than his family and brothers. Each time she popped into his head, his heart smiled and his cock twitched. She was so much more than just a girlfriend.

He took out his phone and sent a text to her.

Muerto: *Thinking bout u.*

When a ping came back he smiled.

Raven: *I was thinking bout u 2. Then u texted. Cool.*

Muerto: *I have tonight off. Want 2 take u for a steak dinner.*

Raven: *Sounds nice. Fancy place?*

Muerto: *Ya.*

Raven: *Even nicer. Get to dress up.*

Muerto: *Pick u up @7.*

Raven: *Can't wait.*

Muerto: *I love u.*

Raven: ♥ *u 2.*

★　★　★

MUERTO SUCKED IN his breath when Raven came out of the bedroom in her high-heeled sandals and black formfitting dress. She was breathtakingly beautiful and elegantly sexy. She spun around. "You like it?"

"Fuck yeah. You look gorgeous. We're gonna have to take your car. I'm pretty sure you don't wanna go on the Harley."

"Not dressed like this." She laughed. "But I have to confess I'm craving another ride on your bike. I loved it."

"Yeah, Harleys have that effect on women."

"And so do the men who ride them." She grabbed her clutch bag. "Are we ready to go?"

He cocked his head to the side. "In a minute. Come over here."

Shaking her head, she giggled. "No way. I know that look and that tone of voice, and it means my makeup getting all messed up, my clothes wrinkled, and my bra and panties ripped. It took me too damn long to get ready for tonight."

"I oughta smack your ass for disobedience," he teased.

"You'll have to wait to do that later. First you need to feed me." She placed her hands on her stomach. "I'm starving."

He winked. "You're absolutely worth the wait. Let's go."

As he backed the car out of the driveway, he saw a figure in his peripheral vision by the tree across the street. He slammed on the brakes and the shadow vanished.

"What's wrong?" Raven said as she braced against the dashboard.

Without answering, he bolted from the car and ran across the street, walking behind the trees. No one was there. He stood quietly, listening to see if he could hear anyone breathing. Nothing, just the normal sounds of the neighborhood: kids squealing, mothers yelling, lawnmowers whirring, cars humming. Ears pricked, he tried to pick up the slight rustle of leaves, or a twig snapping. Nothing.

Reluctantly, he went back to the car. "I thought I saw someone." He started up the car again and drove slowly by the trees, then around the block. He came up from the opposite side and parked halfway down the block, his gaze fixed on the cluster of trees.

Raven laughed. "Take it from me, if you stare too long at the trees, they start morphing into people. I know that from experience."

Still staring at the area, he asked, "What do you mean? Have you seen someone behind the trees staring at the house?"

"A couple of times. It's been at night, and I do just what you're doing. I stare and then move away, pretending to have lost interest, but I'm still looking."

"What happens?"

"Nothing. No one walks away. It's just the same as always. I just chalk it up to my eyes playing tricks on me, or it's the shadow people. I've seen documentaries on that subject. A lot of people think they see someone from the corners of their eyes, but when they look full-on no one's there. It gives me the chills."

"Yeah, well, I know my eyes aren't playing tricks on me. And it's not some damn shadow person. What I saw was real. My gut's telling me the same thing. I can't believe the person disappeared so fast."

For the next twenty minutes they watched the trees, but nothing ever changed except the lighting. The sun was in its final descent. The gurgling of Raven's stomach brought Muerto out of his trance. He turned to her and leaned over, kissing her cheek. "Sorry, sweetie. I get carried away at times. We'll go to the restaurant."

"I'm sure it was just the way the light played on the trees. Sometimes that happens too."

"Yeah, you're probably right." He drove past the trees, taking one last look.

As they headed to the restaurant, a nagging feeling gnawed at him. *Something definitely isn't right.*

Chapter Thirty

WHEN I REALIZED he'd spotted me, I had to think and move quickly. I dashed over to the next house, which was only a few feet away, and dove into the big scratchy bush. The leaves were so dense that sunlight barely filtered through. I thought for sure he was going to come over and check it out, but he was obsessed with the trees and foliage in the small parkway. Good for me.

While he'd watched the trees like a hound dog, the ants and spiders feasted on me, but I didn't move a muscle. Normally, I would've brushed them away and climbed out from under the bush, but I laid there silent and unmoving. I had to. He was out there listening, waiting. One movement, one shout, and it was all over. So I let them crawl on me, let their stings prick at my skin, and I didn't even flinch. And Dr. Clemmons had said I didn't have any self-restraint. *He should see me now. What a fucking quack.*

Brushing off the twigs and dirt from my hair and clothes, I was happy that he'd finally left. I wasn't sure how much longer I could've stood the bugs crawling all over me. That was a close call. Now I knew better than to risk coming over before sunset. It wouldn't happen again.

I walked down the sidewalk, engrossed in thought when I literally bumped into the woman with the dog—Patricia. Again!

"It's you again. Hello. Are you taking advantage of our beautiful Indian summer evening? We won't have too many of them before the cold sets in. I can already feel the chill in the night air."

Turning my head in such a way that she couldn't see my full face, I grunted my agreement, hoping it'd be good enough for her to leave me the hell alone. But it wasn't my night. She kept talking and trying to engage me in conversation.

"It's nice to see people walking in the neighborhood. It makes me think of when I grew up and everyone was out and about on a nice night. We didn't even lock our doors. We didn't have to."

Shut the fuck up! Why did people impose themselves on others? I'd never done that, and I found it extremely rude when people insisted on doing it to me. This old lady had crossed the line. She could also identify me when the cops started asking questions once they found Raven Harris's bloody body.

"Where did you say you lived, ma'am?"

"Across the street in the red brick house with yellow trim. I just painted the trim last summer. I love it. I always wanted it yellow but my husband didn't. He was very conservative and traditional. For him, it was white trim or brown, nothing else. When he died a couple of years ago, I was so sad, and a friend of mine suggested I lose myself in a house project. So I painted the trim yellow. I know a lot of peop—"

"I'm sorry but I have to go. Maybe we'll meet again sometime soon."

"Oh… yes. I'm sure we will. Goodbye."

I mumbled my goodbye and rushed to my car a few blocks away. I'd be back, but I had to wait until it got darker. I decided to grab a bite to eat before I returned.

Three hours later, I waited until the old lady and her dog came out for another walk before she closed up her house for the night. She didn't disappoint me. And that time, I purposely bumped into her. She was elated to see me and we engaged in tortuous chitchat. Then I asked her to come into the alley with me because I wanted to show her something a bit strange that I'd stumbled onto that evening.

Being the busybody that I'd suspected she was, she gladly followed me into the alley.

"What is it you want me to see? It's so dark I don't think I'll be able to see anything. Teddy has good eyesight even though he's going on eleven years. That's not so old for a small dog."

"That's fascinating," I said as I led her deeper into the dark alley.

"Oh… I tripped. I don't think I can go any farther. I don't want to fall and break my hip. People my age have to worry about that."

"We're exactly where we need to be. Come over and look at this. I've got a flashlight."

When she came over and bent down, I went around and stood behind her. Flashing a beacon of light on the concrete, I said, "Do you see it?"

"No. What am I looking for?"

"Eternal silence." And with one blow from my heavy-duty flashlight, I crushed her skull. She didn't even cry out, it was that swift. I then proceeded to beat her to death. I got rid of a lot of anger in that beating, and I felt so much better as I walked down the alley.

Careful not to have anyone see me, I hurried along the shadowed sidewalks until I reached my car. As I drove by the front of the duplex, I saw that they weren't home yet. Staring at it for a few moments, I thought about how far I'd come in taking charge of my life and not letting people bully me around.

I'd eliminated the pesky old woman who could identify me. Now the road was clear.

I was ready to kill Raven Harris.

Chapter Thirty-One

RAVEN RESTED HER head on Muerto's shoulder as they drove home from the restaurant. Their dinner was delicious, and being with him was always amazing. She couldn't get enough of him. The night before, she'd told her dad she'd found a wonderful man, and he was so happy for her. She left out the part that Muerto was an outlaw biker, but when her dad met him and got to know him, she'd tell him.

"I had a great time," she said softly as they approached the duplex.

He kissed the side of her head. "Me too, babe. And I'm gonna show you an even better time in about fifteen minutes." She giggled.

As they pulled into the driveway, she saw a dog on the front lawn. "That's Teddy," she said.

"Who's Teddy?" A frown crossed his forehead.

"Mrs. Kilpatrick's dog. She's always taking him for walks. I think she gets lonely staying in so much." She got out of the car and went to the front yard. Teddy backed up a few steps, his tail wagging. Muerto came up to her and Teddy started to growl.

"It's okay, Teddy. He's with me, and even though he looks rough, he's really a big softie."

"Only with you," Muerto said.

A shudder went through her as she thought about his words. The truth was that she rarely thought about what he and his club members actually did when they went out on "club business." Since finding out that he was in an outlaw club, she'd read a ton of articles, watched many documentaries, and read a few memoirs of government agents who'd infiltrated the clubs, and they made her hair stand on end. So she decided to just not think about it. Muerto was so loving and attentive when they were together that she couldn't imagine him as an outlaw. But every once in a while, when she'd see the hardness in his eyes or see his anger directed at someone, she'd remember what she learned from her research.

Teddy's barking jerked her back to the moment. "He must've broken his leash." She pointed to the powder blue leather leash dragging behind the dog. "I'm sure Mrs. Kilpatrick must be distraught. I have to bring him back to her."

"Who is she again?"

"She's a widow who lives on the next street in the red brick house with yellow trim. Do you see it?" He nodded. "Stay here. I'll go over to Teddy. He knows me." In a soft, friendly voice, she coaxed the dog to come to her. When he came over, she snagged his leash and walked back to Muerto. "I'm going to take him home."

"I'll go with you," he said, and she saw his eyes dart to the trees across from them.

They walked up the stairs to Mrs. Kilpatrick's porch, and Raven rang the doorbell. She waited several seconds, then rang it again. She looked through the window on the side of the door. Lights were on, but there was no sign of Mrs. Kilpatrick. "That's strange." She rang the bell another time.

"Maybe she's out looking for her dog. Let's take him back to our place and wait for her to come back. Do you have her phone number?"

"I do. I insisted she give it to me. She's such a nice lady. I know she must be worried about Teddy. She treats him like he's her son."

They walked back to the duplex and as they neared the front porch, Teddy ran forward, taking Raven by surprise. She dropped the leash and Teddy ran to the alley. "Teddy, come back!" Raven started to take off after him when Muerto pulled her back.

"He'll be back. He's probably looking for his owner."

"I just don't want him to get hit by a car," she said, tears lacing her voice. Then hysterical barking came closer and Teddy rushed over, barking and staring up at her. Before she could grab his leash, he dashed back to the alley, then came back barking. Teddy kept up the pattern for several minutes.

Turning to Muerto, who was checking his phone, she said, "I think Teddy's trying to tell me something. Maybe Mrs. Kilpatrick fell and she's hurt."

He looked up from his phone. "He does seem freaked out. I'll go look, but I don't want you staying on the front lawn or porch. You have to go inside and lock the door."

Before she could argue with him, Walter came out on his porch. "Why does that fucking dog keep barking?"

"He belongs to Mrs. Kilpatrick. Do you know her?" Raven asked. "I think she may be hurt."

"Never heard of her." He swiveled to go back inside.

"She lives a few houses down on the next street. You can see her house from here."

Without looking at her, he growled, "I told you I don't know the old lady." Then he closed his front door.

"He's lying. If he doesn't know her how does he know that she's old? Why would he lie about it?"

"I don't know or give a fuck. Now go in the house and lock the door. I'll be back."

"I'm going with you. And before you tell me no, I'm the one Teddy trusts, not you. If you go alone, he'll just run off." Teddy kept running to her, then to the alley and back to her, his barking filling the expanse of the neighborhood.

"You got a point." He jerked his head toward the alley. "Let's go."

When they entered the passageway, Raven saw Teddy dashing into the darkness. She slipped her hand in Muerto's. "It's so damn dark," she whispered. Taking a small flashlight from his cut, he switched it on and shined it down the alley. She saw Teddy lying down on the pavement, his whines echoing.

As they came closer, she saw a body on the ground. "Oh my God! I'm sure it's Mrs. Kilpatrick. She *has* fallen."

"Stay back." Muerto went up to the body and bent down. "It's an older woman."

"Is she conscious? Should I call for an ambulance?"

Standing up, he held her gaze. "Call 911. The old lady's dead."

The words stabbed her like jagged glass. "Dead? Did she have a heart attack? How do you know?"

He came over to her and embraced her tightly. "She's been murdered," he said softly, as if that would lighten the blow.

"How can that be? What was she doing in the alley? Who would do this to a nice lady like Mrs. Kilpatrick?" Tears stung her eyes.

Muerto took her phone and handed it to her. "Call 911."

Fifteen minutes later, sirens filled the alley. In the darkness, the red and blue flashing lights bounced off the faces of the cops and paramedics, making them look grotesque and eerie. Raven had never seen a dead body before, let alone one that had been badly beaten. Her dad had told her that she'd been at her mother's funeral. He'd said that she'd kept asking for someone to wake up her mommy, but Raven didn't remember, so Mrs. Kilpatrick's lifeless body was her first corpse. She shivered. Muerto pulled her to him, and she felt safe tucked under his arm.

For the next half hour, they answered Sheriff Wexler's questions, and finally they were free to go home. Raven brought Teddy home with her and fed him her leftover steak. Sooty, not thrilled with the new houseguest, lay in the corner, glaring at him. Whenever Teddy came too close for Sooty's liking, she'd hiss, her eyes two glowing emeralds.

After a long hot shower, Raven walked over to the bed and slipped under the covers, her arm around Muerto's waist. "I still can't believe this happened in this neighborhood. And to Mrs. Kilpatrick, of all people." Even though she didn't know her neighbor all that well, the horror of the way she'd died touched a deep chord in Raven. Tears trickled down her cheeks.

"It's gonna be okay, babe. It's always bad when innocent people are killed. She didn't deserve what she got." He kissed her tenderly as he held her close.

"I wonder if who you thought you saw was somehow involved in this."

"I've been thinking the same thing, and I think there's a connection. I'm not sure if the guy was targeting the old lady or if she just happened to be in the wrong place at the wrong time."

"I'm scared."

"I'm here. I'll keep you safe. I'll make it a point to be here before sunset with you every night, and if I can't make it, you'll stay with Ava. Something's going on here, and I need some time to figure it out. I think the vandalism at the pool hall and someone watching the house are somehow related. Not sure how, but I know in my gut they are."

"Do you think it's those guys you and Diablo beat up at the junkyard? The one guy, Cory, was pretty pissed that I hustled him."

"I've thought about it. It could be. Jaime said there were two men."

Mrs. Kilpatrick's bloodied housecoat flashed in her mind. "Poor Mrs. Kilpatrick. What a horrible way to go." She clenched his waist tighter. As long as she lived, she'd never get the image of Mrs. Kilpatrick's face, beaten beyond recognition, out of her mind.

Chapter Thirty-Two

A FEW DAYS after the murder of Mrs. Kilpatrick, Raven sat hunched at her work desk, stringing sea beads for a necklace she'd been commissioned to make. Sooty was curled on an old cushion on the wicker chair, and Teddy was stretched out on his side in the corner where the sunlight didn't reach. She loved the quiet moments in her studio where she could forget about the horrible things in the world and simply create beautiful pieces of art.

After working for a while, satisfaction at completing her job coursed through her. She picked up a vintage broach and began taking it apart when she heard the floor outside her studio creak. *What was that?* Her eyes flew to Teddy and then to Sooty, but neither of them stirred. She breathed in and out several times, quelling the panic threatening to explode inside her.

Focusing back on the necklace, she unhinged the clasp, putting it aside for a possible use one day. Glistening faux pearls and shiny crystals easily fell into her hand and she smiled. She loved the vintage jewelry she found in the antique stores, and she tried to imagine what the women may have been like who'd worn the broaches, necklaces, earrings, and rings she'd bought.

Another creak, louder that time but somehow more distant. Sooty raised her head and Teddy's ears perked up. Raven's hand flew to her throat, fingers trembling, though her muscles and nerves were coiled tight. *What is that? Is someone in the house?* A low growl from Teddy made her jump.

As quietly as she could, she pushed her chair back and stood up, her breathing suspended. The noises of the neighborhood that had been comforting not so long ago were distant and muffled. All she could hear was the floor creaking. The sound pounded in her ears, flowed through her veins, and climbed up her spine. Glancing down at her desk, she cursed herself for leaving her cell phone in the kitchen. She stood up and walked over to the window. She quietly turned the lock, but it wouldn't budge. Frantically, she tried to get the lock to slide but had no luck. *Why the hell is this broken* now *of all times?* She willed herself to stay calm and took several deep breaths.

Her eyes darted around the room, desperately looking for anything she could use to defend herself. Then her gaze landed on her soldering gun. With shaky fingers, she grabbed it. *It's better than nothing.* She took the first step, her bare feet soundless on the wooden floor. Then Teddy scrambled to his feet, barking wildly. She put a hand over her mouth, thinking she might scream, but nothing came out. Fear of attracting whoever was outside her studio kept her quiet.

With frantic scratching, Teddy managed to push the door open further. He rushed out, his nails clacking on the floors.

If I can just get to the kitchen, I can call Muerto. Although... maybe I'm being paranoid.

Gulping in air, she moved closer to the door. Her heart slammed against her breastbone as the ringing in her ears intensified. She grasped the door and opened it slightly, expecting to see a man standing in front of her, his face ugly from evilness, but no one was there.

The silence strangled her. *Why isn't Teddy barking? Where the fuck is he?* With one hand gripping the soldering gun, the other clenched into a fist, her nails digging into the palm of her hand, she walked out into the hallway. *Fuck the phone. I need to get out of here.* She walked to the living room, her aim the front door.

Before she entered the living room, she paused. Nothing out of the ordinary. She crept to the front door, stifling a yelp when she felt something brush against her legs. Eyes wide, she looked down, almost breaking out in hysterics when she saw Sooty next to her bare leg. "You scared the shit out of me," she whispered.

Tiptoeing to the front door, she stopped. *What if he's on the porch?*

She felt her pulse in her throat, but she forced herself to look through the peephole. Nothing as far as she could see. She pulled the curtain aside ever so slightly and peeked out. No one was on her porch. She saw Mr. Davis mowing his lawn, but nothing else. *I have to get out of here.*

With trembling fingers, she unlocked the deadbolt and grasped the door handle. From behind her she heard a rush of footsteps, loud, assaulting her ears. And breathing. Short, chattering bursts.

"Shit!" She whirled around and saw a figure in a ski mask inches from her. From behind, she tried to open the door, but the damn knob wouldn't turn. For a long second, she froze, and that's when her attacker slammed something hard down on her head. Blood gushed from an open wound, flowing into her eye. The attacker lifted the object again, but that time she saw it—a flashlight. In a burst of energy, she hit the person with the soldering gun, but her vision was clouded in red.

The intruder was able to clip her head again with the flashlight, and Raven stumbled and fell down. Then a rag was shoved over her mouth and nose, and her lungs screamed for air. She thrashed, fingers gripping at the rag to jerk it away. The panic was a deluge of ice water surrounding every limb, creeping higher. *Think, Raven. Think!* But her head was pounding and she couldn't think straight.

Her fingers grasped the bottom of the ski mask, and as she struggled for breath, she pulled up on it, exposing the intruder's face. For a moment, confusion sparked through her as she took it in. The exposure seemed to take her attacker by surprise. And when Raven saw the cold, flat eyes and the darkness distorting the facial features, she screamed. It was a scream of hysteria and disbelief, bordering on terror.

"You!" she choked out, pain ripping through her dry throat.

Another hit on her throbbing head.

Then the rag over her mouth and nose again.

The maniacal laughter.

And the blackness. Creeping blackness.

The room was spinning.

Blackness.

She was gone.

Chapter Thirty-Three

MUERTO PLACED A bottle of beer in front of one of the regulars at Balls and Holes. "Hey, Willy. What's shakin'?"

"Not much. Jus' waitin' fer Gator to git his ass in here. He got lucky the last time. I gotta git my money back." Willy's laugh turned into a coughing fit, and the older man grabbed his beer and took a large gulp.

"You should check out that cough. It doesn't sound so good."

"Fuck, Muerto. Don't you start on me. I git enough of that shit from my ol' lady." He took out a pack of cigarettes and tapped one out.

He chuckled. "Fair enough. If you need anything just holler."

As Muerto headed to the bar, he saw Sheriff Wexler coming inside and he immediately tensed. His dislike of badges went back to when he was a kid and saw how many of the people in his neighborhood were treated differently from the ones in the better sections of town. Since joining the Night Rebels, his distrust of anyone wearing a badge had grown.

Glancing sideways at the sheriff, Muerto kept walking to the bar. *Probably here about the strip bar. He's got a lot of balls comin' here to talk to me when we did his fuckin' job. Asshole.* Lining up the glasses for the day, he ignored the cop.

"How're things going?" Wexler asked as he sidled up to the bar.

"Okay." Muerto didn't look up.

"I need to talk to you about someone I think you may know."

Muerto's insides tightened. *There's no way I'm talking to a badge about a brother. I'm no fuckin' snitch.* He kept stacking glasses, never once looking up.

Wexler laughed dryly. "This doesn't have anything to do with the

Night Rebels. I have a situation here and I need to clear some stuff up."

Muerto glanced at him. "I know I can't help you."

"I think you can, and I think you need to because something bad may happen to you or someone you know."

Standing tall, he rested his hands on the counter. "Stop with the cryptic warning. What the fuck are you talking about?" A curl lifted Wexler's lips as he slowly took off his bomber jacket. *He's fuckin' enjoying this. I'm ready to kick his ass.* "I don't have time for this shit. I have a job to do." Muerto turned his back and started arranging the liquor bottles on the shelves.

"Do you know a Penny Leslie Burnside?"

"Nope. Never heard of her," he replied, his back still to the sheriff.

"She works for you."

Muerto turned around. "I don't have anyone working for me by that name. If she told you that, she's a goddamn liar."

"How many women work for you?"

"Only one, but she quit a few days ago. She was with the management company I use, but her name isn't what you said. It's Deanna something. I can't remember her last name just now."

"I'm talking about your businesses."

"The club's businesses? I don't know all the women who work at Lust. I just run this place." *I'm getting real pissed with the game this fuckin' badge is playing.* "I got a feeling you know exactly who the chick is, so stop with the bullshit and just ask me."

"Penny Leslie Burnside is an alias. She goes by Jaime Brandt. Do you know a woman by that name?"

"Jaime? Yeah. She works here. What the fuck did she do? Drive too fast in a school zone? I'm busy here."

"I picked her up the other day for shoplifting over at Randall's. It was a tube of red lipstick. I—"

"I'll pay for it. She's cool. She's been under some stress. Don't you have bigger shit to deal with than a shoplifter?"

"What kind of stress? The pool hall's robbery?" Wexler leaned over the counter. "I knew about that. Figured you guys were gonna take care of it on your own."

"I said I'd pay for the lipstick. Let this one slide."

"It's not the tube of lipstick that I care about. She was a book and release with a future court date. The thing I'm interested in is what I got back when I ran her prints through the automated fingerprint system this morning. It came back that the prints belonged to a Penny Leslie Burnside. And I also got a photo of her from South Dakota law enforcement." He took out a piece of paper and showed it to Muerto. "Is that your employee Jaime Brandt?"

Muerto scanned the black-and-white mug shot of Jaime. He nodded. "That's her. A lot of people use different names. Sometimes they don't want exes to find them. I still don't see why you're making a big fuss about it."

"She has an outstanding warrant out of Pierre, South Dakota… for murder." Wexler stared at him.

Fuck! I wonder who she offed. Stone-faced, he returned the sheriff's stare.

"What time does she come in for her shift?"

Muerto shrugged. *I'm not giving him shit.*

A wry smile brushed Wexler's lips. "You know, when I arrested her she told me she was unemployed."

"How'd you know to come here?"

"When I got the information, me and a few deputies got the judge to sign a search warrant. We went over to her place but she wasn't there. We had the landlord let us in, and I found some real interesting things in her apartment. Did you have a relationship with her?"

"You mean fucking?" Wexler nodded. "No. Why?"

"Ever go out with her?"

"Again… no."

"Well… she's got a whole wall dedicated to you in her bedroom. A bunch of pictures of you alone, with other women, but the disturbing thing is that there's a section of the wall of photos of you and some black-haired woman. There are also photos of the black-haired woman by herself. On the face of the woman, the words 'slut', 'whore', and 'cunt' are written in red marker. And the photos of you with this woman have a black X over your face, and some of them have 'You're dead' written on them."

Is this for fuckin' real? "'You're dead' was graffitied on these walls," he said in a low voice. "Are you sure we're talking about the same Jaime?" He scrubbed his hands over his face. "What the fuck?"

Raven! The world fell away, drained of all color. He grabbed his phone and tapped in her number, the phone shaking slightly in his hands. Straight to voice mail. "Fuck!" His icy fingers tapped the number a second time. Again, voice mail. Sweat dripped into his eyes, and he pulled up his shirt and wiped his face.

"My woman's in trouble. I gotta go." He rushed from behind the bar. "Willy, watch the bar for me," he said as he hurried out.

Wexler panted as he caught up to him. "Wait up, I'm going with you. The woman is dangerous. She spent some time in a mental ward for attacking and vandalizing an ex-boyfriend's house." He turned around and ran back to his SUV.

Jumping on his Harley, Muerto sped away. *Don't let me be too fuckin' late. Hold on for me, babe. I'm coming.*

Chapter Thirty-Four

RAVEN MOANED AND tried to bring her hand to her pounding head. *I can't move. I'm tied up. Oh God… I remember.* Her eyes darted around her living room, but she was alone. Except for the dried blood on the floor and the upside-down entry table, the room looked like it always did: neat, comfy, and inviting.

I have to get out of here. How long have I been out? Is it still the same day? She pulled at the rope binding her hands behind the chair she sat on, a slight give lifting her spirits. *I can work my way out of these. I know I can.* Then she came in, and Raven's eyes grew wide. *Why is she wearing my clothes? What the hell is going on?*

"You've come to. That's good. I've waited a long time for this moment."

"Why are you doing this? I don't even know you." Raven's fingers worked the rope's knot.

"You know me, you bitch!" She rushed over and raised her hand. *Smack!* Raven gasped. "You cunts are all alike."

"I've never done anything to you. I've only talked to you a few times at the pool hall." *Smack!* Another slap across her face. She grimaced at the metallic taste of blood on her cracked lips.

"Keep your fucking mouth shut! You deserve everything I'm going to do to you. Women who steal other women's men away deserve to fucking die!"

Smack! Smack! Smack! Wetness covered her cheeks as her head pounded relentlessly. *I'm going to be sick.* Swallowing, bitterness coated her throat. *And what's she talking about? What man?* Extreme burning in her throat. *I know I'm going to be sick.*

"Did you think I'd let you fuck my boyfriend and not do anything about it? You flaunted it in front of me, ignoring how I felt. Well, bitch, when a cunt sleeps with another woman's man, she has to be ready to suffer the consequences."

"I don't know what you're talking about. Who's your man?"

"Like you don't know. Muerto, bitch. He's been my boyfriend ever since I was hired as a waitress. He adored me, but then you seduced him with your trampy ways. Everything was great between us until you came along."

"Muerto? He's your boyfriend?" She wanted to lie down to stop the jackhammer in her head. *Did she say Muerto? I can't think.*

"Don't act like you don't know. I see through you." She put her face a couple of inches from Raven's. "I know women like you. You don't fool me. Not. One. Bit." She stepped back. "You made him desire you. He couldn't stay away from you. And while I thought he was at work or running errands, he was sneaking off to be with you. Every chance you got, you were fucking like pigs. You disgust me! Do you hear me?" She grabbed Raven's hair and yanked her head up. "You fucking disgust me, you dirty whore!" *Smack!*

The whole side of her face was swelling. "I didn't know you guys dated. He never told me."

"He'd come to me, still smelling of you, and when I took his beautiful cock in my mouth, I tasted you. Then he'd cry and tell me that he loved me... not you, bitch! He hated that he was powerless to resist you. Muerto told me he wanted to break free of you. I told him we had to leave Alina and go somewhere far away. He agreed. He asked me to marry him. He wanted you out of his life, but you wouldn't leave him alone." She walked away, muttering to herself under her breath.

Waves of nausea hit Raven as her body jerked in the chair. The room was spinning; she felt like she was going to topple over. *Muerto was with her? What's her name? I know it. It's....* She closed her eyes, picturing the pool hall, the woman, the bar—*Jaime! That's her name. They never acted like a couple, but why would she be so mad at me if it wasn't true?* She tried to wrap her throbbing head around it. *Muerto was cheating on her with me. How could he do that to me? To her? To us?*

Jaime came back into the room, the crazed look in her eyes replaced with a cold hardness.

"I'm so sorry I've hurt you, Jaime. I had no idea that you and Muerto were dating. I would never date a man who belongs to another woman. That's not the way I am."

"You fucking liar. I saw how you flirted with him. You saw us kissing but you didn't care."

Saw them kissing? Am I missing something? "I never saw anything between you guys."

"You're lying again, but that's what sluts do when they're caught by decent, good women. Muerto wants me to kill you. He told me it's the only way he can be free of you."

What? Muerto wouldn't have a woman do his dirty work. Something isn't adding up. Fuck, my head hurts.

Her lips curled up in a cruel smile. "I've been watching you. He's spent every night with you for the last three weeks. You really are a slut."

She's the one I saw that night. This is too crazy. Wait, the knot's loosening. "I know you don't believe me, but I didn't know you were dating Muerto."

"I don't believe you. I loved Muerto very much, and he would've loved me too if it wasn't for *you*. You stole that chance away from me."

Raven shook her head. "But I thought you told me that you and Muerto were together and he asked you to marry him. What you're saying doesn't make sense."

Baring her teeth, Jaime shook her fist in Raven's face. "Stop confusing me! You're trying to turn everything around. I threw Muerto out when I found out he betrayed me. But he came back to me last night, with an armful of red roses. Beautiful red roses, and he begged me to take him back. I told him he hurt me too deeply, but then he grabbed my shoulders and kissed me so sweetly that it made me cry. He made love to me. He didn't fuck me like he does you but made heavenly love, and I took him back." She had a faraway look in her eyes.

She's a fucking psycho. This is all in her head. I have to get away from her.

Then her attention shifted back to Raven and her gaze was steely. "You deserve to die for what you did to me… to him. You ruined everything. He would've come to me, but you spread your legs, enticing him. A man can't resist a slut. My mother was so right!" *Smack!*

"Stop hitting me! Untie me and let's fight this out on equal ground, or are you too fuckin' scared that I'd beat your ass?"

"Shut. The. Fuck. Up!" Jaime ran out to the kitchen and came back with a large black flashlight. "I'm going to kill you just like I did that nosy bitch with the stupid dog. But this time I'm going to enjoy it."

The bile she'd been forcing down surfaced and spewed from her mouth. The acid scorching her throat and tongue sickened her. *Shit!* Then behind the madwoman, she saw Walter coming in through the kitchen, his eyebrows squished together. *Why's he here? He's here! I have help. Is he going to help me?* Her thoughts were scattered as her heart drummed in her chest.

"Your cat's outside. I was just checking to see if you…. What's going on in here?" Walter's eyes widened.

Jaime whirled around. "Get out of here! We don't want you in here." Walter kept walking in. She turned back to Raven. "You're dead, bitch!" She raised her arm.

Before Jaime could smash her skull, Raven lunged forward and, with her freed hands, punched her captor in the belly. Jaime groaned and bent over. By that time Walter was next to the women, and he pulled the flashlight out of Jaime's hand.

Raven untied her feet and stood up. *Oh shit.* She held her head between her hands and plopped back down on the chair.

"Let go of me!" Jaime struggled in Walter's arms. Through clouded vision, Raven saw her kick Walter hard in the shin and he howled, releasing the crazed woman. Jaime ran off to the kitchen.

"She's probably going to get a knife," Raven said to Walter as he turned to follow her. "Be careful." With her head still in her hands, she tried to get up, but searing pain ripped through her. *I just want to lie down.* Then she heard Jaime scream and a flurry of deep voices. She couldn't even look up, the pain that bad in her head. "Walter?"

Heavy footsteps came toward her, and then black boots entered her field of vision. *They look like Muerto's boots. I must be getting delirious.* Then she smelled the desert and the sunshine. *Muerto!* A beam filled her face.

"Oh, baby." Warm, strong arms embraced her. She breathed in his fresh scent. "I'm so glad you're okay."

He kissed the top of her head and she cried out. "That fuckin' psycho did a number on my head. I think I may have a concussion."

"The paramedics are on their way. I was so worried about you."

"She said that you were her boyfriend."

"She's a very sick woman. When you feel better, I'll tell you all about it."

"How is she?" Sheriff Wexler asked.

"Her head's smashed pretty bad," Muerto replied.

"I'll be okay. I just need to lie down." She forced her chin up a bit and looked up. "She told me she killed Mrs. Kilpatrick. Beat her to death with a flashlight. How horrible." Wet streaks dampened her cheeks.

"We'll look into it. Your neighbor wanted me to tell you that he has your cat and dog. I guess that's what alerted him that something was wrong." Wexler looked toward the window. "Paramedics are here. I'll be around later to get your statement." He went behind her and opened the door.

As the emergency technicians loaded her into the ambulance, she saw Jaime sitting in the back of a police car, beaming at her. For a split second, she felt sorry for her, and then the doors closed and she shut her eyes, relaxing for the first time since the ordeal had begun.

Chapter Thirty-Five

AFTER SEVERAL STICHES and a three-day stint in the hospital, Raven was as good as new. Each time Muerto looked at her, his gut would clench at the memory of how close he'd come to losing her. She was his stability in a world filled with chaos, and with each day, his love for her grew stronger. At times he couldn't remember how he'd functioned without her in his life. She was the light to his darkness, calmness to his storm.

He kissed her. "Did you arrange everything with Breanna for the biker rally next month?"

"Yes. She's so nice. We had a long conversation, and we made plans to have lunch next week. I can see us becoming good friends."

"She's cool. Steel got a good woman, but I have a better one." He fisted her hair and pulled her head back so he could kiss her deeper.

"Do you guys want to go in the back?" Crow joked as he went behind the bar.

"I still can't believe Jaime lied about everything." Brandy sat on the barstool shaking her head. "I mean, she'd sworn me to secrecy last year when she told me that you two had an affair. I totally believed her, and that's why I kept flirting with you." She gazed at Raven. "No offense, but I figured if Muerto broke the rules with Jaime, he might break them with me. But once you came on board, I stopped all flirting. I just can't get over it. I really believed her."

"It's strange as fuck. I never led her on once. Wexler told me that she'd told her friends we were lovers. Made up some elaborate fantasy where we were a couple, living together, and planning to get married. I mean, I suspected she had a crush on me, but I never pictured anything like this."

"She was a fuckin' looney tune. Do you think she believed all that?"

Muerto shook his head. "I guess, but it's hard to imagine someone would be that far out there. The badge said that Jaime's mom is in a mental institution in South Dakota. From what he learned, Jaime did a stint in a mental ward for attacking her ex-boyfriend and vandalizing his house. She's definitely fucked-up."

"So she really believed I took you away from her?" Muerto nodded. "You know, after I found the rose in the blood at my house, I started to wonder if it was Deanna who'd done it. I knew I hadn't left the window unlocked, so I figured it was someone who had a key to my place. Deanna never liked me, so I thought she was messing with me."

"It was Jaime who did it. Wexler found a copy of the keys to my Harley, the pool hall, and your rental. She must've snagged my key ring when she was working. And she was stalking you and me. She had a shitload of pictures of me over the past year. Damn, I never saw that coming."

"And she faked being attacked. I still can't believe it," Brandy said.

"She fuckin' caused a lot of damage around here. I knew something wasn't right about it." Crow scrubbed his hand over his face.

"She wanted it to look like someone was after the pool hall, meaning you or me. So, in her warped mind, after she killed Raven, the suspicion wouldn't be on her. It'd be on the 'guys' who broke in and roughed her up a bit. Fuckin' sick."

"Having a series of similar robberies in the area probably gave her the idea. Spraying that shit on the wall was stupid because the dudes didn't do it at the other businesses. I guess she couldn't help herself. She must've been real pissed at you to spray all that shit around here." Crow shook his head.

"And don't forget the attention she received from you after you rescued her. I know I keep saying this, but I *really* can't believe any of this." Brandy crossed her arms. "And for something like this to happen in Alina. Unbelievable."

"Who'd she kill in South Dakota?" Raven asked softly.

"Some old woman in her apartment building. She must've had a thing about old women." Muerto reached around and grabbed a Coke.

"Poor Mrs. Kilpatrick. I still can't fathom why she would kill such a nice lady," Raven said in a low voice.

"And I hung out with her. We'd go barhopping sometimes. Gives me the chills." Brandy rubbed her arms.

"I guess as long as you were single, she could keep the fantasy alive of you and her having a relationship, but when I came along and we started dating, I threatened all that. It's just too weird. It's almost like it never really happened, you know?"

"Yeah, but now it's behind us and we can move on." Muerto crushed the empty water bottle and tossed it in the recycle bin.

"I hope she pleads guilty. I don't know if I can stand a trial." Raven rested her chin in her hand.

"Aren't they sending her back to South Dakota?" Brandy asked.

"The sheriff said the DA wants to try her for Mrs. Kilpatrick's murder, and the attempted murder and kidnap charges they filed for what she did to me. Since she's here, they'll do all that first, and later she'll have to go to South Dakota and face charges there. It's going to be a long haul, that's for sure." Raven exhaled loudly.

"We'll be by your side," Brandy said. "Jaime needs to be locked up for a very long time. She really needs help."

Raven's phone interrupted the group's conversation. Muerto saw her jaw tighten. "I have to take this. Be right back." She hurried out of the place.

"You got it bad for her, bro." Crow winked at him. "You gonna do something about it?"

"Maybe, but keep your fuckin' mouth shut about it. Sometimes you, Goldie, and Chains gossip worse than a bunch of ladies."

"Are you gonna marry her?" Brandy asked. "I can barely believe you have a girlfriend, but a wife? No way."

"I'm not saying anything. You both need to keep your mouths shut."

Muerto watched Raven as she talked and walked the floor. Her back was to him, but he could see her arm flying around. *I hope everything's okay with her dad.*

When she came back in, her eyes were twinkling and her face was beaming. She rushed over to Muerto and squealed while clapping her hands. "They sold one of my paintings, and he wants a few more." She jiggled in place.

He hugged her. "I'm so proud of you. Fuckin' good job. Which one sold?"

"*Devoradora.*" He threw his head back laughing, and she joined him. Soon they were in hysterics while Crow and Brandy looked on.

"Seems like craziness is catchy around here," Crow said, and the two lovers laughed harder.

"I think you're right," Brandy agreed.

"It's a private joke," Raven sputtered. "I'm just so stoked that I sold a painting at the gallery. This opens all sorts of doors for me."

"Congratulations. I never knew a real artist. That's so cool." Brandy walked over to the bar and poured herself a cup of coffee.

"We're going out to celebrate," Muerto whispered in her ear. "You pick the place."

"Alfonso's. That's where I first met the man behind the attitude, and I liked him a lot."

He wanted to make love to her at that moment, but instead, he held her tight. "Seven work for you?"

"It's perfect. Love you."

"Me too."

WHEN THEY CAME home that night, Raven went over to Walter's and knocked on the door. He flung it open and stared at her. Muerto came up behind her.

"Hi, Muerto," he said, his gaze darting from Muerto's to Raven's.

"Hey." Muerto jerked his chin up.

Raven cleared her throat. "I want to thank you for helping me out a few days ago. If you hadn't come in when you did, I wouldn't be talking to you." Her voice hitched and Muerto put his arm around her. "I just really appreciate what you did for me. You're a good guy."

Walter fidgeted in place and kept looking behind him at his TV. "My program is on."

Muerto held his hand up. "Don't want to keep you from it. Just thanks." He held Raven close to him as they walked away.

"Uh… you're welcome."

They turned around and saw Walter looking at them, his hands shoved into his pockets. Raven smiled at him, and he licked his lips then stepped away from the door. Muerto tugged her along and they went to the front of the duplex.

When they got inside, Teddy barked and jumped in excitement and Sooty slinked over to Raven, her eyes fixed on Muerto. "I think she's getting used to you," Raven said as she took off her jacket.

"That's good because she's going to see a ton of me."

After Raven changed the water bowls for Sooty and Teddy, gave them treats, and played with them for a bit, she sat down next to Muerto. "I'm so tired."

"The doc said you gotta take it easy. You had a concussion and lost a lot of blood. It was just a few days ago."

"It seems like a lifetime ago. Strange. Let's go in the bedroom. I'm beat."

As she took off her clothes, Muerto sat on the bed. "We need to move. This place is too small and has bad memories for you."

"Are you asking me to live with you?" She tied the sash around her short robe.

"We're already doing that. I'm just saying we need a bigger house." He reached out and tugged her to him.

"You're going to give up your room at the clubhouse?" She settled on his lap.

"I'll always have my room there if we want to crash after a party."

"Or a few rounds of pool." A twinkle lit up her eyes.

"Brutus isn't letting up on that."

"I don't want to get rusty." She curled her arm around his neck and kissed him deep, hard, and wet.

"I like that."

"Thanks for coming into my life. I thought I was never going to see you again." She buried her face in his neck.

"You're a fighter, babe." He peppered kisses over the side of her face and she winced. "Sorry, sweetie." He gently rubbed his fingertips over the fading bruises. "I love you."

He looked at her, his dick hardening when he saw the desire in her gaze. She took the initiative and slid his shirt over his head, running her fingernails over his chest and circling her palms over his nipples. He sucked in his breath and looped his arms around her, hugging her to him chest to chest. She moaned and he pushed her back onto the mattress, her robe parting and exposing her breasts. "Fuck," he muttered under his breath, and then he stroked the very tip of her nipple with his finger.

"I love the way you touch me," she rasped as she ran her fingers up and down his arms.

As his hands roamed her curves and his mouth traveled over her body, she whimpered and moaned beneath him, her sounds of pleasure fueling his fire. He was more than ready to bury himself between her legs. Bending down, he swiped his tongue over her pussy, which pulsed in glistening need. As he sucked her wet clit, his tongue flicking against her hardened nub, she arched her back, pushing her mound into his mouth.

"You are my passion, my love, and my life," he said thickly.

"I love you so much," she panted.

The scent of her arousal was so intoxicating that he lost himself to the hunger, licking and sucking her as he brought her to the edge and then withdrew. He rubbed his hard dick over her sopping pussy, then pushed it inside her inch by inch.

"Fuck me," she said hoarsely.

He pushed all the way in, watching his cock slowly disappearing into her warm, tight center as he squeezed her tits. He lay on top of her, kissing her deeply while his dick pulsed and twitched inside her. Pushing up, he pulled out and then plunged back in, her moans surrounding him as he increased his pace. He leaned over and breathed her in, and with the way she wrapped her legs around his waist, whimpering, he knew he'd never have his fill of her. He'd never let her go. She was his.

"You're my woman. I'm claiming you. You belong to me," he rasped as he plunged into her again.

"I'll always be yours." Her face contorted as he pushed in deeper.

Grunts. Moans. Growls. Pants. The sounds of them coming together reached a frenzied pitch, and he felt her ready to come—tight, swollen, gripping his cock. He kept pumping in and out, wanting her pussy squeezing his dick as he exploded in her. Then he shot into her still-pulsating wetness while she screamed her release. He filled her up, and the minute he was finished he wanted to fill her up more; when it came to her, he was never sated.

When their breathing became more even, he rolled off her and tucked her to his side, their legs entwined under the cool sheets.

"That was the best," she whispered, her head pillowed on his shoulder.

"You're the best." He ran his fingers up and down her damp back. "I want you to be by my side for the rest of our lives." She stiffened under his touch. "Do you want that too?"

"Yes. Are you asking me something?"

He licked his lips. "Yeah. I'm asking you to be my old lady and wear my patch."

"That's when I wear the vest thing, right? Is the patch on that?"

He laughed and squeezed her. "Love you, babe. My patch is on your cut. The patch is everything. It binds us together in love, respect, and pride. It's a fuckin' big deal for a brother to ask a woman to wear his patch, and it isn't taken lightly. I never thought I'd meet a woman who

I'd want to wear my patch, but you're everything to me. You make my life complete."

"I'm the yang to your yin." She kissed his chest.

"I think that means what I'm saying."

"It does. And you totally rock my world. I'd love to wear your vest, patch, jacket, and whatever the hell else you want me to wear." She slid up and kissed him hard. "I think I'm going to need some lessons on being an old lady."

"I think you do." He chuckled. "Breanna can help you. We got a couple of other old ladies, Sam and Shannon. They'll teach you the ropes."

"I thought Breanna was the only one."

"She's our president's old lady, so she's the head. You'll be second since I'm an officer. Sam is Tattoo Mike's old lady and Shannon's Rooster's. They're older and been around for as long as I've been with the Night Rebels."

"I'll have to meet them. I like Breanna a lot."

"That's good. You made me happy."

"And you make me ecstatic. I love you," she said against his skin.

"I love you too."

He stroked her hair for a long time. Once she'd fallen asleep, he held her tightly.

She'd entered his life when he wasn't looking for love, and then he'd found it just like that—one flashing, throbbing moment. And he couldn't imagine it any other way.

Chapter Thirty-Six

THE SMOKY AROMA of charred peppers and flank steak tantalized Muerto when he walked into the clubhouse. He glanced to the left and saw sizzling fajitas on a portable grill. Several of the brothers scooped up the mixture, and he ambled over and grabbed a plate.

"Hey," Goldie said as he grabbed a few corn tortillas. "You've been a stranger for the past two weeks."

"I only see you at the pool hall, dude. What gives?" Crow asked as he speared several strips of steak with his fork.

"Been busy." Muerto took a generous portion of fajitas, smothered them in pico de gallo, and headed for a table, jerking his head to the hard beats of Motörhead's "Ace of Spades" playing in the background.

"Has your main squeeze taught you any tricks on hustling? I thought we'd set up a tournament and have her play for our side. Of course, I'd play too. I can kick ass real good...just not hers." Army plopped next to Muerto.

"We don't talk pool. And the—"

"I bet you don't." Snickering, Brutus kicked out a chair and sat in it.

Swatting at the air, Muerto frowned. "I was trying to say that Raven's not my main squeeze, she's my old lady."

The only sound in the room was the shredding guitars from the speakers. Sangre turned the music off, then looked at Muerto. "What the fuck?"

Taking a long gulp of beer, he pushed back from the table and stretched out his legs. "I said Raven's wearing my patch." He scanned the shocked faces around the room. "Fuckin' deal with it."

"I can't wrap my head around you having an ol' lady," Goldie said.

"I mean, you can't focus on a chick longer than a couple of days."

"Raven's different." Muerto gestured Patches for another beer.

"You moving out?" Chains asked.

"Yeah. We found a place we're moving into next weekend. I need some help. Any volunteers?" He brought the beer bottle to his lips.

Most of the brothers voiced their support, and a warm feeling spread through him. He knew they were shocked as hell that he'd asked a woman to wear his patch. Hell, when the thought first came to him, he was just as surprised. He never thought he'd ever have an old lady, but then, he'd never met a woman like Raven. She came barreling into his life and since he first met her, he hadn't had a chance to catch his breath. Life without her just wasn't an option. He knew some of the brothers didn't like her or trust her, but he also knew they'd respect her and defend her with their lives if they had to now that she was his old lady. That's what he loved about the Night Rebels—they were together to the end no matter what.

As the shock of his revelation wore off, the members came up to him and congratulated him by punching his arm or grasping his shoulder. By the time the sun set over the snow-capped peaks of the San Juan Mountains, Muerto was drunker than hell. Most of his brothers didn't fare much better. When his phone pinged, it felt like a bullet through his head. He blinked several times as he tried to focus on his phone.

Raven: *U gonna b home 4 dinner?*

Muerto: *Ate already.*

Raven: *What did Lena make?*

Muerto: *Not sure.*

Looking up, he asked, "What the hell did we eat today?" Goldie, Army, and Brutus met his look with glassy gazes as they shrugged.

Muerto: *We had something.*

Raven: *R u drunk? :)*

Muerto: *Fuckin' trashed. Celebrating u being my old lady.*

Raven: *Sounds like fun until u get the hangover. U probably should stay the night.*

Muerto: *Can u come here? Don't wanna spend the night without u.*

Raven: *Sweet. B there in an hr. ♥ u.*

Muerto: *Me 2.*

"Is your ol' lady comin'?" Goldie asked.

"Yeah."

"What about a pool match?" Brutus said as he scooped up a handful of peanuts. "I've been itching for a game with her for a while."

"You gotta ask her when she gets here." Muerto stood up. "I'll be in my room." He weaved through the doorway and clamored up the stairs.

Once inside, he threw off his clothes and stepped into a cold shower. After he was finished, he heard a knock at his door. With a towel wrapped around his waist, he padded over and opened it. Ruby stood there, her heated gaze fixed on his chest and arms. "Hey," he said as he opened the door wider.

"Hiya. I heard you asked that black-haired chick to be your old lady. Is that true?" She ran her fingers over his chest.

Stepping back, he nodded. "I'm hitched now."

"I can't believe it." Her brow creased slightly.

He laughed. "Neither can I."

"First Steel and now you. I hope it stops there." Ruby pursed her lips.

"Never know. Seems like Steel broke the ice around here."

"So does that mean you're off limits, or are you gonna have some fun sometimes like Rooster Mike does?"

Shaking his head, he smiled. "Off limits. My woman's the only one for me."

"You never know… it can get boring being with the same woman all the time." She stared at him. "If that happens, let me know. I'll always be available for you."

"I'll keep that in mind. We had some fun times. I hope you find someone you can hitch up to."

Ruby shook her head. "No way. I don't want that. I'm having too much fun with all of you. Do you need anything?"

"A pot of black coffee would be great. I'm trying to sober up before my woman comes."

"Got it. I'll be right back with your coffee." She spun around and disappeared around the corner.

An hour later, Muerto was leaning against the bar feeling better. When Raven walked in, he resisted the urge to run up to her and scoop her up in his arms. If he did that, his brothers would rib him about it for a couple months, so he stayed where he was, watching his old lady—it still seemed strange to call her that—sashaying over to him.

"Hey, babe," he said as he pulled her close to him.

"You sobered up nicely," she teased as she pressed tighter against him, smiling when she felt his hardness.

"Feel what you do to me each and every time I see you?" He feathered kisses down her neck.

"You wanna play a game of pool?" Brutus's deep voice startled them.

Raven jerked back and looked at him. "Sure. When do you want to play?"

"What about now?"

"Anxious to lose the money you just made?" Muerto said as his hand rubbed Raven's back.

"More like wanting to make more." Catching her gaze, he said, "I'll meet you at the pool table." He walked away.

"You don't have to play," Muerto said in her ear.

"I want to. I have to admit that I miss the game. It'll be good to play again."

A couple hours later, Raven handed Muerto a stack of bills she'd won from the pool game. Brutus came over and handed her a shot of tequila. "You're a kickass player. It was a fuckin' good game."

"I had a good time. You're a good player. I was starting to sweat. Thanks." She threw back the shot.

"We gotta use you in our fundraiser. We sometimes do pool runs. They're like poker runs except the brothers from different clubs play pool. With you on our team, we could make a lot of money for our charity—Bikers Against Child Abuse," Goldie said.

"I'd love to be a part of that." She snuggled deeper into Muerto's embrace.

"If I know you, Goldie, you'll be betting on the side to line your pockets as well." Muerto raised his eyebrows.

"I gotta pay for the expenses from the run." Fixing his eyes on Raven's, he said, "We'll talk." She nodded.

When Goldie sauntered away, she whispered in Muerto's ear, "I think your brothers are getting used to me."

"You're part of the family now. They'll respect and include you in family and some club activities."

As the night wore on, the party became rowdier: fistfights broke out, club girls openly sucked and fucked the members, and liquor flowed non-stop. "You ready to head upstairs?" Muerto asked.

"Yes. I heard your parties were wild, but nothing like this. Is it always like this around here?"

"On the weekends, yeah. During the week, not so much. Tonight's special 'cause I told them you're my old lady."

"So does this mean they're glad about it?"

He laughed. "Fuck yeah. You'll get used to this world. I know it's a lot to take in, but you got me by your side, so it's all good." He kissed her then grasped her hand and pulled her behind him as he led her up to his room.

Once inside, Raven reclined on the bed, the lamp's light bathing her nakedness in a golden glow. Muerto winked at her as he peeled off his clothes and joined her, his fingers running up and down her arm. "Did you tell your dad about us?"

"Yes. I thought he'd hung up when I told him you were a biker with an outlaw club. He was so quiet, but after the shock passed, he told me that he'd love to meet you. He said he could hear how happy I was in my voice." She gazed out the window, a faraway look in her eyes. "I really miss him."

"Then what's stopping you from seeing him? Vegas is kickass, and I'd like to meet your dad."

Her gray eyes sparkled and he loved the way they picked up the light. "Are you serious? I'd love for you to get to know my dad. That would be beyond awesome."

"Then we'll go. Don't they have like a million chapels there?"

"You mean those cheesy wedding ones?"

"Yeah. Maybe we should visit one of them. I like cheesy."

Her lips turned up, and she moved her face closer to his. "I do too." She kissed him. Then he pressed her close to him and kissed her deeply.

"Make love to me," she said softly as she ran her fingers across his shoulders.

He gently pushed her down and hovered over her, the back of his hand caressing her cheek. Then he slowly and sensuously made love to the woman who'd captured his heart so completely.

Epilogue

Three months later
Las Vegas

FLASHING YELLOW, BLUE, red, and purple neon lights lit up the night as Raven and Muerto walked hand-in-hand down the Vegas Strip toward the brightly illuminated pink-and-orange feather sign. The balmy desert air rustled through the palm trees as they passed a glittering Eiffel Tower.

Raven laughed. "I lived here for almost a year, and I never got used to the over-the-top, surreal feel of the strip. I mean, it's jarring to pass the Statute of Liberty, the Great Pyramid, a medieval castle, and the Eiffel Tower in less than twenty minutes."

Muerto squeezed her hand. "That's what makes it Vegas, babe. It's a place where excess is the norm and the more indulgent it is the better." He winked at her.

She shook her head. "Did you want to join up with your brothers after we have dinner with my dad and Wanda?"

"Maybe. I can check in with them and see if they're somewhere you want to be. Knowing them, they'll be at a strip club. Goldie's crazy for them, and Chains and Army are right behind him. I'm pretty sure Crow and Paco are checking out the chicks, and Diablo's definitely at the blackjack tables."

"Diablo seems real nice. Does he have a woman?"

Muerto chuckled. "Not that any of us know of. He doesn't talk too much about himself. He goes with a couple of the club girls but not on a regular basis. He's a real good guy. He'd give you the shirt off his back. Loyal all the way."

They walked through the entrance of the Flamingo Hotel and made their way to the restaurant. When they entered, Raven spotted her dad and Wanda at a table by the window, Caesar's Palace shimmered in the background.

"Pop!" Raven broke away from Muerto and dashed toward her dad, who had risen to his feet, his arms outstretched. She fell into his embrace and they hugged each other tightly. "I've missed you so much."

"Me too. It's been too long." He kissed her cheek and pulled back a bit, his gaze surveying her. "You're looking really good." He glanced behind her. "Is that young man the one responsible for making you look so happy?"

She nodded while smiling. She reached out her hand and tugged Muerto closer. "Pop, this is Muerto."

Muerto shook the man's hand. "Nice meeting you. Raven talks a lot about you."

"I'm hoping it's all the good stuff. My name's Ed. You've got an unusual name. I don't think I've ever heard it before."

"It's a road name. That's what a lot of the bikers have," Raven said. "And you don't really want to ask why he chose that name."

"You're probably right about that." Ed pulled out a chair for Raven then sat down.

"How're you Wanda?" she asked her dad's partner. Wanda looked very stylish in her St. John black knit dress with a spattering of crystals along the neckline.

"I'm doing great. Your father and I have been having all kinds of fun." The skin around her eyes crinkled when she smiled.

Warmth spread through Raven when she saw her dad grasp Wanda's hand and squeeze it. *Pop's taken care of. After all these years, he's finally found someone to love and settle down with.* She leaned over and kissed her dad's cheek. "I'm happy that you have Wanda in your life," she whispered in his ear.

Ed brushed his fingers against her cheek, then turned to Muerto. With his arm around Raven, he said, "This pretty, intelligent, and sweet woman deserves to be treated like a rare, precious gem her whole life. I'm not as young as I used to be, but if you do wrong by her, I'll come to Colorado and kick your ass good."

"Ed!" Wanda gasped.

Muerto laughed. "You're my kind of man. And if I don't treat this awesome lady good, I deserve to have you kick my ass." His lips brushed against Raven's.

"Fair enough." Ed motioned the waiter. "Now it's time to drink and eat while you tell me why you prefer Harleys over Honda Super Cubs."

Raven groaned. "I don't think we have enough time for that." She leaned against Muerto and smiled up at him.

"You and Wanda talk shoes and purses while I talk bikes with your young man. I always wanted to get a motorcycle. I'd be interested in hearing which ones you think are the best. Raven told me you're a Harley guy, but there must be other bikes you like."

"Nothing's better than a Harley." Muerto picked up his beer and brought it to his lips, but Raven saw the sparkle in his eye. One of his favorite things to do was to talk bikes. Actually, it was a favored topic of conversation for all the brothers.

As they ate, drank, laughed, and talked, Raven was overcome with joy that the two most important people in her life were getting along so well. She'd been worried that her dad might not think Muerto was a suitable husband for her, but he seemed quite taken with the outlaw biker.

As the foursome walked out into the warm, night air, Muerto pulled her against him. "Do you want to join us for a bit of gambling?" she asked her dad and Wanda.

"Nope. I stay away from all that. I don't even hustle anymore." Ed looped his arm in Wanda's.

"I can't say Raven's given it up entirely." Muerto kissed the side of her head.

"You still shooting pool?" Ed's blue-gray eyes shimmered with pride.

Nodding, she said, "Not as much as I used to, but there always seems to be a club member who wants to challenge me. The club had a charity run a month ago, and I made a ton of money for it."

"I miss it real bad sometimes." Ed glanced at Wanda as she cleared her throat. "But it's all behind me. I do different things now."

Raven caught the wistful tone in his voice. "When you come to visit us, you can play pool with the brothers. They seem to like to lose."

Muerto guffawed. "Don't let them hear you say that."

"I'd love to play a few rounds when Wanda and I come to Colorado." Ed's eyes brightened. "Now you go and have a good time. We're going to head home. We'll see you tomorrow at the chapel." He hugged Raven, then grabbed Wanda's hand and walked away.

"You want to hang with Crow and Paco for a bit? Crow texted me that they're at Margaritaville having some drinks on the patio. Crow said they have a great classic rock band playing."

"Sounds fun. The bar's in the Flamingo. Let's go."

They turned around and went back inside the hotel. Soon they were sitting with Crow and Paco. The three guys laughed and talked while she sat back and listened to the tunes of the cover band as they sang classics from the Beatles, Jimmy Buffet, Billy Joel, and many other artists. As she sipped her frozen pineapple daiquiri, she watched Muerto wave his hands as he spoke animatedly about something the three of them had done together a few years back. She noticed the women checking him out as they passed by and how he was oblivious to it. And when he turned to her and winked, her heart fluttered and her legs clenched. *He's so wonderful and he's all mine. Life is so perfect right now.* The moon shone, the breeze caressed, the glittering lights lit up the sky, and she was sipping the most delicious daiquiri she'd ever tasted with the sexiest man she'd ever known on the eve of her wedding.

"You doing good, babe?" Muerto kissed her. "Your lips are cold." He laughed.

"I'm doing great. Don't worry about me. I'm having a good time watching all the people."

"I love you," he breathed against her neck. "I can't wait to take you back to our room."

A shiver of anticipation rolled up her spine. "Me neither."

He ordered another round of drinks for the table, and Raven knew she was playing with fire because the daiquiris tasted too much like a pineapple shake, but the way her eyes weren't focusing, she knew they were lethal.

I'm getting married tomorrow. I can't believe I'll be Muerto's wife—Mrs. Ruiz. She giggled and the three men turned and looked at her. Then she giggled some more until she was laughing heartily, tears running down her cheeks. Through her guffaws, she heard Muerto say, "She's had a few too many." When the other guys agreed, she laughed harder. And it felt so good. Her life was just so damn good at that moment. She leaned her head on Muerto's shoulder, and he instantly wrapped his arm around her, pressing her close.

As the men droned on, she happily sipped her drink and nestled further into her man, her life, her love. The following day she'd no longer be single. She and Muerto would be an "us" forever, and even though she'd been scared by that thought, she wasn't anymore. She wouldn't have it any other way. She had finally found the missing piece in her life's puzzle. And it was fantastic.

"LET ME KNOW if I'm tying your dress too tight," Breanna said as she pulled the ties on the back of Raven's corset dress.

"The tighter the better." Raven sucked in a deep breath as Breanna pulled harder.

"There you go." Breanna caught Raven's gaze in the full length mirror. "You make a sexy bride. I didn't even know you could get a black leather wedding dress. I'm sure Steel would've loved it if I'd worn one."

"What kind of wedding dress did you wear?"

"An ivory one with lace sleeves and pearls. It was pretty traditional, but it was lovely."

"I found this dress online. When I saw a corset leather wedding dress with a matching thong, I was sold. This is the dress for our Vegas wedding, but I'll have the traditional one for the church wedding in Alina. Our marriage is such a huge deal for Muerto's mom and sisters that I couldn't deny them the traditional wedding they want. If it was up to us, this would be it, but Muerto would never do that to his mom."

"I could barely handle one wedding. I can't imagine having to do it twice."

"The one today is fun and relaxed, but the big family wedding will be exhausting."

"Does Muerto's mom know you're getting married in Vegas?"

"Yeah, but she doesn't consider it real without a priest. It's all good. Two honeymoons work for me." Raven laughed and finger-combed her hair.

"I still can't believe Muerto's getting married. Steel just shakes his head every time I bring it up. I mean, he's the last brother I thought would marry. But then again there's Paco and Goldie...oh...and Chains, Crow...."

"Diablo...damn, I can't think of any of them settling down," Raven said. The two women laughed. Raven poured a shot of tequila for both of them. "Thanks for being here with me. I wish my mom could've been here. My pops has been great, and Wanda has helped me with some of the arrangements, but it's not the same as having my mom."

"I know," Breanna said softly. "She's watching you from above, and I know she's beaming." She hugged Raven then pulled back. Lifting her glass she clinked it against Raven's. "To a long and happy life with a moody, sweet, and crazy biker."

"I'll totally drink to that, and to a life of hotter than hell sex. And you know what I'm saying." Raven threw her shot back as Breanna giggled.

"They are hot blooded, aren't they?" Breanna drank her shot.

"Yeah, and we wouldn't want it any other way." They laughed. Looking in the mirror one last time, Raven took a deep breath. "I guess I'm really going to do this."

Breanna handed her a bouquet of red roses with baby's breath and greens. "It's time."

"Let's rock and roll." Raven opened the door and walked into the corridor.

Muerto stood by the doorway to the chapel, surrounded by his brothers. He wore a crisp black shirt with gray pinstripes, his leather cut, black jeans, and his shined up biker boots. His hair was combed back, and she thought he was the most handsome and sexy groom she'd ever seen. Butterflies fluttered inside her as his heated gaze rose slowly up her body. "Gorgeous," he mouthed when his eyes caught hers. She wanted to run to him and wrap herself around him, covering him with kisses as she ground against his hard body, but she merely smiled and winked at him.

The guests took their seats in the small chapel and the director escorted Raven and Muerto outside. A black Harley stood at the entrance, the neon lights from the chapel's sign bouncing off the chrome. Raven sat behind Muerto and he craned his neck as she leaned toward him. They kissed then he revved the motor and rode into the chapel. As they rode up the black aisle runner, the brothers cheered and whistled until Muerto cut the motor and helped Raven off the bike. Steppenwolf's "Born to Be Wild" reverberated against the white walls. The justice of the peace, dressed in jeans and a black leather jacket, smiled at the couple and asked them to hold hands.

During the ceremony, Raven and Muerto held each other's gazes. When he placed the simple white gold band on her finger, her insides exploded and she flung her arms around him and peppered his face with kisses.

Clearing his throat, the officiant said, "We're not quite at that part yet."

Raven pulled away, but Muerto tugged her back into him. "If my woman wants to kiss me, then she can fuckin' do it anytime she wants." Hoots and whistles filled the small room.

After they kissed deeply, Muerto nodded to the justice of the peace.

"Go on."

When they were pronounced husband and wife, the brothers, who were able to come to Vegas for the wedding, stomped their boots, pounded against the wooden pews, and yelled out. The group of twelve people made as much noise as a crowd of a hundred. Raven beamed at her dad, and her heart lurched when she saw tears in his eyes.

"I want to give my dad a hug," she whispered to Muerto. She went over to her dad and held him tightly. "Thanks for being the best pops ever," she said in his ear.

"You don't know how wonderful my life is because you're in it. You make me proud. I love you." His voice hitched.

"Me too." She kissed his cheek.

"Now go to your husband." He gently pushed her away.

She jumped on the back of the Harley and they rode out of the chapel. When Muerto helped her off, he hooked his arm around her waist. "You look so fuckin' sexy in your leather dress. I can't wait to peel it off you. I love you, babe."

"I love you, too. And you're way too handsome right now."

"Is there any damn whiskey around here?" Army asked as he came out of the chapel.

"And I'm wearing a leather thong," she breathed in Muerto's ear before she turned to Army. She giggled when she heard Muerto groan, his fingers digging into her hips. "Army, the reception is in the room to the left. We have cake and booze. We're taking everyone out to dinner later."

AFTER A NIGHT full of food, drink, and laughter, Raven rested her head on Muerto's shoulder as they walked down the hallway to their room. "What an awesome day," she murmured.

"It fuckin' ruled." He slipped the key card in the door. From the floor-to-ceiling windows, the lights of the Strip reflected on the plush carpet of their honeymoon suite. Muerto picked up the bottle of champagne from the bucket and popped the cork.

"How did that get here?" she asked as she accepted the glass he gave her.

"I called ahead and said I wanted it chilled when we got to the room." They clinked their glasses together. The bubbles made her giggle. His arm looped around her, drawing her back against his hard chest. He nuzzled her neck, nipping the soft flesh. "I've had a fuckin' hard-on since I saw you at the chapel."

As he continued lavishing kisses on her neck and shoulder, she rubbed her butt against his hardness. When he cupped her breasts with his hands, a deep moan vibrated against her throat. She reached back and rested her hands on his firm buttocks, her neck cradled against him. He dipped his head down and crushed his lips on hers, his tongue thrusting into her mouth.

"You're the sweetest thing," he rasped against her lips.

"I love you so much. I can't believe you're all mine," she breathed.

"Believe it, babe. We're each other's for life." He pushed her forward slightly and began to untie the leather straps of her dress. "And it's pretty damn amazing."

"It's the best." She whirled around and took his face between her hands and kissed him. Gripping his hand, she led her husband to the bedroom. And as he slowly undressed her, her body tingling with every brush of his fingers, lips, and tongue, she lost herself in his love.

He'd come into her life when she wasn't expecting love. He consumed and devoured her in the most delicious and loving way.

Yeah…it is pretty damn amazing.

He eased her down on the bed and hovered over her. Their life together was just beginning.

And she knew it'd be a long, exciting ride.

Make sure you sign up for my newsletter so you can keep up with my new releases, special sales, free short stories, and other treats only available to newsletter readers. When you sign up, you will receive a FREE hot and steamy novella. Sign up at:

http://eepurl.com/bACCL1

Visit me on Facebook
facebook.com/Chiah-Wilder-1625397261063989

Check out my other books at my Author Page
amazon.com/author/chiahwilder

Notes from Chiah

As always, I have a team behind me making sure I shine and continue on my writing journey. It is their support, encouragement, and dedication that pushes me further in my writing journey. And then, it is my wonderful readers who have supported me, laughed, cried, and understood how these outlaw men live and love in their dark and gritty world. Without you—the readers—an author's words are just letters on a page. The emotions you take away from the words breathe life into the story.

Thank you to my amazing Personal Assistant Amanda Faulkner. I don't know what I'd do without you. I value your suggestions and opinions, and my world is so much saner with you in it. You keep the non-writing part of my indie publishing world running smoothly. I so appreciate it. You are always ready to jump in and fix everything when I'm pulling my hair out. You are so cheerful, and when I hear your bubbling voice, it instantly uplifts me. So happy YOU are on my team!

Thank you to my editor, Kristin, for all your insightful edits, excitement with my new series, Night Rebels MC, and encouragement during the writing and editing process. I truly value your editorial eyes and suggestions as well as the time you spend. You're the best!

Thank you to my wonderful beta readers, Kolleen, Jessica, Paula, and Barbara. Your enthusiasm and suggestions for MUERTO: Night Rebels MC were spot on and helped me to put out a stronger, cleaner novel. Your insight and attention to detail were awesome.

Thank you to the bloggers for your support in reading my book, sharing it, reviewing it, and getting my name out there. I so appreciate all your efforts. You all are so invaluable. I hope you know that. Without you, the indie author would be lost.

Thank you ARC readers you have helped make all my books so much stronger. I appreciate the effort and time you put in to reading, reviewing, and getting the word out about the books. I don't know what I'd do without you. I feel so lucky to have you behind me.

Thank you to my Street Team. Thanks for your input, your support, and your hard work. I appreciate you more than you know. A HUGE hug to all of you!

Thank you to Carrie from Cheeky Covers. You are amazing! I can always count on you. You are the calm to my storm. You totally rock, and I love your artistic vision.

Thank you to my proofreader, Daryl, whose last set of eyes before the last once over I do, is invaluable. I appreciate the time and attention to detail you always give to my books. You ALWAYS deliver, and I love that I can count on you.

Thank you to Ena and Amanda with Enticing Journeys Promotions who have helped garner attention for and visibility to the Night Rebels MC series. Couldn't do it without you! Also a big thank you to Book Club Gone Wrong Blog who is hosting and promoting MUERTO. Totally indebted to you.

Thank you to the readers who continue to support me and read my books. Without you, none of this would be possible. I appreciate your comments and reviews on my books, and I'm dedicated to giving you the best story that I can. I'm always thrilled when you enjoy a book as much as I have in writing it. You definitely make the hours of typing on the computer and the frustrations that come with the territory of writing books so worth it. You make it possible for writers to write because without you reading the books, we wouldn't exist. Thank you, thank you! ♥

MUERTO: Night Rebels Motorcycle Club (Book 2)

Dear Readers,

Thank you for reading my book. I hope you enjoyed the second book in my new Night Rebels MC series as much as I enjoyed writing Muerto and Raven's story. This gritty and rough motorcycle club has a lot more to say, so I hope you will look for the upcoming books in the series. Romance makes life so much more colorful, and a rough, sexy bad boy makes life a whole lot more interesting.

If you enjoyed the book, please consider leaving a review on Amazon. I read all of them and appreciate the time taken out of busy schedules to do that.

I love hearing from my fans, so if you have any comments or questions, please email me at chiahwilder@gmail.com or visit my facebook page.

To receive a **free copy of my novella**, *Summer Heat*, and to hear of **new releases**, **special sales**, **free short stories**, and **ARC opportunities**, please sign up for my **Newsletter** at http://eepurl.com/bACCL1.

Happy Reading,

Chiah

DIABLO
Book 3 in the Night Rebels MC Series
Coming in June, 2017

Diablo, Sergeant-At-Arms of the Night Rebels MC, doesn't chase women the way his fellow brothers do. Women flock to the ripped, bearded, tatted biker but he pushes them away.

His past haunts him and rage burns deep inside him. The club, his Harley, and his shots of whiskey are his only focus. He doesn't want a woman messing with his life. He doesn't trust them.

Then he sees her. Her hazel eyes reflect sadness and regret. He's drawn to the loneliness that fills her up—it haunts him.

She's his employer's daughter. He knows he should stay away from her, but he can't. He wants to take her in his arms and protect her, but she won't even talk to him.

Diablo's not the type to give up. He wants her, and he'll do everything he can to make her his.

Fallon Richardson can't stand a man's touch. Ever since her mother left her when she was a young girl, she's been living in hell. Her father is the kingpin of illegal underground fighting. She tries to make herself inconspicuous so the men won't notice her and the women won't make fun of her, but it never works.

She hates being at the fights, but her father demands her presence.

Then she sees *him* across the room. His penetrating stare pulls her in no matter how hard she resists.

The tall, muscled man stirs feelings in her she has shut off for years. Her body wants him, yet, she can't give herself to him. Men are cruel, animalistic, and not to be trusted. But the tattooed man has a softness beneath his rough exterior that speaks to her.

Then shadows from years ago emerge from the darkness. Someone is determined to leave the past buried even if it means killing her.

Can Diablo and Fallon gain each other's trust in time for him to protect her?

This is the third book in the Night Rebels MC Romance series. This is Diablo's story. It is a standalone. This book contains violence, sexual assault (not graphic), strong language, and steamy/graphic sexual scenes. It describes the life and actions of an outlaw motorcycle club. If any of these issues offend you, please do not read the book. HEA. No cliffhangers! The book is intended for readers over the age of 18.

Other Books by Chiah Wilder

Insurgent MC Series:

Hawk's Property: Insurgents Motorcycle Club Book 1
Jax's Dilemma: Insurgents Motorcycle Club Book 2
Chas's Fervor: Insurgents Motorcycle Club Book 3
Axe's Fall: Insurgents Motorcycle Club Book 4
Banger's Ride: Insurgents Motorcycle Club Book 5
Jerry's Passion: Insurgents Motorcycle Club Book 6
Throttle's Seduction: Insurgents Motorcycle Club Book 7
Rock's Redemption: Insurgents Motorcycle Club Book 8
An Insurgent's Wedding: Insurgents Motorcycle Club Book 9
Insurgents MC Romance Series: Insurgents Motorcycle Club Box Set
(Books 1 – 4)

Night Rebels MC Series:

STEEL: Night Rebels Motorcycle Club Book 1

Find all my books at: amazon.com/author/chiahwilder

I love hearing from my readers. You can email me at:
chiahwilder@gmail.com.

Sign up for my newsletter to receive a FREE Novella, updates on new books, special sales, free short stories, and ARC opportunities at: http://eepurl.com/bACCL1.

Visit me on facebook at:
www.facebook.com/Chiah-Wilder-1625397261063989

Printed in Great Britain
by Amazon

19888349R20142